A NOVEL BASED ON A TRUE STORY

LOVE'S WILL

Faith. Fate. Love.

P. RYAN CAMPBELL

Formatted by Rik Hall, Wild Seas Formatting

(http://www.WildSeasFormatting.com)

Cover Design by Sherwin Soy

**Learn more about the author at
pryancampbell.com**

ACKNOWLEDGMENTS

To Jana, for the guidance from above.
To my Mom and Dad, for the inspiration.

To my wife, for the love and support.
To my brothers, blood and not, for the camaraderie.

To my supporters and doubters, for the motivation.
To my boat and the summer sun, for the memories.

To working hard, playing hard, and praying hard.
To my Savior, for everything.

To all of you, for reading. I truly hope that you can take something from this story. Whether its inspiration, reminiscence, laughter, tears, or pure enjoyment, I hope that it touches you in some way. Let's escape together...

1

"It's over," he says.

His eyes are welled with tears. Of course, I have seen my son cry on many occasions. Tears are rites of passage when growing up. He was crying the moment he came into this world. He cried when he lost his first tooth. He cried when he crashed his bike. Tears can usually be dried with some sort of remedy. But these tears are different. These tears have substance and fear behind them.

She broke up with him two weeks ago. He was devastated as his two-year investment in their relationship came to a sudden crash. There has been a little aftershock communication, but it's apparent that she has moved on. As a grizzled veteran in the game of life, with the scars and bruises to show it, I considered it a shade darker than puppy love in the grand scheme of things, but this has turned out to be much more serious. I know he is upset, but I figured he would get over it quickly, especially with summer approaching and college starting in the fall. There is so much to look forward to, but all he can do is look backwards. He has spent every day sulking in his bedroom, avoiding others, not eating, and bypassing responsibilities. He feels as though he is the only one – like pouring rain is soaking him while others stand next to him basking in the sunlight, like the old cartoon. I let it go on because I felt like he deserved the right to grieve, but it's getting to the point where he needs to move on. But then again, who am I to judge? Sure, many people experience heartbreak, but no two situations are the same. Pain is never carbon-copied. It's always customized.

A father always fears moments like this – moments when you are helpless. Moments when you can't take away the pain. Even though he is almost a full-fledged adult, he still seems so innocent. In my mind, he's still my little boy. But no matter how innocent he appears, I can't protect him from everything. Over the past two weeks, I've tried telling him everything. I can continue to tell him to be strong, give it time, he's better off. All of them sound like clichés, and clichés aren't going to suffice. Words can be powerful, but they rarely ever heal a broken heart. I've consulted with other parents, even my own. Having him see a counselor or psychiatrist even crossed my mind, as that seems to be everyone's answer these days. Fathers are supposed to have all of the answers, but for the first time, I don't know what to do. Just as I admired my father, he admires me. I know the feeling – having a hero, and everything you do is at least indirectly to make him proud. That added to the difficulty of the situation, as he hates that he is showing vulnerability and weakness in front of me. I've taught him everything he knows, including how to be strong. My mind is spinning with different thoughts. It's one of those times where I wish his mother was here to help.

I have to do something. I can't let him continue down this dark path. But I have to choose my next move carefully. This is an extremely delicate situation that could very well affect my son for a long time. Nothing has helped so far. Somehow, I need to get across that his life isn't over. I turned my eyes away from his and peered through his bedroom window. Rain was pouring down and hammering the thinly grown grass. The rain drops raced down the window, splintering off in different directions and at different speeds with no common purpose. A pessimist would view that as a microcosm of our lives. An optimist would say that everything happens for a reason. I needed to find the words of a realist.

The clock keeps ticking and I need to get to work.

"We'll talk about it later, okay, buddy?" I say.

He nods his head slightly. I stumble downstairs to

a quiet living room, with only the rain making a sound. I walk past the kitchen island with mail stacked up and newspaper pages spread over the counter. I throw on my suit jacket and tighten my tie and get in the car. Fighting the traffic downtown, I park in the busy parking garage, make my way up the elevator, and walk through the doors, down the hall, and sit down at my desk.

I'm a lawyer. I know what you're thinking – I don't particularly like them either, and I've probably already heard that joke. Honestly, I don't particularly enjoy my job, although I've been successful and made some money. It provides a good living, but it doesn't provide a good life – a good day's work, but not a good life's work – if that makes sense. I find it mostly unfulfilling. I struggle to leave my work at the office, so I always end up bringing it home. The stress and demands often pour over into my personal life, which often have a negative effect.

When most people hear that I'm a lawyer, they instantly think of a sharp suit and slicked back hair, standing in front of nine wide-eyed jurors at the front of a packed courtroom. An innocent person's life is on the line, and I'm the only one who can possibly bring justice. The client is always innocent and someone inevitably cracks on the stand in a tearful admission thanks to my brilliant questioning. After thirty minutes, justice is served with a not guilty verdict and I'm the hero driving away in my brand new Mercedes. Sometimes I let them think that. After all, that's what we see on TV. The truth is, if a lawyer is lucky, that may happen once in a career.

The majority of my practice consists of estate planning, which rarely ever gets me in the courtroom. The majority of my days are found sitting at this desk, staring at a computer screen and taking phone calls. No, I don't sue people. No, I can't get you out of a DUI. No, not even a speeding ticket. And especially, no, I don't do divorces. What do I do, then? Basically, I do the boring stuff. I make wills, trusts, and estate plans for people. My clients are often older and planning their exit strategies from this world. I have often thought of changing professions over the years, but I got trapped a long time ago, afraid to take a risk to try something new and unknown, and afraid to give up a comfortable job that pays my mortgage and allows me to have a lake cabin, and, I must admit – my Mercedes. Quite frankly, I'm afraid to start over. But at the same time, I go on uninspired by my life's work. It's a trap that many fall into. I just never thought I would.

I go through the motions all morning. I am physically here, but mentally I am still at home concerned about my son. It's Friday of Memorial Day weekend, so the office is closing at noon. After work, I plan to drive up to the lake cabin, which is about three hours northwest of the city. When I get home and pull into the driveway, I realize I can't wait any longer. It's time to deal with this. I walk into the house, throw off my suit jacket and unwind my tie. Work is over. It's time to be a dad. Ironically, at times, being a dad is far more difficult work. I stop for a moment and look out the back-porch window. *What are you going to do*, I ask myself.

"Alright, buddy, lets hit the road!" I yell upstairs as I walk in the door.

I keep going back to the same idea. I thought about it initially, but I didn't want to go there. I still don't. But at this point, he is leaving me with no choice. It's drastic, but it's necessary. It's time to remove the roadblocks from memory lane. I thought about myself at his age, harkening back to my own experience and how he could draw on it. I walk into our storage den which is on the other side of the house. In the corner of the room, covered in papers and books, is an old metal chest. It's an old soldier's chest – army green with rust on the corners. It belonged to my dad, who like so many others of his generation served his country valiantly in the Second World War. He gave it to me since we shared the same name. I open the chest and sort through some old folders and books collecting dust until I find an old yearbook with my graduation year in weathered metallic gold plastered on the cover.

Meanwhile, I hear my son slam the door and walk outside into the car. I look over my shoulder towards the door before sitting down on the floor and resting my back against the chest. I open the first page to find a photo with my senior classmates surrounding the front entrance to the high school. I'm the one in the middle of the five guys proudly sporting letterman's jackets. I turn to the next page slowly, almost nervous to do so. It's a picture of a gorgeous girl with golden-blonde hair in a cheerleading uniform, her smile still capable of taking my breath. She had her own page to herself. Above her picture were the words "In Memory Of."

I run my thumb across the picture slowly. Her smile in the picture endures. My heart skips a beat – something that hasn't happened in a while. I slowly close the album and hold on to it firmly with both of my hands as I stare forward. Leaning back a bit, I ponder for a moment before grabbing a stack of yellow worn and wrinkled papers along with it and closing the chest. I walk briskly through the house and grab my bag, locking the house before walking outside.

He's waiting in the car, already slouched in the

passenger seat. He's waiting. He needs his hero. I get in the car, start it up, and put it in gear. I pull out of the driveway and hit the open road. We remain mostly silent until we get outside of the city limits. I spend the next few miles looking outside at the Minnesota countryside – the green grass, rolling hills of grain and corn, and the little white lines on the blacktop up ahead. I love the feeling I get on the drive to the lake on Fridays. It's a sense of anticipation and optimism. It feels like I'm driving away from all of my worries and cares and straight towards freedom. It serves as a summer haven, escaping the bustle of city life. That feeling helps me garner the courage.

"Hey, buddy," I open the conversation as I take my eye off the road and look over at him, "I want to tell you a story. I want to tell you our story."

2

"Just believe!" I yelled as we marched single-file off the bus.

Living in Shoreham Lake, Minnesota, you don't exactly have the chance to make all of your dreams come true every day. However, dreams had their opportunity to shine on a special night under the blinding lights of the extravagant Minnesota Sports Arena. For my teammates and I, this was the ultimate dream we had worked for our entire lives. It was more than just a high school sports game. It was a special night for a team, a school, and a town. Before I started playing high school hockey, I had been to every state tournament championship game as a fan since I was three years old. It was a tradition for our family, even during the years Shoreham Lake didn't make it. On my last shot, I was determined to be playing in it.

I'll never forget the smell of the rink when I walked through those doors. I tried to focus on the game and block out the noise, but it was impossible.

The place was magical. Almost the entire town of Shoreham Lake was in attendance. Our parents and other fans lined the hallway to cheer us on as we walked down into the basement to our locker room. I walked past Jenna, and although I tried my best to keep my game face on, I couldn't help but crack a smile when our eyes met. The locker room was our bunker where we prepared our attack strategy. Our hockey sticks lined the walls like swords in medieval battles. Our helmets and pads served as our armor. Teammates performed their pregame rituals, some would call them superstitions. Ghosts of Spoiler hockey past made the room stuffy. The pressure of a small-town dream made it hard to breathe. When we ran out onto the ice, the crowd rose to their feet and roared.

The cheerleaders were bouncing up and down with excitement, like maestros leading the boisterous crowd of thousands like a symphony. Their captain, however, was missing from her spot in the middle. Always day-by-day, Jenna wasn't physically able to cheer. It killed her that she couldn't be there with her teammates, cheering on the team. Instead of jumping around with her curls bouncing and her pom-poms waving, she was crouched in a frail state in the stands. To be honest, even though I didn't tell her, I was preoccupied with her in the crowd. However, I think it would have been much worse if she was not there at all. She was determined to be there and, just like everything she set out to do, she made it happen.

The days prior to the state tournament were her lowest points yet. She was on constant bed rest and had her pulse checked regularly. Her doctors recommended that she not make the road trip to Minneapolis, especially in a high-pressure situation with thousands of people screaming and crowding around her. But she had cheered for me at every single game for the past four years, and she wasn't going to miss the biggest one yet. Besides, cheering in that game was a dream for her too. Under her heavy coat, she wore her uniform, with a blanket covering her legs. As she entered the arena, they informed the security staff and the ambulance staff. Her mom checked her pulse literally every five minutes. I probably looked at her up in the crowd just as often. She looked so cold bundled up in her coat and scarf sandwiched between both of our moms. She still managed to clap lightly and event shout a few times at the refs. Throughout the game she constantly would look at her cheer squad at ice level to make sure they were doing their jobs correctly.

Jenna wasn't your stereotypical cheerleader. Sure, she had golden-blonde hair, a slender body with creamy skin, as well as other features desirable to most males. She was five feet of scenic beauty and very impressionable to everyone she encountered. Guys wanted her and girls wanted to be her. With everything she had, she could've gotten away with being arrogant and catty, but she wasn't. She was wholesome and sweet with a kind soul. She basically had it all. She knew that she was a blessed person and always appreciated it. That was probably my favorite trait about her. She could have coasted through life on her physical appearance, but she didn't. She was a people-pleaser and hated when people didn't like her, as rare as that was. She was pretty easy to like, her only defectors were the occasional girls who were envious of her long blonde hair or popularity. Some simply hated the idea that she was beautiful, a cheerleader, and dating the star of the hockey team. In a way, she was quite the cliché, I guess. However, so was their envy.

Jenna and I had been dating since eighth grade, and I was extremely faithful to her. I only had one mistress, and she knew all about it: hockey. Shoreham Lake was a hockey town. We had two seasons: summer and hockey. The sport was a second religion. It brought pride to the town. What football was to Texas, hockey was to Minnesota. And nothing represented that more than Shoreham Lake. It made the town feel a part of something. It provided people with a sense of escapism from their everyday lives, especially during the dark, cold, and snowy winter months. People left their jobs or problems behind for a couple of hours every week and watched the Spoilers play. It was a place where young boys lived vicariously through the players, and so did the older guys who could no longer play but longed for the glory days. Our five state championship titles hung from the rafters and in people's memories. From the time boys were old enough to walk, parents and grandparents bundled up in heavy coats, beanies, and scarves to battle the cold dry air of the hockey arena to see the young ones sliding around on the ice. Usually their coats would proudly advertise their kids on picture buttons fastened with safety pins. We constantly had exhibition battles out on the frozen lake that would often go into the late hours of the night. We would trek through the deep snow and fight the bitter cold. At times those games got more serious than our real games.

Being a Shoreham Lake Spoiler was a prestigious honor in the town and even across the state. What's a "Spoiler" you may ask? Good question. It was our nickname, if you want to call it that. In fact, no one truly knew what "Spoilers" meant. Most people would tell you that it originates from the 1950s, when our basketball team was the underdog and upset Red River High School in the state semifinals, putting an end to their undefeated season. Even though we lost in the state championship game the following day, legend has it that we were forever branded the "Spoilers." The school officially adopted the name a few years later. We've been the Spoilers in crimson and gold ever since. Over the years we have lived up to the nickname, often defeating much larger schools and more talented teams in big games. Once again, we were faced with a better team in the state semifinal game. And once again, we weren't going to back down.

Jenna loved hockey, too. When I made the varsity team as a freshman, she made the cheerleading team as well, so we shared in the entire journey. That was a dream come true to finally put that jersey on and play for the Spoilers. Because I had two older brothers, I knew of the tradition that came with it. Most people knew that I was good enough to make the team and supported my decision. There were a few detractors, but they were parents of the youth team I was leaving or parents of seniors on the varsity team worried I was going to take their kid's spot. The politics of small town hockey rivaled the United States Congress at times. The next four years were a rollercoaster that I could have never expected.

My freshman year we made it to the state semifinal game and lost in a blowout to the eventual state champion. My sophomore year we made it back to the state tournament, but got bumped out in the first round. My junior year was a breakout year, as I led the region in scoring and we made it back to the state semifinal. Unfortunately, we lost a heartbreaker in overtime. That loss took a lot of out of me. I was convinced we were destined to win the championship, and I took the loss personally. But I still had one more year left, and we were returning a lot of our key players. I still had one more shot.

My senior year we were one of the favorites to win the state championship. I was voted team captain and Jenna was voted captain of the cheerleading team. Talk about that cliché, again. It was our year. We knocked on the door the previous year. It was our time to finally win it. We had a successful season and scratched and crawled our way back to the state semifinal game. The stage was set.

Sitting next to Jenna in the stands was my mom, who was the epitome of a hockey mom – caring yet fierce. She sacrificed what seemed like an infinite amount of time, money, and nerves so that I had a chance to live my dream. By day, she was a first grade teacher and absolutely loved every minute of it. She was a master with kids and could break open even the most shy or combative kid into cooperation, eventually turning into full-blow engagement. It was a gift. She was gentle and affectionate to others. But make no mistake, she could be tough and stood her ground when necessary.

My old man wasn't sitting next to them. Like always, he was standing by the glass at ice level in the corner behind the opposing team's goalie. It turns out players aren't the only ones with superstitions. My dad was the captain for the first state championship team for Shoreham Lake as a senior thirty years prior. Before that game, someone spray painted on the highway overpass, which still remained, "Last one to leave town, turn off the lights!" His two brothers played hockey as well, one of them earning a state title a couple of years later. His two sons before me played in state championship games, one ending in victory, one in defeat. But he was equally as proud of both of them.

Together, my mom and dad were always there for me and my brothers. They provided for us in the early years when they probably couldn't, and didn't spoil us as we got older when they probably could have. I couldn't even pretend that I had a tough childhood, because my parents did all they could to make sure I didn't. And they both adored Jenna. They were always excited when she walked through the door and usually greeted her enthusiastically.

"Haven't you found anyone better yet?" My old man would often joke when she would come over to our house.

"I keep looking," Jenna would humor him. "It's a small town!"

My dad would let out a deep belly laugh as he went back to watching the evening news. Those two constantly traded joking barbs. I was usually the subject of their jest. Often when she came over, she would visit with my mom before coming to greet me. They were very close, as my mom was like a second mom to Jenna. And because my mom had all boys, she treated Jenna like the daughter she never had. I always loved when Jenna got along with my parents. For some reason it meant a lot to me. Their relationship was so sincere. Both approved of each other. When we first started dating, Jenna constantly inquired about how my parents felt about her. I was also nervous about it. But just like me, it didn't take them long to fall in love with her.

Since I had two older brothers who played, I was always dragged to the rink for their games and practices. Consequently, I took my first steps in a hockey rink – literally. During my formative years, my diet consisted of arena food which was the finest hot dogs, pizza, nachos, and candy known to man. I went on every road trip. I was at the front of the line at every "Skate with the Spoilers" event. From the time I was a year old, hockey was all I could think about. At age three, my dad put me in skates, against the wishes of my mother and the advice of pretty much everyone around town. We went on the frozen-over lake in our backyard. When he let me go, I pedaled my legs fast and never looked back.

I was somewhat of a child prodigy from day one, at least for Shoreham Lake. Growing up watching my brothers play every day, I learned by example and tried to emulate them. Every day as a child, I pretended I was scoring the game winning goal to win a state championship. I played hockey on the floor in the basement, on the pavement in the driveway, on the frozen lake behind our house, and even in my head. I would play entire games, start to finish, playing every position on both teams. I would even play commentator out loud, including instant replay. I can't imagine what the neighbors thought, especially when I would jump in the snowbank to celebrate with my imaginary teammates. I would trek through the snowy yard, often knee deep, to the frozen lake and spend hours fighting the bitter cold and skating on the ice. When it snowed, I had to shovel it off. It was a lot of work and required a lot of energy, but nothing brought me more joy – whether it was with a dozen friends in a competitive game or just myself gliding across my winter paradise.

I could lift the puck off the ice with my shot before anyone else. I think my record of seventeen goals in one scrimmage is still a Mites league record. That's unofficial of course. At age ten, I entered an international hockey camp in Minneapolis where I competed against kids who were twelve and thirteen years old. My mom feared for my life and begged my dad not to send me. After the week, I was named Most Valuable Player of the camp. National traveling teams bombarded my parents with phone calls and letters offering me a position on their teams. More importantly, they wanted my parents to pay thousands of dollars to fund it. Although flattered with the attention, my parents politely declined the offers. Keeping our family together and keeping me with my friends in a regular school environment was important to them. My parents were passionate about hockey, but they also were cognizant that there was more to life than just hockey, especially when it would inevitably come to an end.

***

The puck dropped to start the game as my heart pounded and my palms perspired. We jumped out and put the pressure on early, our first goal coming just three minutes into the game. The crowd erupted and gave us momentum. We added a second goal towards the end of the first period. Our opponent, St. Mary's High School, cut the lead in half with a power play goal midway through the second period as our momentum slowed. After that, it was a rare defensive battle. We held our one-goal lead heading into the third period. In the locker room during intermission, I made an impassioned speech, stressing to the team that we were only one period away from our lifelong dream. Twenty minutes away.

The defense of both teams continued their strong play to start the third period. We got a tripping penalty midway through, which was a highly debatable call by the referee. St. Mary's controlled the puck in our zone, passing it around to set up the perfect play. A St. Mary's defenseman wound up and let a slap shot fly from the blue line into the crowd of players in front of our goaltender. Goal. Tie game. Our lead was gone and the momentum had shifted away from us.

The clock was ticking down. Four minutes, three minutes. It felt like it was taking forever. We needed a hero. I can't even begin to guess how many times I had envisioned this scenario growing up, a chance to score the game-winning goal to send my team to the championship game. If you believed in fate, this was it. Two minutes left. It appeared that we were heading to overtime for the second year in a row. With a face-off in St. Mary's zone, I was exhausted from logging so many minutes throughout the game. But this was too big of a moment to forfeit by changing lines and taking a rest. Not now.

It was a play that Mark and I had worked on over and over for years. He wins the face-off back to me and I skate in and shoot. They say practice makes perfect. We were hoping this was the place where it would pay off. The face-off was won in my direction. I pulled the puck towards my body and made a move around the defender. I skated deeper into the zone until I was about even with the goal line, just to the left of the net. After briefly considering passing it across the crease area in front of the net, I corralled the puck on my backhand and took a shot. The puck soared over the goaltender's shoulder and into the top shelf of the net. The crowd roared with excitement. My heart almost beat out of my chest. I felt like butterflies were flying out of my stomach. Did this just happen? I skated towards the glass to our fans going wild in the crowd. I raised my arms in celebration as my teammates swarmed around me. We skated towards our team's bench and took a seat for a rest while the team hugged and gave me high fives. "Great shot, Will!" Mark yelled. "We did it!"

"It's not over yet," I warned, even though I thought to myself it was.

We finally punched our ticket to the state championship game. The crowd continued to cheer. I was living my dream. I turned around and looked up into the crowd at Jenna. She had a huge smile on her face as we locked eyes. She had one hand holding her mom's and one hand holding my mom's. That was an incredible moment. Tears started to well in my eyes as my body filled up with emotion. As the puck dropped and the game continued, I quickly told myself to snap out of it.

Shifting into panic mode, St. Mary's took control. They kept the puck deep in our zone and pressured our defensemen. They got a few quick shots on our goaltender, which he turned away. The atmosphere was intense. One minute remaining. The puck remained in our zone. My teammates and coaches on the bench kept screaming to get the puck out at all costs. A St. Mary's defenseman kept the puck in at the blue line and fired it on net. Despite being screened by all of the people crowded in front of the net, our goaltender made a huge stop. The puck bounced off his pads as he flopped out of position. The net was wide open. A St. Mary's forward slapped at the puck desperately as it crossed the goal line. Tie game, again. We were stunned. All we had to do was hold them off for a little over a minute and we couldn't do it. I went from hero to zero within seconds. It was a new game. The final buzzer rang. For the second year in a row, we were heading to overtime in the state semifinal game.

The puck dropped to start overtime. We lost the face-off and St. Mary's gained control. Their all-star defenseman picked up the puck and started rushing it up ice. He got around one of our guys, then another. He had a burst of speed as he crossed into our zone. Our defensemen started clutching onto his arm. He fended him off and skated around him and cut in towards the net. All I could do was watch from afar. He moved in towards our goalie, made a move and deeked around him. As I saw was his arms fly in the air in celebration, people in the crowd rose to their feet and St. Mary's fans roared. St. Mary's players jumped off the bench and flooded the ice. They were like a monsoon charging at the game winner. *Was this possible? Did this just happen?* I couldn't believe it. I looked around to see if I could find a referee, hoping for some reason he would signal no goal. I looked towards our coaches on the bench to see if there was anything we could do. Their heads hung. It was over.

We put up an epic fight in that game.

Unfortunately, once again, it was not quite good enough. I was devastated. I worked relentlessly for fifteen years to get to that point. I felt as though my dream was taken from me. I failed. When the game ended, I was still in shock physically, but mentally I knew that we had lost the game. Our season, and my career as a Shoreham Lake Spoiler, was over. I always knew that day would come. I just imagined it would be accompanied with a celebration, not mourning.

I wanted to look up at Jenna in the crowd, but couldn't bring myself to do it. I was too ashamed. After every game, no matter if we won or lost, I had a tradition of being the last player off the ice on our team. I hunched over in a disappointing state as I waited for all of my teammates to exit the ice. Mark, my best friend and fellow senior, came over to me and embraced me with a big hug. We both started to cry. We both knew what that moment meant, but we couldn't come to grips with it. It was a heavy moment. We walked off the ice and into the locker room together.

As I walked back in the locker room, the last to enter, my brain was frozen, it was surreal, like a dream, like it didn't just happen. As I sat in my locker stall, I could feel the guys' eyes looking upon me for guidance, as they always did. I could hear them wondering, "what now?" I had nothing for them. I had let them down. I had instilled this sense of hope in them. I thought of everyone affected – my teammates, my coaches, my family, Jenna, my friends, my idols who I aspired to impress, the kids that idolized me. But most of all, I thought of myself. How could this have happened? Other people work hard and strive for a goal and achieve it. You see it all the time in newspapers, books, and movies. I heard stories from my elders and even witnessed it with my own two eyes. I had worked and wanted it twice as bad as some of those people, so why hadn't it come true? In years past, I always had the next year to look forward to. Not that year. That was it.

During the hockey season, I usually went to see Jenna right after games and practices. Until senior year, I was always one of the last to leave the locker room. I enjoyed hanging with the boys, escaping whatever we considered reality at the time. My mom wasn't the biggest fan of my loitering. She made dinner every evening and I was always the last one to arrive to a cold plate. But my reality changed that year. I made rare appearances at mom's dinner table during my senior year. I would usually join Jenna for dinner at the hospital or at her house. I must admit, my mother's cooking was much better than the valiant efforts of the hospital cooking staff. But that was a sacrifice I was willing to make.

After the devastating loss, I didn't want to face the people upstairs. I waited it out, hoping everyone would leave before I came out. As the last one to leave the locker room, I took full responsibility for the loss. I was the captain, and I chose to go down with the ship. I put on my shoes and stuffed my bag full of sweaty equipment. As I opened the door to the hallway, I expected it to be empty from people running out of patience. Hundreds of people started clapping when I walked out. Everyone had waited – all of my teammates and their parents, and all of our fans. That's the power of a small town. Win or lose, they were there. Jenna was waiting in the front for me. She walked slowly towards me. I looked away as tears flowed. My throat choked. We hugged as I buried my face in her coat.

"I love you, baby." She whispered into my ear, which only made me cry harder.

All I could do was nod my head. Her embrace was comforting.

That was the quietest bus ride I've ever experienced. Everyone was exhausted, drained mentally and emotionally. It was the end of a fifteen year journey, as most of us had been teammates almost the entire way. In an instant, it was over, gone. I imagine it's a similar feeling of any senior in any sport that loses their final game – a forced closure with an empty feeling remaining.

The next night was the state championship game. I was a finalist for the Mr. Hockey Award, one of three seniors, which was given out during the awards ceremony after the game to the most outstanding player of the year. I didn't want to go to the game because it was painful to watch. I showed up late to the game and waited for the ending. It didn't compare to the state title, but I figured it would be a decent consolation prize to be recognized individually. As I stood on the ice waiting for my name to be called, they announced the winner was the captain of the St. Mary's team, the same player who scored the game-winning goal against us in the semifinals and led his team to the championship title.

After the game, I made the late night drive back home with my parents. We finally pulled into our dark driveway a long three hours later. My dad put the car in park as my mom opened the door and stepped outside.

"Darling, give us a minute," my dad requested as my mom shut the door and walked inside the house.

I couldn't bring myself to look at him. I could see that he wanted to make a big speech, but nothing came out but a few tears.

Finally, he mustered with a crack in his voice, "I'm

proud of you."

The next few days after the state tournament were filled with reflection. It was a very emotional time. It wasn't just a game to me, it was my life. It was my dream. No one understood that better than Jenna. I spent the Sunday after lying in bed with her all day and watching TV. The emotions we shared with each other that day were profound. She helped me from completely falling off a mental cliff. She was sad, too, not only because she knew how much it meant to me, but she was also a part of the team. She was also a part of the dream.

I didn't want to go to school the next Monday, but my parents forced me into it. I woke up just in time, threw on a hoodie and sweatpants, and forgot about a shower. I basically spent the entire day staring into space and daydreaming. After I got done with class, I drove right over to Jenna's house. I no longer had practice after school. After playing the sport constantly for the last fifteen years, it was actually nice to have a break. It was nice to get out of school and not have to worry about rushing to practice. That obligation wasn't something that I missed. When the hockey season ended the past couple of years, that time was spent going on a beer drinking binge with all of my teammates. I never drank during the hockey season, and most of my teammates followed suit.

However, when the season ended, we made up for lost time. Mark would usually pick me up right outside of school with a case of beer in the trunk, and usually with a fresh can waiting for me in the cup holder.

Senior year was different, for me anyway. While Mark and the other boys continued the tradition, I had other priorities. I had Jenna. In her defense, she often encouraged me to go join them. She knew how important my friends were. It was my decision to decline the offers and stay with her. I liked going out with my boys, but I loved Jenna. I could live without a cold beer, but I couldn't live without seeing Jenna's smile when I walked into her room.

It may not make sense, but what I enjoyed with Jenna most was when we just laid and did as close to nothing as possible. That's basically all we did for the next month. I avoided most social situations. I ignored phone calls and letters from colleges and junior hockey programs. We just laid around together, watching TV or playing board games. Even though I valued my friendships and my future, nothing was more important to me than Jenna. Since we were together for so long, we experienced pretty much everything together. She was my best friend and the love of my life. At that point, she was all I had and all I cared about.

***

"How are you doing?" I asked her with concern.

"You know, you don't have to ask me that every single minute. I'm just fine." She responded while she grabbed my hand and locked our fingers together.

She clutched my hand firmly as if she never wanted to let go.

"Why did you want to meet the reporter here?" I asked.

I was referring to the Swanson cabin. It had been listed for sale for over two years now. It was a gorgeous property sitting atop the tallest point overlooking Shoreham Lake. It was on the east shore, so it was a front row seat to some of the best sunsets in Minnesota. It was especially picturesque that evening. Even so, the cabin couldn't find a taker. Most people in the area speculated that the price was much too high. Some thought that people didn't like being so elevated above the beach, perhaps too lazy to walk down a bunch of stairs. As for my theory, I always thought he was just a stubborn old man. Like anything else, everyone had their opinion. Andrew Swanson III, the property's owner, felt it was worth the steep price and hadn't budged on his number at all. Perhaps it just meant too much to him. It had been in his family since his father built it with his bare callused hands, leaving a rustic and nostalgic feel. His kids were all grown and moved away and his wife had recently passed away from breast cancer. The cabin was too big for one person and he was becoming too weary to maintain it.

Jenna and I had stopped there once a week, usually on Sundays, and sat in the yard on top of the hill. Because it was listed for sale, we felt safe trespassing on the property, even though no one would ever believe we were serious buyers. Mr. Swanson caught us once, but didn't say anything. He just waived and hauled a few things out of the garage down the path into his truck and drove away.

Like all couples who have been together for years, Jenna and I discussed our dreams together – lofty, if not grand illusions – and buying the Swanson cabin was part of ours. We shared and compared fantasies, hoping they would match. Jenna's theory on the steep price was because Mr. Swanson really didn't want to sell it and let go of all the memories. She thought that by the time we saved enough money to buy it, Mr. Swanson would be ready to part ways with it. For some reason, she boasted that she could convince him to sell it to us. With her charm, she was probably right.

"I want the interview here because he's bringing a photographer too. This sunset is beautiful." She answered confidently. "Besides, how often do we get a day like this?" She said with appreciation.

It was a rare warm and sunny day for early April in Minnesota. It was almost seventy degrees and the wind was perfectly still. She made me dress up in a gray cardigan and khakis, usually reserved for church functions. She was wearing her favorite pearl white sun dress, which was baggy from all of the weight she had lost, with brown cowboy boots that lined her calves. As she sat in my lap resting against a tall oak tree in the lake-side yard, we continued the small-talk.

A small lake town in central Minnesota, Shoreham Lake was nothing special from September through April. It was fairly dormant, with all of the common aspects of a small town. Home cooking and gossip were never in short supply, yet finding something to do other than drinking beer or going to church was sometimes a challenge. There were people who swore by just one, and some who seemed to worship both, ironically. However, from Memorial Day to Labor Day, the ice from the lake and hockey rink thawed and Shoreham Lake shot to life as a vibrant summer getaway. The population more than doubled in the summertime as city folks from all over Minnesota, the Dakotas, and beyond migrated to their cabins and cottages, usually passed down through generations in their families. People shed their clothing and occupied the sugar sand beaches in their bare feet. Kids worked on making sandcastles while adults worked on making hangovers. Girls caught a tan and guys caught footballs. It epitomized the summer life.

The town itself was built around Shoreham Lake, but a bunch of other lakes surrounded it – Minnesota is, after all, the land of ten thousand lakes. Shoreham Lake was surrounded by the seven sister lakes: Melissa, Sallie, Maud, Lizzy, Ida, Eunice, and Lida. Although it's impossible to prove or disprove, legend has it that an area farmer named the seven area lakes after his seven daughters many years ago in settlers' times. At the least, it's a good story, so people go with it. Shoreham Lake was farthest north, and served as the patriarch who looked over the seven sisters.

Jenna lived in town, just a few blocks away from the high school. Our houses were about five miles away, and it only took my trusty white pickup truck a few minutes to make the cruise. In the grand scheme of things Jenna and I came from the same side of the metaphorical tracks. We weren't a story about the haves and the have-nots, but my family had a little more than her's did. Jenna lived a charmed yet blue collar life. Her father, Walt, owned his own mechanic shop on Main Street, from which he made a decent living, but it required constant sweat and aching muscles to churn a profit. He provided a decent living for his family, especially his oldest daughter, Jenna, who he liked to spoil, but never admitted that she got preferential treatment over her siblings.

I lived on the south shore of Shoreham Lake. My family had a big wooden cabin style year-round home with the lakeshore on one side and vast rolling prairie and farmland across the road on the other side. The land was originally owned by my grandfather. After he passed away, my dad demolished the old house and built a newer and bigger house that covered the old lot plus the neighboring one. Our house was two stories with tall windows on the lake side. A balcony wrapped all the way around the house connected to a porch that expanded out towards the lake. It was a beautiful home. Like every home, ours had a unique smell to it. Ours was the smell of cedar wood, even years after it was built. Across the lake, you could see the Swanson cabin on top of the hill.

"Hi guys!" The reporter shouted as he marched up the lawn with his young colleague running to catch up behind him, trying his best not to strangle himself with his camera strap around his neck.

He was a tall man with jet black hair, oily and slicked straight back. He was wearing a dark blue suit and tie, with old light brown leather shoes which he tried his best to preserve by buffing every morning before leaving home. His protégé was young, probably no more than a year out of school.

I quickly stood up and helped my girlfriend do the same.

"Jim Callahan, pleasure to meet you." He said as he shook my hand firmly to make an impression and was noticeably gentler with Jenna.

We went and sat down at the wooden picnic table that rested on the porch. Jim had driven a few hours from Minneapolis. He heard about Jenna's story from his college friend who worked at the local paper in Shoreham Lake. You could tell he was ambitious, trying his best to make a name for himself in the journalism business, and he saw an opportunity for a human interest piece on Jenna. I didn't mind that he wanted to write about her. In fact, it was sort of exciting in a way. After all, Jenna's story was very unique, especially for our small town.

"How are you doing, Jenna?" Jim asked with what seemed like a manufactured sympathetic tone.

"You sound like my boyfriend!" Jenna replied as she rolled her eyes toward me with a smirk. "I've been doing well. There have been good days and bad days, but that's life," she continued. "Will, here, has been amazing," she said as she nudged her elbow in my direction. "He's been with me every single day in the hospital."

"So what do you guys do there every day?" Jim questioned, jumping right into the interview as he scratched notes onto his pad.

I shrugged my shoulders like the humble small town Midwestern boy that I was. I listened defensively to his questions, as I was kind of nervous for her.

"Well, we watch a lot of TV!" She said as we both laughed out loud and the reporter smiled and continued jotting in his notepad.

He continued to toss softball questions about her everyday life – cheerleading, school, and her boyfriend. He asked me a few questions, mostly about Jenna and a few about hockey. I tried my best to paint her in the best light possible, which wasn't very difficult to do. After about a half hour of questions, he wanted to get a little deeper.

"Jenna, pardon my bluntness, but do you ever wonder 'why you?'" He asked, trying to be as polite as possible.

This question made me more nervous. I wanted to interrupt because I didn't want to subject her to it.

"Honestly, I don't. I have an awesome family and

great friends. I have a boyfriend who loves me. People have been so supportive of me from day one. I think it would be kind of selfish to ask that." She responded.

My love for that girl beamed. Her words were so perfect. I wondered where they came from, as Jenna rarely spoke that deeply about her feelings or emotions. Then again, she never really had to. Jim smiled in admiration.

"Should we get a picture?" He asked as he wrapped up his questions.

"Sure," Jenna said as we both stood up and pressed our clothes.

"How's my hair?" She whispered to me quietly so the others didn't hear her insecurity.

"Perfect. You are perfect." I said.

I drove away with the Swanson cabin in the rear view mirror and Jenna in the shotgun seat. Because of her condition, she wasn't allowed to drive a car in fear for her safety. Therefore, I would drive everywhere we went. But on that day, she had no intention of following the rules.

"Pull over," she instructed.

Even after questioning her why and not getting an answer, I gave in. When I pulled over my truck, I looked over at her.

"What are we doing?" I asked again.

"Scoot over," she instructed with a devilish smile.

Even though I knew she shouldn't, I could rarely say no to her. I slipped over towards her as she climbed over me and into the driver's seat. Then she slammed it into drive and peeled away with gravel and dust flying up behind us. Later on during our road trip, as the sun disappeared and the moon replaced it, we pulled over and broke the rules yet again.

***

Over the next week, Jenna's health seemed to improve significantly. She had more energy as the spring air came through and the flowers started to bloom. As the lake thawed in certain spots, we couldn't wait to get on the water, so we dropped the canoe between the ice holes by the shore and just floated around. I couldn't count how many times we went on the lake together every summer. We both loved it out there. Even though it wasn't the same as on my pontoon boat, floating with her on that canoe with her head resting on my shoulder was all I needed. And later on that night, per usual, I went to her house to see that smile.

"Well, hello there, ma'am," I said with my best southern drawl impression as I peered into the doorway of her bedroom.

Jenna was laying in her bed reading a book. As I walked in, she smiled at me while she folded a piece of paper and used it to mark her page.

"Hi, babe," she said with a soft tired voice as she sat up straighter.

I walked over to her bed and got down on my knees. I put my arms and hands flat on the bed and rested my chin on my hands.

"How are you doing?" I asked as I always did, matching the softness of her voice.

"Better now," she answered with a smile.

I looked over at her nightstand and saw a copy of the article.

"Don't you know you're not supposed to read your own press?" I joked as she smiled along.

Picking it up, I looked at the picture under the headline, which featured me standing behind Jenna with my arms wrapped around her. I was slouched a bit with my chin resting on her shoulder. It could easily have been mistaken for an engagement picture. She had her perfect smile, one part of her that hadn't faded. In the background, although in black and white, was that sunset that she wanted, perfectly crafted by Mother Nature.

After staring at it for a few seconds, I commented, "You look beautiful."

"Well, you're no slouch, yourself." She answered.

"Happy Days?" I asked her.

"Happy Days," she agreed as she reached for the remote control.

We watched reruns of the show almost every night. Jenna had a TV in her room, which was rare back then. But her parents thought since she spent so much time in her bedroom, she should have a TV to keep her occupied. Jenna's room used to be in the basement, but they turned the upstairs den into her bedroom so it was easier to keep an eye on her upstairs right across the hall from her parents' room, and so she didn't have to walk up and down the stairs every day. We cuddled up for a couple of hours, reading the article and watching TV before she eventually fell asleep on my shoulder. Whenever she did that it made me feel so powerful, like I was watching over her, protecting her. I didn't want to wake her up, but in order to leave I had to move.

"Well, I should get going, it's getting late." I said as I sat up and stretched out my arms.

"Okay, have a goodnight, babe." She said as she woke up with sleepy eyes.

I leaned in and we shared a soft kiss before I climbed out of bed.

I grabbed her hand and slowly pulled it away as she tried to grasp it to make me stay. She always did that to me, and even though she did it playfully, it always made it difficult to leave her.

"I love you," I said as I turned and walked towards the door.

"I love you, too," she replied.

"Baby," she raised her voice so I could hear from the hallway.

I walked back into the doorway and asked, "Yeah?"

"I love you more than you love me. Always remember that."

I furrowed my brow a bit and smiled as I looked into her eyes.

"No chance. I'll see you tomorrow." I said as I walked out and made the drive home.

That was something that we said to each other since the first time I told her I loved her. We were fourteen years old and watching a movie in her basement. She said she loved me, too, one of the most exhilarating moments I can remember. After, out of pure nervousness, I blurted out "I love you more than you love me." Ever since then, we always had that battle back and forth like a game of tag. Until that night, we hadn't said it to each other in quite some time.

***

The next day I woke up later than usual. I dragged

myself to school, suffering from a bad case of senioritis, but I wanted to get to the library early to read the article again. It turned out to be very well done. It was centered on Jenna's unique battle. "While most students at Shoreham Lake High School were fighting to finish a paper before it was due, Jenna Johnson was fighting for her life," was the opening line of the article. It was nice to see her courage and unwavering optimism recognized.

Surprisingly I was included in the article multiple times. Jim was intrigued by our relationship. He referred to us as a "classic American love story" of a beautiful cheerleader and star athlete. Although I thought it was a little over-the-top, it was sort of flattering. Our relationship did in fact make perfect sense. We had been dating since Jenna moved to town in the eighth grade. We were high school sweethearts. It was a kind of relationship that looked and sounded right. We had common objectives. She was the first and only girl I ever kissed, and hopefully my last. Our relationship was admired by most and envied by a select few.

Just before the bell rang, I returned the newspaper to the shelf and walked through the hallway to my locker.

"Dude, we're going to be late for History." I said anxiously as I leaned against the lockers.

"Dude, it is History. It already happened and it's not going to change. It can wait," Mark quipped back.

I just shook my head, thinking of how he always had a justification for his antics. He was probably the sharpest dumb person I knew.

"I can't find my notebook. Maybe I left it at Scarlett's," he continued, seemingly ignoring my concern.

"Whatever, I can't be late so I'm going," I said as I walked away.

As I walked down the hallway with my usual swagger, I gave a few nods and smiles to my classmates. I quickly looked down at my watch and checked the time as I approached my classroom. When I looked up, Mrs. Erickson, the guidance counselor, was walking briskly towards me. As she approached, she had a serious look on her face.

"Will, can you come to my office?" She asked.

"Sure? But I'm going to be late for class." I said in a state of confusion.

"That's fine. Just come with me." She assured.

It quickly upgraded to a state of worry. I followed her to her office, wondering what I did wrong. As I followed her down the hall, a couple of my classmates stared, probably wondering the same thing. We approached her office and stepped inside.

"Have a seat," she said as she pointed to the chair.

I reluctantly sat down. Mrs. Erickson glanced out in the hallway and then walked towards her desk. She grabbed her chair and just before she sat down, she let the chair go and walked back towards the door.

"I'll be right back, give me a second," she said as she left the room.

What was going on here, I thought? I tried thinking back to anything I could've possibly done to find myself in her office. I thought it must be disciplinary since it was an unscheduled meeting. If it dealt with class schedule or future education plans, that was usually setup in advance. I was a good kid for the most part. I was an athlete and still managed to carry an almost perfect grade point average. I had never been arrested, although I did have a few run-ins with the police, but that ended by simply outrunning the blue lights or by pouring our beers out if we got caught. I had never been suspended from school, or even come close. I only had to serve detention once, and that was in fourth grade for having a friendly snowball fight at recess. I sat there trying to guess. Maybe it was something that Mark did.

Mrs. Erickson came in about five minutes later.

"Sorry about the wait," she said as she sat down

in her chair.

"I have class right now, so…" I began.

She interrupted, "I know, don't worry about it, we let Mrs. Jahraus know."

"Oh, okay," I said.

She sat there silent for a moment and I could tell she was thinking. At that point, I was downright baffled with confusion.

"Am I in trouble or something?" I asked as I sat up in my chair and shrugged my shoulders.

"No, heaven's no. Certainly not," she responded.

"Okay…" I said with a sense of relief.

"Will, I've never had to do anything like this before," she continued.

She was young and she had only been on the job for a couple of months and seemed in over her head at the moment.

"We just got a call from the hospital," she said.

My heart skipped a beat. I could see that she was nervous and her eyes started to well.

"Jenna passed away this morning."

3

"You are such a serious driver!" Jenna said with a sarcastic tone to her voice, not yet sure if we knew each other well enough to poke fun at me.

"What do you mean?" I quipped back with a little smirk, trying to hide my insecurity.

"Your hands are literally right at two and ten and your back looks like a stiff piece of plywood!" She replied with a laugh.

"They are not!" I said as I released one hand from the wheel and sort of slumped in my seat. "For your information, I happen to be a very good driver," I responded.

"Well that's great to know, my father would be so happy to hear that!" She continued with her sarcastic tone. "This is the first date he's ever let me go on."

"I'll stop this car right now and you can walk to the movie, how about that?" I said with a smile, joining in on her fun antics.

She smiled and turned to look out the window at the bright street lights. I kept looking forward, focused on the road even more closely after hearing about her father's *apprehension. All of a sudden, I felt her hand reach across the middle seat and grab mine. She interlocked our fingers and clenched like she never wanted to let go.*

***

My eyes opened. Both of my hands were gripped firmly at two and ten on the steering wheel, loosening quickly by my moist palms. My entire body was frozen. My mind was stuck on autopilot. The entire world around me was in slow motion. Or possibly paused altogether. I found myself sitting in my car outside of the school. Although it was still a little brisk outside, my pickup truck was hot inside because of the bright sun beating down on the windshield and the heat pouring from the vents from the cool early morning drive to school. My heart was racing and my gut was sunken. It was hard to breath. Beads of sweat fermented on my forehead. I felt light-headed, as though I was about to faint.

After Mrs. Erickson told me the news, I sprinted through the hallway, passed the commons area and out through the front doors to my truck. I ran as if the ground beneath me was cracking and splitting while trying to catch up with my steps. I didn't know what to do. I didn't know where to go. I didn't know what to do when I got there. No protocol is in place for a situation like this, especially for an eighteen-year-old kid. The ignition in my truck was on, but there was total silence. For a brief second I wondered if the entire thing was a dream. I was quickly reminded that it was not and snapped back to reality. But I still wasn't convinced it was true. It couldn't be. I just saw her the night before and she was doing great. Even though we knew it was a possibility that she could die within months, we all expected her to live a full life.

Eventually I forced myself to become present enough to drive. I drove carelessly down the four or five blocks to the Shoreham Lake Hospital, running a couple of stop signs at intersections that were empty. I drove right to the front doors of the emergency entrance and parked under the awning, swung open my door and ran inside while the swivel door slowed me down a bit. The woman at the reception counter stood up from her chair when she looked up and saw me walking quickly towards her. She could sense my panic by my breathing and sweating. Of course, she knew me from all the times I had been there.

"Second floor. Room 212," she guided.

I didn't even bother to thank her as I sprinted full-speed down the hall and turned the corner. I pressed the elevator button and it lit up. One second, two seconds, three seconds. Every second mattered. I pressed it again and again quickly, as if that would make the elevator move faster. Running out of patience, I pushed open the door to the stairs and sprinted up both flights, skipping a step on each stride.I sprinted again down the hallway, dodging one maintenance cart and a nurse sitting on a stool at a hallway station. All of a sudden, I saw Jenna's brother Rick standing partly in the hallway. His fist was covering his chin and mouth. He looked up towards me and his eyes opened wider. We didn't say a word to each other. He just grabbed and squeezed my bicep gently as I walked past him and into the room.

And as I walked slowly, almost tip-toed into the room, there she was. Nothing had ever been more real. My eyes opened wide, my eyebrows raised, and my face went ghostly white. I completely lost all feeling in my body. Her eyes were closed. She was hooked up to a machine. She was in a gown that covered her frail body. She looked so thin. Her hair looked dry and frizzy. It didn't have the fullness and bouncy curls that everyone was used to. Her mom, Mary, was sitting right next to her bed, holding her hand with one hand and massaging her arm with the other. She was crying. As soon as she saw me walk in, she stood up and started crying heavier as she covered her mouth with her hand. She was shaking.

She was shaking so much. She walked towards me and nodded her head before embracing me with a hug. At first, I didn't hug her back. My arms just laid at my side.

"When?" I asked.

After finally seeing her lying there, I had the answer to my first question.

"Almost an hour ago," Mary said, "she's at peace now, we are saying our goodbyes."

My face grimaced and shriveled. All of a sudden, I got a sick feeling in my stomach. My upper body collapsed and I put my hands on my knees to prop myself up. Mary pulled me up and hugged me again. I opened my eyes and looked at Jenna again.

"No," I said in disbelief.

"Yes, darling. Yes." Mary said while she tried to comfort me. "We'll give you a few minutes, darling."

She walked out of the room. Jenna's dad, Walt, walked past and put his hand on my shoulder. He didn't say anything, just nodded at me. I could see the tears behind his eyes and his fight to keep them back. He walked out with his family. It was just me and Jenna. For some reason, I was afraid to be with her alone. I didn't know what to do. I didn't know what to say. It was an eerie feeling, like she wasn't present, but hadn't quite left.

I was so scared. So alone. That was my sweetheart

lying there, lifeless. I gently touched her hand with my finger. It was a cold, almost rubber-like feel. I pulled my hand away and ran my hands through my hair. It was surreal, a twilight zone. I shouldn't be alone in this room, I thought. I couldn't get there fast enough and now I couldn't wait to leave. I could not stand to see her like this. Not like this. I hovered over her body and moved in slowly. I kissed her softly on the lips and then laid my cheek on her stomach. I embraced her. When I got up and began walking towards the door, I suddenly became light-headed and dizzy. Nausea came over me. Then suddenly, nothing but black.

***

Jenna was diagnosed with Cardiomyopathy a week before Thanksgiving of our senior year. The day after, she began doing most of her school work from a hospital bed or from home. She quickly traded in jumping up and down and waving her pom-poms for daily blood testing and reading sympathy cards.

Her battle lasted 140 days. A few weeks prior to her diagnosis, Jenna fainted while shooting hoops in gym class after complaining of spells of dizziness. No one thought anything of it and she came back the next day normal as can be. Over the next few days, the dizziness and light-headedness continued as she began to feel sharp pains in her chest. She had to skip a few cheerleading practices after school because her body was too achy and tired. We all figured she was battling a common flu or perhaps just fatigue and dehydration. She liked to keep busy and always had quite a bit on her plate with school, cheerleading, dance, and other extra-curriculars. Perhaps it was just stress that was transferring from her mind to the rest of her body, some speculated. After she fainted a second time a week later, we knew something wasn't right.

It happened at lunchtime. Jenna collapsed suddenly and hit the cafeteria floor while she was carrying her food tray to the garbage. Fortunately and unfortunately, I was not there to witness her lying on the ground with her tray and leftover food spilled around her. Immediately her friends gathered around her, followed quickly by the entire cafeteria. A teacher on supervising duty ran to the principal's office and called 9-1-1. It took her longer to gain consciousness the second time. She also seemed to remember less of what happened before she blacked out. She woke up in a daze while the emergency medical technicians were lifting her body onto a stretcher. They rolled her out of the cafeteria, through the commons area and the doors to the driveway where an ambulance was waiting. Before she could ask any questions, an EMT informed her that she had fainted and they were bringing her to the hospital.

Jenna was so confused and exhausted that she couldn't physically panic. But through the haze in her mind she was terribly worried. She just laid back and tried to stay calm as the EMT recommended. The back doors to the ambulance closed and the emergency lights and siren ignited. Within minutes, she was in a hospital bed with countless questions and zero answers. I drove to the hospital to be with her after I got word after class. After that, it was decided that it was best if she didn't go back to school for a while as a precaution.

The first thing the doctor noticed was how irregular her heartbeat was. It was no reason to panic, as irregular heartbeats are caused by all sorts of things. After some initial tests at the hospital in Shoreham Lake, she was sent to a larger hospital in nearby Fargo for further tests. Still so many questions. Still no answers. The doctors in Fargo referred her to Rochester, Minnesota, home of one of the largest hospitals in the country. I took the day off of school and made the drive down to Rochester with Jenna and her family. It was only a four-hour drive and I wanted to be there for her. Besides, I had built up enough goodwill with all of my teachers by that point that they excused me without even thinking about it. Jenna slept most of the drive. It wasn't out of the ordinary for her to take naps for three or four hours a day during those weeks.

The first day in Rochester consisted of more tests. I thought to myself, *How many more tests could she possibly go through? Why was it taking so long to figure out what was wrong?* It was irritating. The doctor told us that it would take about a day to get some results back, so we decided to stay the night. It didn't make sense to drive all the way home just to turn around and come back the next day. And rarely do doctors give results over the phone. So we stayed at the hotel across the street. We went out to dinner at the local diner. Jenna didn't eat much. I, on the other hand, devoured my only meal of the day. Earlier in the day we grabbed a snack for lunch at the hospital cafeteria, but that was about it. Jenna stayed in a room with her parents. I slept on a cot in the other room with Jenna's older brother Rick and her little sister Stacey.

Rick was the oldest sibling. He was three years older than Jenna and me. He worked at Walt's shop while he attended the local technical college. From a very young age, Walt was molding Rick as his eventual successor – for good reason, as Rick was a hell of a mechanic like his father. Not only was he naturally talented with his hands, he was educated.

Much to Walt's dismay, Rick occasionally would prove him wrong at work. At the same time, Walt was proud when it happened – a common dichotomy among master and apprentice. He was a great guy to have as your girlfriend's older brother. He wasn't the strict protective type. He was super cool. Of course he played hockey when he was in high school. In fact, we played together during his senior year when I was a freshman. He was also in my older brother Noah's class. They weren't best friends or anything, but they were decent pals. In a small town classroom, everyone is friends to some degree. Rick would occasionally hang out with Jenna and me at their house. He even bought us beer a few times and brought us to a few parties. He was a tall guy with thin blonde hair. He was a spitting image of his dad, minus the silver hair. But that would more than likely come with age.

Stacey was the last in line after Rick and Jenna and didn't come until three years later. Stacey was innocent and fairly quiet. She looked up to Jenna and they were close. But their relationship was more of a mother-daughter type than sisters. Jenna was protective of Stacey and was always looking out for her best interest. Jenna would dress her, do her hair, teach her how to apply make-up, and warn her off of boys entirely. Since Jenna was diagnosed, Stacey seemed a bit lost. And I know it hurt Jenna not being able to look after her as much.

All three children were obviously shaped by their parents. Mary stayed at home and raised Jenna and her two siblings. She kept the books for the shop and sometimes dealt with customers, since she had the niceness and sincerity that Walt lacked. But for the last few months, staying at home to take care of Jenna was a full-time job. Mary and I got along very well. She was an extremely nice woman. She was innocent and even a little naïve, which wasn't necessarily a bad thing. The truth is, in the crazy world we lived in, it was probably a good thing. Mary was always a joy to be around, always positive and upbeat and shelling compliments to people. Her face would light up when I came over. She was always looking for a fun activity, often times board and card games. When it came to more serious matters, she would defer to Walt.

Walt and I were not very close, but we were close enough to get by. Rarely did we have in-depth conversations; therefore we resorted to typical small talk. Perhaps our distance was because Walt had a son of his own and he had no room for another boy in his family. Perhaps he saw me as a threat to his first-born daughter, who was the prize of his eye whether he liked to admit it or not. Walt was a traditional protective father who thought his daughter deserved the best. Deep down he had a feeling of regret that at times he couldn't provide her with what she deserved. Although I was always respectful to everyone, I always felt he had his doubts about me. Even after a big game where I scored a few goals in hockey, it never seemed to impress him. He was mostly a cold, unemotional man who seemed to live his life with some sort of a chip on his shoulder. One could even go as far to say that he was bitter about something, which possibly had some connection to the calluses on his hands and the dirt in his fingernails. He was a blue-collar man – the type of man who built America. His tired demeanor followed him everywhere. His forehead was wrinkly and beard was usually un-kept. From what I was told, he was a former hockey star across the river in North Dakota, but didn't talk much about it. You would think that because a hockey player was dating his daughter, he would be excited to talk about the game he once played. Come to think of it, maybe that was it – maybe he didn't like being reminded of something he once was.

Jenna's parents and mine were cordial to each other and got along just fine, but I always had the impression that Walt seemed leery about becoming too close to my parents for some reason. My old man, the talker that he was, would constantly try to pry conversation out of Walt. It rarely worked. It was almost as if Walt would intentionally fight it. At times it was even painful to watch. Our families didn't spend holidays together or anything of that nature. But we all got together for our birthdays or random events such as Jenna's confirmation ceremony last year. It was usually my parents attending things for Jenna, rarely the other way around. Other than that, our families, especially our fathers, kept their distance for whatever reason. As long as they got along it didn't really matter to me.

The next day, we all gathered in the doctor's office. We waited and waited. Finally, the doctor came in breathing hard with flushed cheeks. He appeared busy. The job was obviously stressful on him.

"Okay, thanks for waiting folks, I'm sorry it took so long . . . " he said as he sat down.

No one in Jenna's family had ever heard of Cardiomyopathy, but they sat and listened to the doctor as he explained that it was a rare heart disease. Shock and disbelief filled the room as the doctor tried making a complicated subject less so. We were scared of the condition, but probably more scared of the unknown. He explained that Cardiomyopathy made Jenna's heart larger, which made it difficult for it to pump blood to the rest of her body. Eventually, it could lead to complete heart failure. At that point in Jenna's case, the disease had no cure. The doctor went on to explain that medication could help, but the optimism in his voice waned with every new sentence.

I was much too uneducated and perhaps naïve to understand the severity of Jenna's condition. Then again, maybe I just didn't want to understand it. At eighteen years old, I felt invincible. Problems were far and few between and if so were minor and temporary. Although I knew it was serious, I didn't know what to think. Maybe I wasn't thinking altogether. My biggest worry up until that point was my next hockey practice. When it came to stuff like this I was below novice level. Mary couldn't hide her deep concern. Her face tightened with worry.

"Doctor, is she going to be okay?" Mary asked as if she expected an answer in the affirmative.

I took Jenna's hand and squeezed her palm. It was my best defense at the time.

"Unfortunately, Mrs. Johnson, at this point there is no cure for Jenna's condition," the doctor replied in the most politically correct way possible.

"Well . . . what does that mean?" Mary asked, her concern escalating.

"Mrs. Johnson, there's no easy way to tell you this. Jenna will eventually succumb to this condition," the doctor inched closer to the truth.

"Well . . . what . . . " Mary tried to respond before Walt interrupted.

"Doc, shoot it to us straight. Please. What are we looking at here?" Walt put it on the table.

"Folks, Jenna is going to die from this," the doctor finally came clean. "It could be months, it could be years, it could even be sixty or seventy years from now, but eventually she will die from this."

The room went silent. The room went still. It was like a movie in slow motion with no sound. What did he just say? Die? This had to be a mistake. Was I dreaming? What on earth was going on?

Mary began to cry. Upon seeing her mother's tears, Stacey began to cry. Walt didn't flinch. He had to appear strong in front of his family, but there had to be fear behind those eyes. He was human. He was a father. Jenna was surprisingly quiet. She let her family ask most of the questions. We were both scared. All I could do was hold her hand.

Throughout the next five months or so, I didn't miss one day with Jenna, with many of those days taking place at the local hospital. Some would call it an obsession, some would call it crazy. I called it love. Truth be told, it was probably a combination of all three. I didn't realize it, but quickly my life changed drastically. My life shifted from playing hockey, going to school, and hanging out with the boys to solely Jenna's well-being. Everything I did, everything I thought about, was with her in mind. Those five months were the most difficult and challenging I ever experienced – or so I thought at the time. It was nothing compared to what I was to face ahead.

***

Suddenly, a bright white light came into focus. Where was I? Was this heaven? For a brief moment, I honestly thought it was. I honestly hoped it was. As crazy as that sounds, I hoped that I was dead. I hoped that somehow God knew that I couldn't live without Jenna, that just a few hours without her was too long, and it was time to rejoin her. Or at the very least, it would save me from this excruciating pain. Mary came in and quickly kneeled down by my side and helped me up. I was still dizzy and queasy. She walked me out and into the waiting room. I sat down and tried to gather myself. I was parched and needed water. Mentally I wasn't in the moment. I was somewhere else, but not sure where. It definitely wasn't heaven, but it didn't feel like earth. I was in emotional purgatory.

"Let's get you home, darling," Mary said as she helped me walk out.

Mary drove me home in Walt's truck. I was silent the entire ride. Walt followed us driving my truck. When we pulled into the driveway, I was still in shock.

"I called your parents from the hospital." Mary informed.

"They're in Minneapolis with my brother," I responded, with my first sign of sanity since I fainted.

"I know, we got a hold of them. They're on their way home," she responded.

I nodded my head with wide eyes as I stared out the front windshield.

"Do you want to come home with us until they get back?" She offered.

"No. I'll be fine." I assured her.

I stepped out of the car and walked into my house. I kicked my boots off and walked into the living room. It was silent. I was still dizzy, now tired. I plopped onto the couch and just sat. I just sat and stared. I wasn't even thinking. Just sitting. Just staring. Our dog, Colby, came in the room as his collar jingled. He sat at my feet with his chin resting on the floor. Even he had a sad face, almost as if he understood what had happened.

That was the longest car ride of my parents' lives. They felt so helpless. Their baby boy was in despair and they couldn't be there to console him. My dad drove about ninety-five miles per hour the entire way. He peeled into the driveway and slammed on the brakes. I heard them barge into the door behind me. They walked in and saw the back of my head behind the couch – sitting and staring. I didn't even turn my head. I just kept staring forward in complete shock. They walked towards me cautiously. My mom got on her knees on the floor and stared into my eyes. My dad sat next to me. My mom touched my cheek. There was something about my mom's touch that always told me it was okay to cry. I lost it. I completely lost it. I started shaking and tears started pouring out of my eyes. My body got the chills. My mom embraced me fully as my dad hugged us both. We huddled together and cried. We cried for me. We cried for them. We cried for Jenna. We cried for the world.

My mom tucked me into bed that night like I was a baby. She put a full glass of water on my nightstand, kissed me on the forehead, and shut off the lights. That was the longest night of my entire life. I dozed off for a few minutes at a time, waking up constantly. My stomach was sick and I often woke up in a pool of sweat. Fatigue eventually took over and I fell asleep for only a couple of hours.

***

I awoke the next morning early to the voices of my parents downstairs. Their voices were raised which concerned me a bit. I thought and hoped the whole previous day was a dream again, but the feeling in my gut reminded me it wasn't. I slowly got out of bed, my back and knees aching. I walked out of my room to the hallway at the top of the stairs.

"Do you have to go to work today, of all days?" My mom said in an angry voice.

"Yes, I do!" My dad responded.

"For God's sake, Bill, your son is heartbroken and he needs you," she said more sternly.

"I don't know what to tell you, I have to work," he responded.

"Bill, you are out of line," she fired back.

"I need to work because he needs to realize that life goes on and we need to get up when we get knocked down, that's what he needs." He said in a raised voice back to her.

"The day that my dad died, my brothers and I got up for work the next day. We worked the day of his funeral. Because that's what he preached to us," he continued.

"You are ridiculous! There are more important things in life than work." She said.

"You just don't get it. This isn't about work. This is about family. This is about my boys. And nothing is more important than that." He preached.

He stormed out of the house and slammed the door behind him. I turned around and went back into my bed. I laid back down, staring at the ceiling, which featured glow-in-the-dark stars that we stuck up there when I was a little boy. Those stars provided me with a light in the middle of the dark night. I thought back to those days. I was a kid with an imagination, simple and creative at the same time. My favorite book was *The Little Engine That Could* by Watty Piper, the tale of the under-sized and underdog train engine who, against all odds, believes in himself to pull a train over an insurmountable mountain while all the other powerful engines refused the mission. My mother would read it to me every night before bed – in this very bed, actually – sometimes multiple times over. On one night in particular, she became tired as she hunched over on the side of the bed while I lay in preparation of my dreams. Because I had heard the tale a thousand times at that point, she felt she could skip over a few pages to save some time. Even though I was falling asleep, I caught her immediately because of my familiarity and called her out. I needed to hear the whole story. Bless her soul, she went back and read every word.

Throughout the years, whenever I have faced

adverse times, my mother brings up that story. She relates that train's "I think I can" mentality to me. See, I have always been somewhat of an underdog, a dark horse if you will. I was never the biggest nor the fastest. I was never the favorite. Yet I've always felt something inside of me that was different than most – a burning passion perhaps, or a sentimental tendon that most don't have. It's often been a curse as much as a blessing. I just saw things differently. I felt things differently. I truly believed that I could do anything. I knew that I had to work twice as hard as others at times, but I did. I had a passionate and even obsessive personality when it came to things I wanted. It all started with that train. That train made me believe – not only in myself, but also in something bigger than myself. Getting out of that bed was the biggest mountain I had faced yet.

I turned my head to the picture of Jenna and me at last year's prom that stood on my nightstand. Senior prom was in a few weeks. Never in a million years did I imagine I wouldn't have a date. Senior prom is a notable event for anyone, let alone Jenna. She loved prom. She loved those type of events where she could dress up and socialize with people. Prom and homecoming were two of those events that Jenna always looked forward to. My gut wrenched thinking of her not being able to go. Finally, I got up, threw on a t-shirt and shorts, and walked downstairs.

"Did someone get a hold of John?" I asked as I sat down for breakfast.

"We're working on it, darling." My mom said as she poured me some orange juice. "Noah will be here tomorrow sometime."

John was serving our country overseas in the Middle East. He had been there for a year and a half. Before that, he was working for the family business, but eventually felt a calling into military service. It was a shock to all of us, but we were incredibly supportive of him. My mom was on edge and prayed for him every day twice a day. He and I sent letters every week. In one of his letters, he wrote that his biggest regret was missing my state tournament. He also said he was proud of me. I couldn't even begin to write how proud I was of him. My biggest regret was not standing next to him in his mission. John and I had a special relationship. We were both dreamers and we shared our dreams with each other often. We got that from our mom. He was maybe the only person who I could share my wildest dreams to without having him laugh, and vice versa. We had an emotional relationship and were very close. He was due to come home in just a few weeks for Easter vacation, so we weren't sure if he would be able to make it to the funeral. Even though I wanted him home, I understood. He had a job to finish.

My middle brother, Noah, was the brains of the family. He was a banker in Minneapolis. He was sharp as a tack, quick with numbers and finance. Noah and I were also very close. We had a very different type of relationship than John and I. Noah and I were very alike with practical things. We shared a common sense. We got that from our dad. We talked several times a week on the phone. Since he was just a few hours away, he called me immediately after hearing of Jenna and said he would be there as soon as he could.

My brothers were always there for me. They were my best friends, advisors, supporters, and idols. For some reason, they always let their little brother tag along. So I would. It often lead me into trouble, but, for the most part, it helped me grow up fast and tough. They always let me play hockey and other sports with their friends, but made it well know that if I cried, I was going home. Consequently, I ended up holding back a lot of tears when I was growing up. They never eased up or let me score. I played under the same rules as everyone else. That forced me to always compete with people who were bigger and faster than I was, which gave me an advantage as I got older. I learned more from them and their friends than I ever did in a classroom. I was fortunate to have one brother who encouraged me to dream and another who reminded me to wake up and pursue my dreams. Both were equally as cherished.

Mary stopped over later in the day to check on me and to grieve with my family. My mom fixed her a sandwich since she told us that she hadn't eaten anything since before Jenna died. We all sat in the kitchen and talked about Jenna. Even though it was still raw, we managed to talk about some funeral plans as well. The funeral was to be set for Friday. No funeral home or church in town was big enough to hold the wake the night before. The only place with enough seating was the high school gym, so that's where it was held. The funeral service was to be held at our church.

"Will, do you think you could say a few words at the service on Friday?" Mary asked.

"Like give the eulogy, you mean?" I replied with my eyebrows slightly raised.

"Well, if that's what you want to call it. I'm going to say a few words at the wake on Thursday night . . . and you know Walt, he isn't exactly a talker. You would be perfect. Jenna would want you to be the one standing up there," Mary continued.

I was caught off guard. I hadn't even thought about the eulogy, much less me giving it. Why would I think about something like that? Everything still seemed so surreal. My first thought was I didn't really want to stand up there and talk. I'm also an emotional guy, so I knew it was a long shot to get through the speech without choking up.

"I certainly can if no one else wants to, but are you sure it shouldn't be a family member?" I asked.

"Will, you know you are part of our family," Mary said as she put her hand on my shoulder. "You have been for years. At least think about it. It was Walt's idea."

It was Walt's idea? That pretty much blew me away. When she told me the request came from Walt himself, I could not turn it down. Even though we were never very close, I had a deep respect for Walt and felt extremely honored that he chose me to speak about his daughter's life. Considering our arm's length relationship, I was very surprised that he wanted me to do it. I always found myself seeking his approval.

"Okay, I'll do it," I decided right then and there as Mary smiled with sympathetic appreciation.

I had spoken in public before. I had given speeches in class on the Revolutionary War and a riveting biography of Johnny Cash for English class. We were told to pick a historical figure and I picked the man in black. I had given plenty of locker room speeches. I was a fairly outgoing person, so I wasn't that afraid of speaking in public. But I had never done anything quite like this. The funeral was in three days. I had three days to muster up a summary of someone's life. Not just someone, but someone as special as Jenna. The task seemed monumental, but I wasn't about to let everyone down. I felt as though I had done enough of that already. I was tired of letting others down, especially the ones closest to me. So I accepted the challenge. As we continued to talk for a while, all I could think about was that speech. I was completely focused on it. I was determined to deliver. In a way, it gave my life purpose again, if only for a few days.

The next couple of days were full of mourning. Jenna's family received countless sympathy cards. People brought over home cooked food. Flowers were delivered to their door and piled up in their living room. I never left the house, skipping school and basically everything else. I constantly had a sick feeling in my stomach and was overwhelmed with anxiety. The only thing that temporarily eased the pain was sleeping, so I laid in bed most of the time trying to fall asleep. That would screw up my sleeping schedule at night, so I stayed up a lot in the dark.

The night before the funeral was the wake service. It was extremely emotional, as hundreds attended and more than a dozen people shared their memories of Jenna. Members of her family, my family, our friends, and even a few unexpected people talked at the podium. I couldn't bring myself to do it. Besides, I was saving my words for the next day. I've never seen so many tears. I slept about an hour total that night. I thought about all of the memories shared and how Jenna had such an effect on so many people.

Since I was up anyway, I used the time to write the eulogy. Come to think of it, that probably contributed to my inability to sleep. I was nervous about it. The anticipation of the speech was unbearable. Where does someone start with a eulogy? How am I supposed to summarize Jenna's life in just a few minutes? What is appropriate to say? Should it have a sad, somber tone or one of appreciation and a celebration of her life? Would she be listening from up above? The expectations were weighing heavy on my heart. I've heard some eulogies basically give a history lesson on the person's life. I heard others that were more personal to the speaker. I'm not sure I was comfortable enough to speak about my emotions in public, especially something as personal as the love of my life. I knew of at least a couple of things that I wanted to share. I had to figure out how to fill in the rest. One thing I could do was write. I had always been a good writer, ever since I was little. I always preferred to write papers instead of taking exams. Once I got going, the words flowed.

I wrote for hours. I wrote about how we met, where we first kissed, our favorite places to go, our favorite things to do, the first time I told her I loved her, our loving, our fighting, our dreams. I think it served as therapy for me, writing things that I couldn't find the confidence to say aloud. By the time the morning came, I had about a dozen pages.

The morning came with dark overcast skies and fog. My mom knocked on my door to wake me up, only to find me sitting up in bed still writing. I snapped out of my writing coma and rubbed my eyes.

"You're up?" My mom asked in surprise.

"Yeah, I couldn't sleep," I responded.

"How are you doing?" She asked as she crawled into bed and sat up next to me.

"I'm okay," I said.

"How is the eulogy coming?" She asked.

"I don't know. I have a lot of material, but I'm not sure if it's what people want to hear," I replied.

"It doesn't matter what people want to hear. Just speak from the heart and tell them what they need to hear. You're going to do great," she assured me.

I appreciated my mom's encouragement, but it didn't help calm my nerves. I had a general idea of what I wanted to say in my head. The rest I finally decided to take my mom's advice and speak from the heart. I climbed out of bed and hit the shower. I stayed in there entirely too long as I just stared at the wall and let the water massage my head. I put on the hand-me-down suit from my brother, navy in color and far from form fitting. As the baby of the family, at least half of my entire wardrobe was hand-me-downs. I tied my tie as good as I knew how and combed my hair as I always had. It was time to face this. I went downstairs. My aunt was over helping my mom prepare breakfast. I joined my brother, Noah, at the table.

"Where's dad?' I asked.

"Oh you know, he had to do some work this morning," my mom responded as she put a plate of roasted breakfast potatoes on the table, one of my comfort foods.

"He should be back soon," she added.

We all sat down and ate while we talked about the day. A few minutes later, we heard my dad pull up in his truck on the gravel driveway. My mom got up and went outside for a moment. She came back inside and asked me to help him carry some boxes inside. I rolled my eyes and threw on some shoes and walked out the door. As I looked up, I saw my brother, John, unloading his bag from the back of the truck. He walked up towards me and we embraced. I was elated to see him. It was exactly what I needed at the moment.

Once inside, John and my dad joined us at the table. Apparently, John was granted a leave to come home for the funeral and jumped on a plane and flew across the globe to be home. He was only home for the weekend, but it was a God-send to have him there. It was really nice to have the whole family back together again sitting around the dinner table. It was a silver lining.

School was let out for the funeral. I sat up in the front row with Jenna's family, with my parents sitting right behind me, looking over my shoulder in support. The pews in the old church were narrow and uncomfortable. The oak seat bottoms were stiff. When you knelt down, your feet hit the kneeler in the pew behind. The altar was showered with all types of flowers and arrangements. It was like a beautiful greenhouse. In the middle of it all was her black casket, with a picture on an easel of Jenna hugging a picture of me in her hospital bed. No one told me that it was going to be on display, and it certainly didn't help calm my emotions. Although it was a generous act, it only made me think of how I could no longer have her back. The intentions were well-founded, but it actually made things worse.

When I stood up, the entire church was echoing with silence. All eyes were squarely on my back as I walked up the step to the altar area and onto the podium perch. My hands were shaking as I grabbed the folded piece of paper with my notes out of the inside pocket of my suit coat. I put the paper down and tried flattening it on the surface of the podium. My heart was beating out of my chest. For a second I thought I could hear my heartbeat through the microphone so I grabbed it to make it stop as it made a muffling sound throughout the church. I remained silent for a few seconds. I looked at my parents. They looked so worried. I looked at Jenna's parents. They looked so sad. I could feel a hot sensation running through my body that extracted through my clammy palms. The responsibility given to speak the last words of someone's life is a powerful and pressure-filled task. All eyes were on me and it put me in an extremely vulnerable position.

"'I love you more than you love me. Always remember that,' were the last words I ever heard Jenna Johnson say to me. No one else could have exited this world so gracefully. For those of you who don't know me, I'm the guy in that picture. I'm the guy she will always love." I said into the microphone.

The more I talked, the more I felt comfortable. In a

weird way, I slowly started to enjoy speaking on her behalf. I laughed when people laughed, and I shed tears when I saw other peoples' tears. The audience's engagement brought me comfort.

"No one in this room will ever be the same after knowing Jenna Johnson," I concluded, "This world won't ever be the same. But it's a better place because of her. I love you more than you love me, Jenna."

The cemetery was on the outskirts of town. The hearse led a caravan of vehicles through downtown, around the north side of the lake, and continued toward the edge of town. The last time I was escorted like that was just a few months earlier. On our way to the state hockey tournament, we had police and fire vehicles leading our bus out of town with their sirens blaring. People lined the streets cheering. Cars pulled over to wave and take pictures. The entire town was so supportive. We all felt like kings with that treatment. I loved that feeling. But this had a much different feel. It was a cryptic feel. It was a ghost town. The streets and sidewalks were empty. The entire town was probably at the funeral, most of them part of the caravan. I rode with my parents and brothers. Our car was third in line behind Jenna's family.

It was overcast with fog clouds dancing close to the ground and hovering over the gravestones. We walked across the dewy grass, passing gravestones with familiar last names. I think I recognized every single one of them. A rectangular hole was already dug in the ground. Jenna's brother and cousins served as pallbearers and they carried her casket towards the site and gently let it down on the springs that went across the hole. Everyone crowded around the site. A couple of kids were chasing each other around as their parents reached to rein them in.

Our priest, Father Mike, held out his arms and motioned for everyone to gather closely.

"Let us pray for our departed sister, Jenna," he said as he bowed his head.

Everyone followed suit by bowing their heads to the ground. I didn't. While Father Mike said the prayer aloud, I stood frozen. I looked around the site and examined everyone that was there. I looked at their faces. I wondered how they were feeling. Were they feeling the same pain as I was? I thought about their relationships with Jenna. The inner ring of the circle consisted of her close family. Her little sister Stacey stood there crying, clearly old enough to grasp the situation. Holding her hand was her cousin Hannah. Jenna and Hannah were best friends growing up in Oakwood, North Dakota until Jenna moved to Shoreham Lake the summer before eighth grade. Jenna's grandparents stood there, agonizing that it wasn't the other way around with Jenna standing by their graves. All of her friends stood there, still stunned, but trying to get as close as possible to the casket to say one more goodbye.

Eventually I tilted my head down and stared at her casket. Light reflected on the surface today, but what happens when it's dark? What happens when it rains? I thought about the prospect of rain falling down on her grave when no one was around. Sure, we were all here now. But after the service people would return to their lives. They may think of her occasionally, some more often than others. But we won't physically be here. We couldn't be. I closed my eyes for the prayer.

***

"Do you feel that?" Jenna asked.

"Feel what?" I responded.

"I felt a few raindrops. Maybe this was a bad idea." She continued.

"I don't feel anything," I responded as a couple big drops landed on my nose.

She started giggling. All of sudden a boom of thunder rolled. The skies threatened. Jenna yelped as showers started to sprinkle. We'll wait it out, I thought. I sure was wrong. My idea of a romantic picnic was a bust. Thunder rolled again as the rain picked up steam.

"Okay, I feel it now!" I admitted.

We quickly gathered the basket and our plates with wet sandwiches and set them on the grass. Our napkins fell to the ground and began to soak into the grass. I grabbed the blanket we had been sitting on and shifted closer to her and wrapped it around the both of us, covering our heads and protecting us from the rain. The rain poured on top of us. We put our foreheads together and smiled. I kissed her with my tongue, and I could taste the rain water rolling off her lips. Thunder rolled again and this time we saw lightning strike close by.

"Let's get out of here!" I exclaimed and she agreed.

We left everything behind and ran towards my truck hand-in-hand. When we got in, we climbed in the back seat and kissed and passionately lost ourselves in one another. It wasn't a bust after all.

***

My eyes opened as the prayer concluded. I could no longer protect her from the rain falling on her. That feeling of helplessness absolutely killed me. As the crowd broke, people gave each other hugs and some put roses on her casket before the undertaker lowered it down. I stayed until she was lowered to the bottom. My mom stood with me, taking hugs and handshakes, thanking people for coming. Father Mike also stayed. He stood across the grave and talked with folks but I noticed that he kept an eye on me. He walked over.

"Will, God bless you, my friend." He said with complete sincerity as he grabbed my shoulder. "Keep the faith."

I didn't know how to respond. I was still in shock over everything. I nodded my head in acknowledgment and walked away to catch up to my mom. My suit jacket waved in a wind gust that came through. I didn't look back.

Some family and friends gathered at the church parish center for lunch. I always found it kind of strange that people took the time to eat a meal together after a funeral. Someone just died and we sat and ate good food like it was some sort of a holiday. The ladies of the parish slaved away in the kitchen all morning to cook their usual hotdish and corn after spending the last few days baking every dessert imaginable. The entrance to the parish center had poster boards made by her friends with picture collages of Jenna, her friends, and her family. I didn't take the time to look at the pictures, but I imagine I was in a fair share of them. I walked with my mom to find a table amidst the clumps of people socializing and talking about how nice the service was. When I found a table in the center of the floor, I pulled out the steel folding chair as it scraped over the floor and took a seat. The last thing I wanted to do was work the crowd and small talk with everyone, collecting their pity. I had received enough over the past few days.

After eating, Mary and Walt asked me if I wanted my clothes and other stuff that was at their house. That was a very profound moment. It became clear that this was all real, and that my time as being part of their family was coming to an end. At first, I was sort of offended by the gesture. My fury boiled at the thought of taking back memories and pretending like they never happened. But as I thought about it more, what else were they supposed to do with my stuff? I often made the mistake of thinking that I was the only one struggling with her loss. I thought that no one could possibly understand what I was going through, when in reality there were other people suffering as well. When I walked outside to their car and grabbed the box from them, the sweatshirt that she always wore gave off her scent. The scent of a woman is powerful, and it's the damnedest thing to get out. It lingers. It evokes feelings you think you'll only feel once, yet they return with the scent every time.

The luncheon eventually came to a close. I was physically and emotionally exhausted from talking to people. My buddies came over and said their goodbyes. It was tough watching them leave because it made me feel even more alone. I could tell they wanted to get out of there. I don't blame them. I wanted to as well. I looked up at the old crooked clock that hadn't worked in years hanging between the heavy rug-like flags of the United States and the State of Minnesota. We finally left about a half hour later. The parish ladies were busy doing dishes and throwing away the uneaten food they slaved over hours earlier. My mom took some home to be courteous. We didn't talk much on the drive home. My mom made a few comments on people she hadn't seen in a while. When we finally pulled up to the house, we walked in the door and my dad threw his keys on the counter. I untied my tie and threw it on the couch. I unbuttoned the top button of my shirt that was choking me all day.

I was so exhausted. I walked upstairs and threw my suit jacket on the floor and flopped on my bed. As I laid on my stomach and the right side of my face, I looked at our prom picture again. Now what, I thought? When she died, at least people thought of her, almost as if she was still in people's lives. Now that the funeral was over, people would move on quickly with their busy lives. That is what depressed me the most. They say you don't know what you have until it's gone. Not in this situation. I always knew what I had and never took it for granted. I cherished every moment with Jenna, especially the last six months.

My mom came in and dropped off the box that Mary and Walt had given me. I got up and grabbed the sweatshirt and brought it back in bed with me. I put it up to my face and inhaled her scent. It brought me back in time and chills came over my body. I wondered what was next for me. I didn't have Jenna to look forward to seeing the next day. I didn't have hockey practice anymore. School was basically over as senioritis was in full form. I didn't even have the eulogy to focus on anymore. It was an empty feeling. I was on my way to a very dark place, a type of emotional prison. Against my will, I was being dragged in shackles down a long dark hallway to my cell. I couldn't stop it. The closer I got to my cell, the darker it got. The worst part about it was that I had no idea if I would ever get out. I didn't know my sentence. I didn't know my fate. The only thing I had was faith, as Father Mike told me to keep with me. Faith provided me with a faint light, but it was flickering and dimming more and more with every step. I finally got to my cell and laid on the concrete floor. In hopes of easing the pain for the moment, I closed my eyes and tried to fall asleep. It took me a while, but after the iron bars slammed shut, eventually I did.

4

"Marietta." Said Jenna.

"What?" I asked as I pulled my sunglasses down on my nose.

"That's what we should name our first daughter." She responded. "We can call her 'Mary' for short," she continued.

She was always planning for our future, which included coming up with names for our unborn children. She talked about having ten kids. I always thought two was enough, given that my mom had a handful with just three boys.

"Whatever you want," I said with a smile.

I always wanted her to be happy, so I frequently deferred to her desires. Even though we were sitting on our old lawn chairs on the beach outside my cabin, in our minds we were on a vacation on an exotic beach somewhere in Mexico, just the two of us.

"Marietta it is," I continued as I lifted my sunglasses back over my eyes.

"We call her Mary," Jenna responded with a smile before she closed her eyes again and soaked up the sun.

***

My eyes suddenly flipped open. I felt sick. My stomach was tight. My face constantly felt hot. My hands shook, my palms sweaty. Two weeks had gone by, and it felt like all I had done was lay around and sleep. Despite that, I was constantly tired. Sleeping was an escape from reality and escape from the pain. It also helped pass the time. I was on mental autopilot and I had no physical energy. Having already conquered my mind, Jenna's memory was sinking into my bones. I constantly used the bathroom yet rarely ate. I already lost eight pounds. Depression was sinking in and anxiety was pouring out. I often found myself hallucinating that Jenna was there. At night, during the rare times where I did sleep, she would appear in my dreams. It was a recurring dream, with Jenna and I sitting on old Adirondack chairs on the beach. Those dreams drove me absolutely mad every time I woke up and realized they weren't real.

I was completely broken.

For the first time in my life, I didn't know how to fix it. Jenna was always there to help me fix it. She grounded me. She provided direction. Jenna was my other half, and she was the reason I did anything. Everything I did was to please or impress her. She was my motivation. Without her, there was no fuel.

I'd never felt more alone. It felt like I was floating through the air with no gravity and no purpose. I completely lost any purpose for living. I had no identity. Demons were attacking me on multiple fronts. I always identified myself as two things: Jenna Johnson's boyfriend and a hockey player. At that moment, I realized I no longer fit either category.

My mind then drifted to hockey. From as early as I could remember, I was a hockey player. I was that boy who looked up to older players and then I was that leader that people looked up to. Growing up in Shoreham Lake, I was always aware of the ex-athlete whose glory days were behind him. Some of them were parents of my friends. Some of them were guys who graduated a couple of years before. Some were driving the Zamboni at the hockey rink. Some worked on area farms or factories. But after years of being the center of attention in an arena full of people, suddenly they had to pay for a ticket to get in. They often wallowed in those days and conceded early on that it would never get better. So often they didn't even try. It's a feeling I imagine every good former athlete, prize winner, record breaker, and even former presidents have. You're no longer a celebrity and people are less excited to see you. I was quickly finding out that the greatest enemy of accomplishment is time. Success diminishes as days goes by. I always thought that would never happen to me. Was I already becoming that stereotype? I was scared to death that the best days of my life were behind me. Perhaps it was unavoidable. Perhaps it's a phenomenon too powerful, and that's why it had so many victims. Who was I to think I could be different?

My mom knocked on the door but it was locked. I didn't answer, pretending I was asleep. I always wanted to be alone, but at the same time hated being lonely. I slowly became somewhat of an introvert. A few more hours went by. I played some music on my record player. I always enjoyed listening to music before, but it was during those weeks where I became passionate about music. I listened to a lot of my dad's old country records about life, women, drinking, and heartbreak – all things I could relate to. The lyrics made me feel the emotion of the singer. That connection was powerful.

"Will! The boys are here!" I heard my mom yell through the door.

My eyes popped open. I had avoided them for the past couple of weeks. I looked outside the window and the sky was a little dimmer. I had slept all afternoon. I heard heavy footsteps running up the stairs. I quickly got up, unlocked the door, and went back into bed.

"Sleep good, champ?" Mark asked as he and the boys stormed into my room.

I rolled over on my stomach and groaned into the pillow.

"Get up!" He continued as he slapped my foot hanging off the bed.

Nick went into my closet, grabbed a tee shirt and pair of jeans and threw them on top of me.

"You look like hell, man." Mark said.

"Gee, thanks," I replied with a groggy voice and my middle finger in the air.

I didn't like looking vulnerable or weak in front of them.

"You're welcome. Look, it's time to party. Let's get you out of here," Mark went on as the others agreed.

"No chance," I responded assertively.

"Dude, you can't stay in here forever," Mark proclaimed with a disgusted look on his face as he picked up a pair of dirty underwear from the foot of my bed and flung them on the floor.

At first, I thought it was a bad idea. It didn't feel right and I didn't think it would look right. But my room had become so stuffy. I thought it might be nice to get out and loosen up a little. Mark was right, I needed a release. I remembered how Jenna encouraged me during the last few months to join my buddies occasionally, so I figured maybe it was alright. I still factored her into my decision-making, wondering if she would approve of things.

"Alright, alright," I said as I sat up.

The three of us piled downstairs as I was still adjusting my shirt. My mom was sitting at the kitchen counter.

"Bye Mrs. Camps!" Mark yelled as I pushed him out the door.

Mark drove. In fact, Mark always drove. He was the first one of us to get his driver's license. That license was a ticket to paradise, a license to do whatever we wanted. And we cashed it in. We would cruise up and down Main Street, park it under the canopy at Eastside Drive-In, and cruise the back gravel roads to all the outdoor country parties. I'm convinced that Mark picked up girls just because he could drive. I always had Jenna, so even though I participated in the road trips, I was merely a spectator unless she came with. We made some great memories in that car, but it also got us in plenty of trouble. It got me grounded a few different times for missing curfew or coming home with beer on my breath. We had a few different run-ins with the police, but they didn't do much. They usually made us pour the beer out on the side of the road and sent us home. We would drive around with no rhyme or reason. The best part about his car was that the back seat had access to his trunk, where there was usually a cooler full of beer. Some called it booze cruising. We called it road-tripping. Whatever you called it, it consisted of driving around the back country roads drinking beer. It may sound boring, but there was nothing like it. It was just you and your buddies in a car, talking and jamming out to music – George Strait, Bruce Springsteen, Alan Jackson – you name it, all perfectly off-key. We were more worried about running out of beer than gas out there. A lot of our parties were held outdoors, usually in a field somewhere, so we would drive and have more than a few beers on the way there to warm-up. I usually enjoyed the road trips with the buddies more than the actual parties, except the couple of times Mark drove us straight into the ditch and got us stuck.

We pulled up to Pelican Point, a popular party spot in the middle of an abandoned farmstead. The bonfire was already going and we were already buzzing. There were about a hundred people already there, pickups backed up to the fire to provide tailgate seating. We walked up to the party with our usual swagger. I always had more confidence when I was with my boys. I was greeted with hugs and high fives. People expressed their sympathies, which was nice, but I also hated that type of attention. Nevertheless, it felt good to dip back into the social scene.

Later in the night, across the fire, I noticed Alisha Anderson. In between taking pulls from the community Vodka bottle and stealing a guy's cowboy hat, she would peer over at me curiously from the corner of her eye. She was wearing her usual tight jeans and cowboy boots. Alisha was in our class, so I had known her since we were little. Jenna and Alisha were never very fond of each other, but they got along to each other's faces. Alisha always seemed to want everything that Jenna had, which included me. Jenna and her friends envied Alisha a bit as well even though they would never admit it. Alisha's father was a wealthy farmer who owned land all over the tri-state area. Her dad and my dad were good friends, and they often joked in the early days that their son and daughter would marry someday. Alisha seemed to buy in to the potential arrangement. I never did. Alisha always had the newest and most expensive clothes and jewelry. She drove a brand new Ford Mustang, quite the scene when she rolled up to a small town high school. I don't think she had ever heard the word "no" in her life. Girls also envied the fact that she developed physically before all of them and continued to flaunt it through high school. She spent most of the summer days in her bikini, lying out on the back of different guys' boats. She was a fun girl, but she was trouble. A lot of different guys experienced both with her. One thing that no one could deny, though – she was really hot.

We made eye contact and she started to strut around the fire over to me.

"Hey, Will." She said as she hopped up and sat down next to me on the tailgate.

"Alisha, how goes it?" I said with a drunken slur.

"Not great. I miss Jenna. How are you doing? I've been thinking about you so much." She said.

I knew she was lying about the former but probably not the latter.

"I'm hangin' in there," I answered as I raised my beer and took a drink.

"Oh my gosh, I can't imagine what you are going through." She said as she took a drink out of the liter of vodka and then motioned the bottle over to me.

I declined politely by shaking my head. I didn't want to tell her that the last inch of it was mostly backwash. I just looked at her. Her platinum blonde hair was parted in the middle and waved along the curves of her face. Her cheek bones were defined and she had a slight dimple in her chin. She looked at me and we locked eyes. Her green eyes were seductive and her raspy voice was tempting. She had full pouty lips with a small mole on the tip of her nose. She cracked a little smirk. I knew she wanted to be seen talking to me.

"I'll be just fine," I assured her.

"If you need anything from me, just let me know." She said as her hand touched my thigh. She grabbed my cup out of my hand and took a drink, her eyes peering over the cup.

The buzz from the beer was starting to really kick in. Or maybe it was her spell of lust. Either way, I just looked at her and didn't say anything. She hopped down off of the tailgate and started walking away.

"And Will . . . " she turned her head and looked back.

I nodded towards her in response.

"Anything, anytime," she said with a smile and walked away as her legs bounced in those tight jeans.

I raised my eyebrows, shook my head, and took a large gulp of my beer. Right after, Mark came over and leaned up against the tailgate with his devilish smile.

"I couldn't help but notice . . ." he started.

"No." I interrupted.

"What?" He exclaimed.

"No." I repeated. "Don't even start."

"Okay, okay!" He said, continuing to smile. "Well if you're not going to pursue God's work of physical perfection, then you won't mind if yours truly gave it an ol' try."

"Go for it. Be my guest." I offered.

"Watch and learn, champ." Mark said as he walked briskly towards her.

Of course, he knew that I knew that they had a brief history – a few different times. But Mark didn't have enough money to satisfy her expensive taste. A couple of experiments with the underprivileged resident bad boy was all she wanted. I watched as he whispered in Alisha's ear, no doubt a recycled cheesy line. She playfully pushed him away before turning to one of her girlfriends. It appeared she intended to leave their history as just that. I couldn't help but laugh inside. He would probably end up sealing the deal later, I thought. Rejection didn't faze Mark. And come around three o'clock in the morning and a few drinks later, Alisha would probably be coming around.

We continued to party for a few more hours. I'd be lying if I said I didn't have at least a little fun. It was sort of a breath, albeit small, of fresh air. I caught up with some friends that I hadn't seen in weeks. Everyone seemed genuinely happy to see me out and about. We played cards and quarters. I lost a few games, shotgunning a beer for my penance. I talked hockey with the boys and school with the girls. My cousin, Vanessa, was there and it was great to get a hug from her. I took a shot with Cliff, the much older guy who somehow always seemed to find his way to our parties. We didn't mind it, since he usually bought alcohol for half the party and he was a good guy. Since a lot of the older guys had moved away, he found friends in us younger folk. During the hockey season, I only saw him at our games, but during the summer, we actually hung out a decent amount.

As three o'clock in the morning rolled around, we were still going strong. People were starting to pass out and cars were starting to drive out. We kept throwing pallets on the fire, sparks flying up as the flames got higher. Around four o'clock, most of the others left. Mark, Cliff, Nick, TJ, and I stuck around. We sat around the fire, polishing off a few more beers and listened to Mark play a few songs on his guitar. We talked more about hockey. At times the talks got emotional as we looked back at all of the good times we had the past four years. Cliff had gone through what we were experiencing, so he chimed in about how he dealt with it. We all seemed to be avoiding the future at that point.

"You want to head out, champ?" Mark asked from across the fire.

"No, I don't." I responded as I threw a wood chip into the fire and gulped my beer.

It was a rare answer from me, as I was usually the one who liked to go home early. I always had Jenna as a reason to go home. But I just didn't want to go back to my depressing bedroom alone. I was like a convict escaped from prison, and I didn't want to go back. My buzz was in full force, my eyes glossy and speech slurred.

"Neither do I," Mark said with a smile.

"Man, Will, you're a lot more fun without Jenna around," said TJ.

The other guys went silent. I squinted my eyes as I looked over at him in disbelief.

"Oh, shit, dude, I didn't mean it like that." TJ said right away. "I was just . . . shit."

I took the last couple drinks of my beer and tossed the bottle into the fire. I stood up and started walking away. I put my hands in the front pockets of my jeans and walked.

"Dude, come back!" TJ said.

"You're an idiot," Cliff said shaking his head at TJ.

"Let him be for a bit, we'll pick him up on our way out," said Mark.

TJ buried his head in his hands in shame. In his defense, he probably didn't mean anything by it. That was just TJ. No one ever accused him of being the smartest guy in the room, and he frequently made gaffs like that. But he was an innocent guy.

Nonetheless, it snapped me back to reality – Jenna was gone. No matter how much I drank and partied, she was never coming back. A feeling of guilt came over me for having fun and not thinking about her for a while. I knew the boys would eventually come pick me up. I just needed to be alone for a while.

"Champ, get in," Mark said as they pulled up alongside of me a few minutes later.

I kept walking, not knowing where I was going. I knew that Mark wouldn't leave me walking in the middle of the country by myself, so I eventually gave in farther down the road. TJ gave me the front seat and handed me a bottle of whiskey. No one said anything as I got in and took a pull. Mark turned up the radio and we cruised towards town.

"I don't want to go home," I said as we were approaching town.

"You want to crash at my place?" Mark offered.

"No. Bring me to her." I demanded.

Mark took his eyes off the road and looked over at me.

"Her?" He asked.

"Yeah, her." I responded as I turned and looked at him with my bloodshot eyes.

"I don't think that's a good idea right now," Mark responded with a rare moment of clarity.

"Bring me to her," I insisted as I looked forward.

"Alright, champ," he conceded, but with hesitation.

We drove around the west side of town and slowly pulled into the cemetery. Mark turned off his headlights so no one would see us. We drove past the gravestones. The other guys were leery.

"Over there," I instructed.

We pulled up and stopped next to the site, with fresh sod planted around the newly minted stone. Grabbing a couple of fresh beers out of the cooler from the trunk, Mark and I stumbled up to the gravestone as the others stayed in the car. At this point, I was a little nervous. My face was ghostly white. I was so drunk that I could barely walk on my own. I grabbed my buck knife from my pocket and flipped the blade open. Mark backed up a step and was on guard. My hand was shaking with the blade in my grasp.

"Will, what are you doing?" He asked as I stood at him with my glossy eyes.

***

Turning and looking towards the gravestone, I punctured the bottom of my beer can and handed the knife over to Mark. He did the same. We both raised our cans slightly and looked at each other. We both put them up to our mouths and cracked them open.

The beer flowed down my throat as I closed my eyes. I chugged the whole thing within a few seconds. I became extremely light headed as the beer flowed into my body. I dropped the empty can onto the ground and fell down behind it. I crawled close to the gravestone, barely awake. The grass was cold. After a brief moment, I passed out.

Mark looked at me and didn't know what to do. His eyes grew wide with fright. He walked back to his car and rummaged through his dirty trunk. He pulled out his sleeping bag that he kept in his trunk so he could crash anywhere on any given night.

"Take my car home, I'm staying with him," he told the others.

"We'll crash in the car," Nick said, "TJ is already passed out back here, anyway."

Mark unzipped the sleeping bag and laid down next to my limp body. He put the sleeping bag over both of us. Mark was worried for his friend. He knew that I was troubled. He didn't know what to do, but he knew that he had to help me somehow. For the first time since he was forced at Sunday school as a kid, he prayed. He wasn't religious, and he certainly never prayed. But now when he had no other hope, he turned to God. It's amazing how people turn to God and prayer when they have nowhere else to turn.

"Please, God. Help my friend." He said to himself.

"Help my friend." He repeated as he slowly fell asleep.

***

Mark was my best friend since we were in kindergarten. We were in the same class and we did pretty much everything together. I was always the more straightened arrow and he was a little rough around the edges. Ironically, I was the one who usually had it figured out and he was the one constantly searching. That was probably because we had very different upbringings. Unlike me, Mark came from very little money, and his parents didn't exactly exude family values.

For much of his childhood, his dad, Mark Sr., was a struggling farmer. He never could quite make it work. He barely made ends meet, but eventually he hit a few unbearable years and ultimately surrendered it to bankruptcy. Mark Sr. never fully recovered from that day.

During the farming years, Mark's mom, Candace, stayed home and took care of Mark and his sister. She put Mark in piano and guitar lessons and encouraged him to pursue music. He took to it at a young age and was really good. He would perform all over the area – at bars, county fairs, his living room – wherever someone would listen.

But as Mark Sr. and Candace's relationship strained, it was often contentious, and when the farm went under and fighting became a daily occurrence, Candace had enough. Mark and his sister often got caught in the middle of it and probably saw some things they shouldn't have around that time. During the four days surrounding the last broken straw in the relationship, Mark was nowhere to be found. He didn't come to school. He didn't show up for hockey practice. He disappeared. I tried calling the house a couple of times and no one answered. Both our teachers and coaches asked me where he was every day because they figured I was the one who knew, if anyone did. I gave the same response every time as I shrugged my shoulders, raised my eyebrows, and told them I didn't know. When he eventually resurfaced, he never said a word about it. He just showed up for school in the morning and went about his business as usual. And as much as I wanted to know what happened in those days, I never asked. Come to think of it, it's probably for the best that I didn't know. We just went on with our lives. Three days later, his mom filed for divorce.

After the breakup, Mark would bounce around from both of their houses, but probably logged the most hours at our house. My parents were his secondary parents, often times serving as primary. Mark and I played hockey together since we started as young kids, even though his family had to borrow money to put him in the sport. My family would take him on many road games when Mark Sr. and Candace were absent. Mark Sr. would disappear for days at a time. When he was home, he was busy drinking or searching for jobs. Candace, who turned to smoking cigarettes and watching TV, would occasionally tend to her kids when it was convenient for her. After sulking in her own pity for a while, she finally got a job selling houses.

Mark played hockey and took it seriously, but never poured everything into it like I did. His main passion was music. When things with his family went sour, he continued to play guitar and write songs. He mastered the craft all through high school, as playing music consumed most of his spare time. Women were attracted to him as the bad boy athlete with a guitar, and he took advantage of it. In between the other girls, he dated Scarlett on and off throughout high school, but it never got very serious, if you ask him anyway.

Even though we came from different places, our friendship fit together perfectly. He pushed me over the edge when I needed it, and I pulled him back when he needed it. Mark and I would find trouble occasionally, but it was innocent and minor for the most part. When we were in eighth grade, we had our first beers together. It was mainly Mark's idea. It wasn't exactly a well-organized heist, but we managed to steal six beers from Mark Sr.'s basement fridge. Mark Sr. was passed out on the couch watching TV, and we quickly grabbed some cans of Grain Belt Premium Beer, stuffed them in our sweatshirts and skirted quietly up the stairs and out the door. Whether Mark Sr. didn't know or simply didn't care, we got away with it. In fact, later on, he sometimes let it happen in order to win Mark over. I had two older brothers who drank beer, so I didn't see anything wrong with it. Although because of them, I probably started out a lot earlier than they did. On the flip side, I tried my best to keep Mark in line when it came to school and overall manners. But no matter what, through good times and bad, Mark was always by my side – even if it was on a cold, wet ground in the middle of a dark cemetery.

***

The next few weeks were more of the same. There was no doubt I was suffering from some degree of clinical depression, which sank in deeper and deeper. However, I was trained by the school of hard knocks. My father did not believe in such a thing. He had an alternative diagnosis for depression – life. His remedy was being tough and getting over it. He had an old school, boot strap mentality. Nevertheless, I would mope around the house and school. I didn't do much socializing. I didn't talk to my buddies very often. I would sometimes skip classes and then go home and lay in my bed. My buddies invited me to do things and I had no interest. I was always too tired. I ate very little and was losing more weight by the day. Sometimes I would lay in pure silence, sometimes I would play some records. I had so many thoughts and feelings that I would write some of them down in a pseudo-journal. I was crying for help on the inside, and then wondered why no one heard me.

After a couple of weekends without hanging out with my friends, or doing anything really, my mom got concerned. The following Saturday, Mark called the house and asked if I wanted to come over to his house, as he was having a few people over. I politely declined and my mom overheard me. After I walked upstairs and crawled back into bed, I heard knocks on my door.

"Yeah?" I answered.

"Will, can I talk to you?" My mom asked as she walked in and sat down on my bed.

"What's up?" I asked.

"I see Mark called. Why aren't you going over there? It's Saturday night." She said.

"No, I don't really feel like doing anything tonight." I responded.

"You haven't done much in weeks, honey. I am worried about you." She stated.

"I'm fine. I just don't feel like going out tonight." I said.

"You can't keep doing this to yourself, you need to try get back to a normal life." She demanded.

"Normal? Nothing about my life is normal anymore," I shot back.

"Honey, I understand you are hurt. But you have to try." She reiterated.

"No. You don't understand!" I raised my voice as I climbed out of bed. "You want me to try? Well guess what, I am trying. I'm trying to figure out what I have that is worth living for anymore." I continued as I stormed out.

"Will, get back here!" My mom yelled.

I ran down the stairs and slammed the door behind me. I hopped into my truck and peeled away as I turned up the radio. If my mom wanted me to go out, I was going out.

I pulled into the yard and parked on the grass. There were a handful of cars in the driveway. I knocked on the door. I could hear music coming from inside. No answer. I walked around to the living room window. I saw Cliff in the window dancing with a few girls. I knocked on the window and he finally heard me. I motioned to the front door.

"Willy!" He said with cheer.

"What's going on, my man?" He asked.

"Hey man, I don't want to bother you, but could you pick me up a case of beer?" I asked as I peeked inside at his little party.

"Sure, I can do that for you. Or you could just come in and join the party," he offered, "plenty of beer here."

"Na, I don't want to crash the party. I just need a case and I'll get out of your hair." I politely declined.

"Nonsense. At least come in and have a few and then we'll go get you some beer." He countered.

I looked around outside as I pondered his offer.

"Alright, that's cool." I finally gave in.

I walked in and recognized a few people. A couple of the guys were around my brother's age. They were hockey players so I knew them. I grew up watching them play. I didn't recognize any of the girls.

"Will Camps," said one of the guys as he handed me a beer.

"We're just about to take a shot of tequila. You in?" He asked.

I had to make a decision on whether I was going

to fit in or not. *I have nowhere else to go*, I thought. Besides, a part of me still looked up to these guys. I wanted to impress them.

"Line 'em up," I said.

What was supposed to be one shot turned into about a dozen. When I wasn't taking shots or getting another beer, I would just sit on the couch and watched the baseball game on TV and the older girls dancing. We took shot after shot of tequila. The guys shared old hockey stories and lit up smokes. I passed on both the memories and the smokes. I just drank and listened. After a few hours, I was beyond drunk.

"The End?" One of the guys yelled from across the room.

All of the girls cheered and started walking towards the door.

"Absolutely!" Said Cliff.

I figured that was my cue to leave. I got up off the couch and could barely stand. I looked at the clock, and even though my vision was blurry I could see that it was almost eleven o'clock. I had been there for hours.

"Willy, you in?" Cliff asked.

"Na, I better get rolling. Besides, I can't get in the bar anyway," I said.

"Don't worry about it, bro. Janet works there. She will get you in." He responded.

"Oh definitely, just stick with me, cutie," said a girl by the door, who I assumed was Janet.

I was about as drunk as I had ever been in my life. I usually tried to stick to only beer, so the tequila was another level. And I didn't eat dinner. My judgment was clouded and I didn't care.

"Shotgun," I proclaimed.

"You son of a bitch!" Cliff said in a joking tone. "Let's rock & roll, boys!"

The End was a dive bar off of County Highway 11, just off of the lake. Even though the neon light turned off at two o'clock in the morning, it was the bar that never closed. It had a pool table and not much else. The crowd was anything but mainstream. I tailed Cliff and the crew inside and no one even blinked an eye. We took over the pool table and set up camp at the big round table in the corner. It had a spinning table top. Cliff ordered a round of shots and beers to kick it off. Then we played a game where a shot was placed on the round table top, a person spun it around, and whoever it landed in front of had to drink it and then buy the next shot of his or her choice. It was essentially a more sophisticated spin the bottle, although it didn't have much sophistication to it. We must have played fifteen rounds, and I was the winner – or loser, however you looked at it – about five or six times. Luckily, I didn't know anyone in the bar so I could be discrete, or so I thought.

My local celebrity status did me in. Multiple people came up and talked to me, mostly about hockey. They knew I was underage, but they didn't seem to care. In fact, a few of them bought me drinks. Some were old farmers, some were old hockey players. One older gentlemen brought up Jenna and how tragic it was. He looked sort of familiar but I couldn't quite put my finger on it. I didn't really want to engage in that type of conversation at the time, so I thanked him for his sympathies and went on my way.

After another hour, I could barely walk or talk. I had never been that intoxicated. I stumbled from the bar back to the corner table and fell into a chair and onto the ground. Everyone laughed as someone helped me up into the chair. I had no choice but to join the crowd and laugh at myself. All of a sudden, a new pack of people stumbled in the door. Even though I was inebriated, I could recognize that body from a mile away. It was Alisha Anderson. She spotted me right away and had a surprised look on her face. She screamed my name and ran towards me before plopping onto my lap and taking a swig of my beer.

"I'm so happy to see you!" She said as she came in

close and nuzzled her nose against mine.

I must admit that I was sort of relieved to see someone that I knew, especially my age. She had also been drinking quite a bit from the looks of it.

"What are you doing here? I've never seen you in here before." She said.

"Just partying," I answered with a slur, pretending it wasn't a big deal.

We exchanged a few more drunken pleasantries. At one point, I looked across the table and Cliff winked at me in encouragement. I passed out for a few seconds and Alisha woke me up by grabbing my jaw.

"Hey sleepy head, wake up," she whispered.

She lifted my chin with her hand and leaned in for a wet kiss. By this point, all of my judgment and feeling went out the window. We made out on the chair for a few minutes until she pulled me up and I followed her to a random door with an "Employees Only" sign on it. We stumbled down the stairs to the basement storage room. She jumped up on a pallet full of cases of beer and pulled my head in as she leaned towards me. We continued for a few minutes. She pulled her shirt over her head and threw it on the ground. I just stared at her with my glazed eyes as she ran her hands threw my hair. It felt so good to feel something again, even if it was just lust. At least it was something. She lifted my shirt off and we continued for another few minutes, feeling each other up and down. She began to unbuckle my belt.

All of the movement suddenly started to make me dizzy. I could barely keep my eyes open, the spinning sensation suddenly making me violently sick. I was losing control. I had to get out of there. I backed away a few steps and looked around for a bathroom. I didn't see anything. I quickly stumbled up the stairs and busted open the door to the bar and ran outside, presumably quite the sight running outside with my shirt off and belt unbuckled. The second I was outside, I immediately went to my knees and started puking. I didn't think it was humanly possible to puke that much. I couldn't stop, with one heave after another. Cliff came outside with one of his buddies and laughed at the sight. They encouraged me to get it all out and Cliff took off his shirt and put it around me. He had a beater tank top on underneath so he didn't care. I let out one last hurl and finally gave up. I fell to the ground and rolled over on my back. I caught a quick glimpse of the stars, and after a moment, I blacked out.

***

"I thought you said we were supposed to be able to see the Northern Lights tonight. I don't see anything." I

complained.

The sky was midnight blue and clear of clouds. The stars were so bright they were almost blinding if you looked straight at one. But the rare, explosive green and pink lights in the sky were nowhere to be found.

"Just be patient," Jenna lectured.

"You know that's not one of my talents," I responded.

We laid on our backs on my pontoon in the middle of the lake, looking at the sky. We waited for a couple of hours. The only sound was the gentle water bumping against the bottom of the boat.

"This is a waste of time," I complained again.

"No, it's not," Jenna responded as she grabbed my hand and rested her head on my chest.

Like usual, she was right.

***

I awoke with my face buried in my pillow. My left eye was sticking out and it took a few seconds for it to get into focus, like a camera lens adjusting to get a clear picture. Where was I? It took me a second, but I recognized I was in my bed. My forehead had a rhythmic pounding. It was if I had just awoken into a brand new world of the unknown. I was hot and sweaty, still fully dressed in an unbuttoned shirt that wasn't mine and jeans with my belt unbuckled. I had one boot on with the other nowhere to be found. I sat up slowly and peeled off the shirt, struggling as it stuck to my body. I stepped out of bed and my head pounded harder. I got so light headed I almost fell back in bed. I had no idea how I got home.

As I went into the bathroom, I slouched my back and braced my hands on the sink. I stared into the mirror for a few seconds, my eyes bloodshot, hair matted on one side, and the lines from my pillow impressed on my face. I wiped off what appeared to be lipstick from the corner of my mouth and what I was positive was puke from my chin. I dazed out for a few seconds and then snapped back to reality. I bumped the sink on and put my head under to catch a drink, too lazy to go get a glass. As I drank, I turned my head into the stream and washed the side of my face. Then I stood back up and stared at the mirror once again with water streaming down my face and onto my bare chest.

Afterward, I walked down the hall and into the living room. My parents were at church so the house was empty. A feeling of guilt settled into my gut. They didn't wake me up for church, so I knew it was bad. If they were just mad, they would've woke me up and made me go. Although I probably didn't want them to see me in the state I was in, I also didn't want to be alone. I walked into the kitchen and noticed a stack of mail on the counter. I sifted through it to see if any was for me. There were a few letters from college hockey programs that I left unopened. The envelope at the bottom of the pile did not have a return address, but it had my name written on it. With my curiosity sparked, I tore it open with my index finger. Inside was a handwritten letter.

> *"Hello my friend. I read the touching story of your girlfriend in the newspaper. I am very sorry for your loss. God also took the love of my life far too soon. There are no words that I can write or anyone can say to make you feel better. Yet I promise you, this will eventually make sense. You may think your life is over, but it's really just beginning again. Keep the faith and God bless.*
>
> *Sincerely, Drew."*

Who the hell is Drew? I didn't know a Drew. And there was that word "faith" again. I found the letter random and strange. I re-read it a few times. I had no idea what to make of it. I looked outside as if someone was watching me. In the process, I thankfully didn't see my car. I had been dumb that night, but thankfully not dumb enough to drive home. Cliff and the guys must have driven me home and carried me inside. If I knew my parents well enough, they would go out for lunch after church. I was on my own. I also didn't want them to give me a ride to Cliff's house and bring them to the scene of the crime. I couldn't call any of my friends because I ditched Mark's party. My hangover was unbearable, but I knew there was only one way to get my car. I had to run.

It was about a five-mile run, and I made it with only puking twice along the way in the ditch. I got into my truck, dripping in sweat. It flowed down like tributaries on my skin. I could literally smell the alcohol coming out of my pores. The cab of my truck was a hot box and I was trapped inside. I was still breathing hard and sweat dripped down my forehead and got caught in my eyebrows. I felt so alone at that moment. I contemplated my current situation. I had lost the love of my life. I had lost my life's passion of playing hockey. I avoided my friends. I disappointed my parents. I even betrayed God by skipping church, something I never did. I had a feeling of guilt but, most of all, loneliness.

I wanted to cry so bad, but couldn't for some reason. How in the hell did I get here? I thought of people who I could blame. I pointed to people in my head and they shook their heads and walked away. They went on living their lives. The truth is, I had no one else to blame but myself. I was envious of those who lost love when the person broke up with them. In that case, at least they had someone to blame, someone to hate. The only person I could blame was myself.

That realization coupled with my guilt inspired me to do an apology tour. I drove to The End and apologized to the owner for how I had acted. He appreciated it and even jokingly offered me a shot of tequila. I settled for a water. He also gave me my shirt back. I faced my parents and apologized to them for storming out and not letting them know where I went. They didn't need to know all the details. I didn't remember half of them, anyway. I didn't remember enough, but then again, I remembered too much.

Last but not least, I needed to apologize to God. I drove to the church that night and sat in the back pew. It was dark inside, with just the candles along the walls shining some light. I pulled out my old rosary that my grandma Marietta gave me for my first communion and spent the next while praying and reflecting. I asked God why, over and over. I didn't get an answer. I then remembered what Jenna said to the reporter when she was asked if she ever asked herself why. Her response was so much more admirable than mine. All of a sudden, a noise came from the front of the church. I became a little frightened, given the time of the day and darkness of the church. A door opened from beside the altar and a light shined through. I could see the outline of a man.

"Hello?" The voice echoed through the empty church.

I was a bit startled. Should I hide? Should I quickly leave? Should I respond? I didn't think it was against the rules to be in the church at that time of day, especially when the doors were unlocked. Not to be accused of an intruder or homeless, I responded.

"Yes," I said as I stood up.

I could hear the footsteps from the man's shoes clink on the marble floor. His shadow blocked each candle as he walked up the aisle. His identity became clear as he approached.

"Hello, son," he said.

"Hello, Father," I said as I began to exit the pew and greet him.

It was Father Mike, the priest of our church.

"No, no, please remain seated," he said as he waived me back into the pew.

I sat down and he did as well. Father Mike had been at our parish for about a year. I probably only exchanged small pleasantries with Father Mike since he arrived, typically before or after a church service and after Jenna's funeral. He was a tall man with a big frame and a burly beard peppered with gray hairs to compensate for his balding scalp. He hailed from New Jersey, a far cry from a small Midwest town like Shoreham Lake. His east coast accent stood out among us Minnesotans. He was a gifted orator, and quite frankly didn't seem like your typical priest. Perhaps it was because he became a priest later in life, already forty years old. He worked an array of jobs prior to entering the seminary and had the life experiences to go with them. Those life experiences allowed him to relate to his parishioners, not just with God. That connection served him well not only on Sundays, but in the work he did within our community. My parents spoke highly of him for his work, and his short sermons of course.

"What brings you to the Lord's house this evening, Will Camps?" He asked in his deep Jersey accent.

I was surprised he remembered my name. But then again, it's a small town.

"Nothing really, I was just driving by and figured I would come say a prayer," I said.

He laughed a little under his breath while he crossed his legs and folded his hands onto his knee.

"Son, from my experience, no one comes to a church at this hour and at your age just because he happened to be driving by," he explained.

I was a bit surprised by his bluntness. Thinking back to my reason provided I can't blame him for calling my bluff. Yet still, I wasn't ready to open up to him about why I was there. I didn't know him for one, and for two, I wasn't ready to open up to anyone.

He looked at me with his tired eyes, challenging me to talk next. Something came over me – call it anger or just plain curiosity – but something gave me the courage to accept his challenge.

"You're a priest, so I'm assuming you believe in heaven, huh?" I asked.

"That would be a fair assumption," he said as he nodded his head.

I could tell he was surprised by my bluntness back to him, and he instantly became more engaged.

"And do you think that as long as you are good, you will go to heaven?" I continued.

"Good being a relative term, but, in general, yes, I do," he responded with another nod.

"I guess my main question is, how do you know?" I asked. "How do you really know?"

"Are you asking for yourself or for a friend?" He answered my question with a question.

I found his response interesting. Would his answer be different, I thought to myself?

"Both," I answered, this time looking directly into

his eyes.

"That's a fair question. I'm afraid I only have an unfair answer," he began. "See, none of us can be sure because we've never been there. We haven't seen it with our own eyes. We haven't touched it with our own hands. That's what makes the question so difficult. And the answer isn't truly an answer. It's a challenge. We call that challenge 'faith.'"

There was that word again. I heard it a lot lately, but didn't really understand what it meant. I nodded my head as if I understood, not to appear dumb. He grabbed a Bible from the back shelf and started paging through it as he sat back down.

"Have you come to believe because you have seen me? Blessed are those who have not seen yet have come to believe," he read aloud from the book of John, closing the Bible before he continued, "That's faith – believing in something you can't see. We must take that principle and apply it to things in our lives, especially what happens after our lives."

I nodded again.

"Son, no one knows for sure that heaven exists. But those who have faith are bound to find out." He added.

There was a long awkward pause. I looked down at my watch and saw it was getting late.

"Thank you, Father. I better get home." I said as I

stood up.

"Of course," he added as he remained seated and tucked his legs in so I could walk around him.

"I'll see you next Sunday," I said as I walked towards the doors.

"Have faith, and you will see her again," his voice echoed as he remained facing the front of the church with his back to me.

I stopped and looked back. He didn't turn around. I opened the door and walked out of the church towards my truck. Meanwhile, Father Mike got down on his knees and prayed for me.

The thought of not knowing if Jenna was in heaven killed me, as did not knowing if I'd ever see her again. It absolutely killed me. I wanted to see her so badly. I wanted to touch her face. I wanted to kiss her soft lips. I wanted to hear her sweet voice. I wanted to witness my pet peeves that bothered me about her, as infrequent as they were. I would've taken anything. The worst day with her was immensely better than my best day without her. I saw her everywhere in my mind. Everywhere I went reminded me of her –the Dairy Queen where we had our first kiss, the movie theatre where we had our first real date, the empty shotgun seat in my truck. She had an adorable habit of calling "shotgun" even though she was the only passenger. She left her mark on everything. And every time it made my stomach churn.

At that moment, I was willing to do anything to be with her again. On the drive home, I contemplated the only way I could potentially find out – by taking my own life. It wasn't so much to stop the pain I had on earth, but just to have the slightest chance of seeing her again. Literally the only thing that kept me alive on that drive home was the thought of the pain it would cause my family. I thought of the pain I was experiencing, and if I were to take my own life, that pain would transfer to them. I couldn't handle the thought of that. So, as I went to bed that night, I knew I had no choice but to keep going. I didn't know how exactly, but I knew I must continue living. I guess that's the faith that Father Mike was talking about.

***

Another week went by, more of the same of wallowing in my depression. Spring was starting to bloom and prom was approaching. I had no intentions of going since I didn't have a date. Prom was special to Jenna. Her mom was prom queen and she loved getting dressed up and walking out in front of everyone. We had gone together the past three years. It always took her months to find the perfect dress. She was preoccupied our senior year, so the search got put on hold and eventually never materialized. I'm sure I could've found a date, but I felt as though I couldn't betray her by going with someone else.

But prom was also special to my mom. She had dreamed of seeing her baby boy going to his senior prom. I was caught between emotions. My dad was actually the one who finally convinced me to go. He explained that it would make my mom proud and it's what Jenna would have wanted. It was a way to honor her, he said. I wasn't wild about going, and I wish I could've stayed home and laid in bed by myself. But a couple of days before, I decided to go.

The day had arrived. My mom cried when she pinned a flower to my tuxedo. I couldn't tell if she was crying because Jenna wasn't there with me or just because it was my last prom and her baby was all grown up. It was probably both. All of us were emotional that day. The boys let me tag along with them and their dates, so they picked me up in their rented limousine.

Prom at Shoreham Lake High School was a big event. It started with a social hour where everyone gathered and took pictures with friends and families in the commons area. The main event was the grand march, where all couples took their turn walking in front of the crowded gymnasium full of people cheering and flashing pictures. After everyone walked through, they crowned the year's king and queen. Then everyone gathered for the dance behind the stage and the guests filtered out.

The social hour was somewhat enjoyable. I got to talk to people I hadn't seen in a while. Little boys wanted pictures with me because I still had the hockey spotlight. I dodged a few questions about my future. At one point, a little girl who Jenna used to babysit asked me where she was. The girl's parents apologized. I told them that an apology certainly wasn't necessary. But looking into that little girl's eyes and telling her that Jenna wasn't there was agonizing. We took a group picture with all of my buddies. I didn't participate in the grand march, instead I sat in the crowd with my parents. I consciously kept an eye out for Jenna's parents the whole night, but they never showed up. I couldn't blame them for not going, but it kind of made me feel a little uncomfortable for going.

After the grand march, it was time for the crowning. I knew there was a good chance I could be announced as king. I was one of the more popular guys in school. I was the star athlete, but I also got along with pretty much everyone. My parents preached to us at a very young age to treat everyone the same, no matter who they are or where they come from. One of my favorite teachers, Mrs. Richards, took the stage. After some pleasantries, she paused for a second.

"It is now time to announce this year's Shoreham Lake High School prom king and queen." She announced to the crowd.

The gymnasium suddenly went quiet. Like the Oscars, she opened a white envelope.

"This year's prom king is . . . Will Camps." She announced.

The crowd started cheering. I sat there motionless and without much feeling. I wasn't surprised. I wasn't quite excited. I didn't know how to feel. I didn't know how to react. For the first time in my life, I didn't want the attention I used to thrive on.

My mom stood up and put her hands together and put them up to her lips as if she was fighting back emotion. I gave her a hug and shook my dad's hand. I walked on the stage and stood there as last year's prom king set the crown on my head. I awkwardly waived to the crowd in acknowledgment. As I started to walk off the stage, Mrs. Richards instructed me to stay.

"And now for this year's prom queen," she continued as she opened a new envelope.

She paused for a moment and looked down at the floor.

"This year's prom queen is in memory of someone very dear to our hearts…our angel in heaven…Jenna Johnson." She said with a soft and sympathetic tone.

My heart sank into my stomach. I went from feeling nothing to being overcome with emotion. I knew it was Jenna's dream to become prom queen. She didn't keep it a secret. It's almost as if the crowd didn't know how to react either – some cheered, some were silent. Mrs. Richards gave me a hug and handed me her crown. It was tradition for the prom king and queen to share a dance right after they were crowned. When the song started playing, it was like razorblade cuts to my heart with every guitar chord. I couldn't handle it. I took off my crown and threw it to the ground and then stormed off stage, through the crowd, and power walked into the back hallway.

I walked into the hall pacing back and forth – short of breath and short of patience. I had nowhere to go. I saw the bathroom door and walked towards it. I shoved the door open with one hand as it slammed the wall and swung back. I walked towards the stalls and opened up the large handicap stall, walked in and closed it shut. Putting my forehead against the wall and slowly raising my fists above my head, I hit them gently against the concrete wall. A couple of tears streamed down my face and gently splashed on the floor. I turned around, rested my back against the wall, and started to slide my body down. As I hit the floor, I put my head down between my knees and completely broke down.

I can't imagine a lower rock bottom. The floor was dirty and wet in spots. A few strips of toilet paper were on the floor, soaking in the water and urine right next to me. That bathroom was like a prison with concrete walls. I was all alone with nothing but my regrets. I must have cried for a good five minutes – an all-out cry. Uncontrollably, emotions poured out. My eyes were foggy, puffy, and red, becoming itchier every time I rubbed them. *How did I get here*, I thought once again. Not too long ago, I thought I had it all. I had everything that an eighteen-year-old kid could want. As I sat on the dirty bathroom floor, I felt as though I had nothing. I lost it all.

"Will?" A voice echoed through the bathroom. I was startled and looked up, quickly wiping my eyes and cheeks with the back of my hand.

"Will? Are you in here?" The voice asked again as I recognized it.

"Yeah," I responded with a choked throat as I sniffled. I cleared my throat. "Yeah," I tried again.

I saw Mark's boots walk up to the door under the stall.

"Dude, are you okay?" He asked.

"I'm fine, man. Just kind of want to be alone." I

started crying again and it showed in my words.

Mark tried opening the door, pushing it in a few times with no luck. He bent down, got on his hands and knees and crawled under the door and into the stall. I can't even imagine what he was thinking when he saw the shape I was in. I was unsightly to say the least. He took a few slow steps towards me and sat down right next to me. I looked down at the floor and he looked at me.

"You know me better than that. I'm not going to let you be alone." He responded.

I breathed hard through my nose and shook my head.

"Dude, I don't think you are okay," he continued.

"No, I'm really, really not." I said with an almost hysterical tone.

For the first time, I admitted it out loud.

I had never been so vulnerable. Mark had never been so serious and honest.

"I get it. She was my friend, too. I get it, champ," he said.

I nodded my head, gently indicating that I understood. Even though mine was to a much higher degree, I wasn't the only one going through this.

"I think you can stop calling me 'champ' now," I said. "I'm not a champ."

"Do you know why I call you that?" He asked me.

I shrugged my shoulders.

"It's not because of the state championship. It's because you are my champ. You're the best guy I know. If it wasn't for you, I'd be on the street somewhere. I'd be a mess like the rest of my family. Hell, maybe I'd be in jail. You saved me from all of that. You're probably the only good I have in my life." He said.

I started crying more as I rested my head on the wall.

"What can I do?" He asked.

"Get me out of here." I requested.

"You got it, champ." He responded.

We sat for a couple of minutes and didn't say much to each other. We just stared forward, thinking of the intensity of the moment, reflecting on how we got to that point. It was not something a couple of eighteen-year-old kids should be going through during their senior prom.

"Man, I hate to see the shape of the guy who was runner-up for prom king tonight." He said with a soft sarcastic tone.

He always knew how to break the ice. I couldn't help but crack a smile. Only Mark could make me smile in my darkest moment. That's why we were such good friends. He got up on his feet, knees bent and his back hunched over so he was still on my level. He put out his hand.

"Just believe." He said confidently.

I looked up.

"Just believe." I said confirming our pact.

That's what we told each other before every hockey game. That's what we told each other before our last hockey game together. At that point, we had been eliminated from the state playoffs and were playing for third place. We had nothing left to play for besides pride and each other. At that moment on the cold bathroom floor, all we had was our pride and each other.

We pulled each other up. Mark handed me his sunglasses to hide my eyes that gave away that I had been crying.

"Let's get out of here." He said.

As reality crept back in, a feeling of extreme embarrassment overcame me. Pretty much the entire town saw me crying and storming into the bathroom. These were people who used to respect and admire me. I put on his sunglasses as we walked out.

I nervously followed Mark back into the gym. It was the only way out of the building. I just wanted to be invisible. As we approached the entry way into the gym, Mark stepped to the side and started clapping loudly with a few of our buddies joining in. I shook my head and put my hand out telling them to stop. Within seconds the entire gym joined in on the applause. They all rose to their feet. All eyes were on me again. I stopped in my tracks and looked at the faces in the crowd. They were my family, friends, coaches, teachers, heroes, and strangers. I curled both my lips in and nodded my head up and down, as if I was thanking everyone on behalf of both Jenna and myself. I took off the sunglasses and put my hand on my heart and scaled the room with my eyes, back and forth. There was no need to be embarrassed. Everyone understood. It was an outpouring of support from the school and community. It was a powerful moment.

Mark walked towards me, put his arm around me and motioned to a few of the other guys to follow. We walked out of the building, with our arms around each other to face the world together. They left their dates behind. I left my crowns behind.

"I love this town." Mark said with a smile.

5

I rolled over into the sunlight shining through the window adjacent to my bed. It was nature's alarm clock, and it was a new day. It was the Monday after graduation which officially marked the first day of summer. For some kids that meant the first day of freedom. For anyone in our family, it marked the first day of full-time work. All that had happened to us in the past few months didn't stop the changing of the seasons or the bills coming in the mail.

My family owned and operated a successful resort on Shoreham Lake – the Shoreham Hills Resort. It was located just down the road from our cabin, and it included a big hotel and restaurant on the beach, indoor and outdoor pools, and a golf course and ranch across the road. My dad bought the place when it was just a little hotel on the lake, and had a bigger vision which eventually, thanks to his relentless hard work and perseverance sprinkled with a little prayer, came to fruition.

Even though our family was well-off, my dad

believed in making his boys work every summer. He believed in a good education and getting good grades, so he didn't make us work much during the school year. That time was designated for homework and hockey. But when school ended, he knew it was critical for us to learn the value of a hard day's work and a real dollar earned. From an early age, we started out mowing fairways and roughs on the golf course, washing golf carts, working the counter, raking the beach, and helping out with maintenance and cleaning the hotel rooms. It wasn't glamorous, but he felt it was important for us to grow up in a similar way that he did.

His dad was a farmer – a comfortable man, but by no means wealthy. Born and raised in Shoreham Lake, my dad was the youngest of eight children. He and his siblings all worked their butts off to help provide for the family. It was a team effort to make life click. They were forced to grow up faster than my brothers and me, which seems to be the trend with each new generation. He was known as "Baby Billy" by most until he graduated years later to just "Billy." As the youngest in the family, he was forced to grow up quick and grow up tough. It also forced him to communicate with people of all ages beginning at a very young age. And he did it well – very well in fact. As good as my mom was with kids, my dad was with adults. If there was a Mr. Congeniality award in the area, my old man would've won it hands down.

He was the best people-person that I knew, always handing out jokes, shaking hands, talking shop, and kissing babies. He could bend and mold people in a conversation like no other. Old ladies would swoon over his comments about their "young age" and old men at the café breakfast table looked to him for whit about farming, business, politics, and everything in between. This trait served him well in business too. The man was a born negotiator and saw it as a sport. He always sniffed out the best deal and often would trip over a dollar to save a penny. He would say he negotiated to save money but we all knew it was mainly for the love of the joust. He always got the best price and usually left the salesman feeling great about it. How did that happen? I have no clue. Among many other things, I admired my old man in this regard. He could run for mayor without lifting a finger, but he was too smart to get into politics – another quality I admired. As my dad experienced some success later in life, he never forgot those origins and how that experience fueled his success. He wanted to preach that to his boys. At the time, we simply didn't know any different. Oh, and we also didn't have a choice. So, we worked and he made sure we worked damn hard.

I got up and threw on some old jeans, stained with grass and dirt spots from last summer. I put on an old Shoreham Hills Resort shirt, brushed my teeth, and stumbled downstairs. Most work mornings I didn't see the point in showering since I was about to get dirty all day anyway. I saved it for the evenings after work and dinner. Not showering in the morning also bought me an extra fifteen minutes of sleep, which seemed much more valuable on those early mornings. My mom was already up and at it, eating breakfast.

"Will, there's a plate for you in the oven." She graciously offered.

"Thanks, mom." I said as I walked over and pulled out a fresh, warm plate of eggs, bacon, and hash browns.

Of course, my dad already had a few hours chalked up at work as he always did. I couldn't remember a time when I was up before him. The guy was a machine with no off button. I quickly downed breakfast and left the plate on the table. I pulled on my work boots, stiff from months of nonuse.

"Will, come put your plate away!" My mom yelled.

I stumbled back into the kitchen with one boot on and quickly scraped my plate into the garbage and put it in the sink along with my empty orange juice glass. I scurried back into the entry way, put my other boot on, and headed out the door. Our resort was just up the road, so I hopped into my truck and peeled out of the driveway. My dad was in his office buried in paperwork, which he tried to take care of before his employees showed up for their daily assignments. I worked at the resort every summer growing up. I was the floating guy, which meant I didn't have a firm position and was put to work pretty much anywhere they needed on any given day. It gave me a good variety, which I liked. My dad felt that it gave me experience in every area of the resort, which was necessary if I ever planned on taking the reins of the operation someday. He didn't believe in favoritism, so he treated me just like every other employee. In fact, my status as his son often worked against me, as more was expected of me and he didn't want to give his employees the slightest appearance of nepotism. So, I started from the bottom. Early on, I swept floors, cleaned hotel rooms, washed dishes in the restaurant, washed golf carts and other machinery, mowed pasture areas, cleaned kennels, fed animals, pulled weeds – you name it. I enjoyed mowing the grounds the best because I loved the smell of fresh cut grass. Years later I continued those tasks, but more meaningful ones were added on top of it, including mowing fairways and greens on the golf course and manning the front desk of the hotel.

It was the first day of our busy season, which extended all summer long. That time of year represented a sense of beginning, a sense of renewal. It wasn't just the weather that I loved, but also the anticipation and energy it brought. Thankfully the ice had thawed off the lake early that year, so docks and boats could go in early, and the golf course was turning green early, as well. Our main season was from May to September, but we kept busy in the fall and winter as well thanks to hunting, snowmobiling, and ice fishing guests. The hotel was three stories and was picket-fence white with navy blue trim. It had a community dock where slips filled up with all kinds of boats, including our massive pontoon which gave guests tours around the lake multiple times a day, the most popular being the sunset cocktail cruise. The restaurant was on the beach side, with a patio overlooking the water. It was a somewhat fancy restaurant with a lot of history to it. It had an aura about it. I imagine back in the day, patrons of women in big hats gossiping and men in polos smoking big cigars on the patio after drinking too much wine and feasting on the fresh catch of the day, our specialty. The golf course was across the road and featured eighteen holes of links-style play with rolling hills, deep sand bunkers, and thick fescue grass outside of the fairways. Finally, the ranch had a sprawling fence line with a big red barn that served as the stable housing our horses for people to ride, along with other livestock grazing for agritourism as well as production. It was a playground for anyone looking for a summer getaway, and it had something for everyone.

I walked into my dad's office as he was on the phone. He put his index finger up in the air, indicating he would be off the phone soon. He was a busy man. Not only did he operate the hotel, restaurant, golf course, and ranch, but he also owned some local real estate and was a partner in the boat dealership in town. I sat down on the worn leather chair in front of his desk. The arms were completely picked and peeled off down to the metal. His prize caught walleye donned the wall above his chair. Pictures of his family were scattered on the shelves. With how hard he worked, the quality I most admired about him was how much he adored my mom and us boys.

"How are you, bud?" He asked after he hung up.

"Fine, just ready to get to work," I said.

"Are you sure?" He asked.

"I'm sure, just tell me what you need me to do," I assured him.

He looked at me with curiosity for a moment and then grabbed his list.

"Ok, sounds good. Here you go. Start by heading up to Laker Sports to pick up some parts." He instructed as he handed me the list.

He could have had anyone do jobs like that, but it wasn't all about getting the job done. It was about keeping me busy and putting me to work.

"Ten-four," I responded as I sat up to get my day started.

Laker Sports was the lake supply and hardware store in downtown Shoreham Lake. Mark worked the counter that summer. It was owned by his uncle, Greg, which is probably the only reason he got the job. As a kid, Mark worked on his dad's farm until it folded and he was forced to find other means to pay for his food and booze. He even picked up shifts working at our resort once in a while since he was around so often anyway. We were one of his uncle's biggest customers, and I always stretched my trip to Laker Sports longer than necessary, sometimes sitting for a while and talking with Mark, Greg, or the other employees. They usually gave me free candy bars and soda, and we would talk about what was going on around town. Often there were guys just hanging out there, whether they were retired or just lazy.

"Champ! What's the good word today?" Mark asked in his usual upbeat tone as I walked in the door.

He was wearing a forest green button up dress shirt with short sleeves and his name tag. He had khaki pants to cap off his uniform. Even though I've seen him in his work attire before, I never got used to it. He looked more natural in his casual shirts and light jeans.

"Work." I replied in a much less upbeat way.

"That's not exactly a good word. What can I do for you on this fine Monday?" He asked.

"First you can wipe that smile off your face, then I need a few of these for my old man." I responded.

"Yeah, whatever," Mark smiled and walked into the back room.

I wandered around the store a bit, reading random labels on boxes of screws, duct tape, and fishing tackle.

"Here you go, only the best for a loyal customer." He quipped as he walked back out and threw the box up on the counter. "I'll give you a discount if you agree to co-host my party on Friday," he offered.

"Ahhh . . . I don't know, man." I replied.

"Champ, you have to come. First one of the summer – first of many." He pointed his finger at me and tilted his head like an infomercial salesman.

"Where's your old man?" I asked.

"Who the hell knows? The palace is all ours." He proclaimed.

The palace he referred to was his dad's cabin on the west side of Shoreham Lake. Since his dad would often disappear for extended lengths of time, the palace served as the venue to many parties over the years, first orchestrated by Mark's older sister and then taken over by him. I attended the majority of them, but successfully resisted a few in which the cops showed up and closed it down. Call it dumb luck, I guess. Mark knew he needed me there to make the party legitimate.

I looked down at the floor and rested my hands on the counter.

"You know I'll be there," I conceded as I looked up at him.

"Yes! That's what I'm talking about!" He said as he raised his hand for a high-five.

"Yeah, yeah, stay out of trouble until then," I said as I slapped his hand, grabbed the box, and headed out the door.

"No guarantees!" He yelled as I walked out.

***

The week flew by. I played golf on Thursday evening with my dad and a few of his friends. I always enjoyed playing with the older guys. It was an opportunity to learn from them, the way they talked just as much as what they said. I also enjoyed the opportunity to impress them with my golf game, even if that wasn't always the case. I think they enjoyed my presence once in a while, too, getting the input of a young guy. Fridays were always a little bit more laid back compared to the rest of the week. Morning and afternoon breaks usually lasted a little longer. My dad was usually more relaxed. Even though I expressed agony to Mark earlier in the week about his party, I became a little more excited as the week went by. I was usually crabby on Mondays, Tuesdays, and Wednesdays. But once Thursdays rolled around I usually turned a corner. I thought it will be nice to get back out with the boys, have a few drinks, and relax.

It was finally quitting time as five o'clock on Friday rolled around. I hopped in the shower and scrubbed the dirt and grease from my body. I threw on a comfortable t-shirt and jeans, ate a quick bite for dinner, and drove over to Mark's. A few of us usually went to his parties early, before everyone else got there. We would play cards or dice and get loosened up before the crowd showed up. Sometimes we would go on the lake. Once again, the pre-gaming activities were usually more fun than the actual party.

People began to pour in a few hours later. The house filled up and the party spilled outside into the yard. Mark had a wooden tiki bar that he built himself on the patio, and he loved playing bartender. It was a fun night. There was a horseshoe tournament, where Mark and I emerged victorious. Everyone used those parties to escape. Their worries went up in smoke with the bonfire. Except mine. I was different. I always had something on my mind that I could never forget. I could ignore it for a few moments here and there, but it always came back.

When Alisha walked outside and joined the party with some other people, I became nervous. It was that feeling when you see your ex, when your heart sinks into your stomach and memories rise to the front of your mind. Even though we never dated, it was the same feeling. I hadn't seen her since the night at the End. She had called a couple of times, but I ignored them. I knew I'd eventually have to face her, but I wasn't ready. I snuck away from the party and I could feel her eyes watching me.

I walked out past the porch and onto the grass towards the water. It was still. You could see lights from cottages around the lake. I wanted to get away from it all, so I walked onto the dock and sat down, with my legs folded and my knees pulled into my chest. My arms wrapped around my legs to keep them in place. I just stared at the dark water. It seemed like a big dark hole. It represented my life as I saw it. I wasn't at rock bottom like I was a few weeks earlier, but I was still in a dark hole. The moon reflected to show a few small ripples in the water. I took another gulp of my beer and set it back down to resume my position.

"Hey," said a soft voice from behind me on shore.

The dock began to sway slightly and I could feel the steps coming towards me.

I quickly leaned back and looked behind me. I couldn't make out who it was in the dark, but I knew it was Alisha. I was trapped.

"Who's there?" I asked.

"Just me," she said as she came into sight.

It was Hannah Johnson. I was pleasantly surprised. She was Jenna's cousin and childhood best friend. I knew her, but not well. After Jenna moved to Shoreham Lake in junior high, they remained friends, but didn't get to see each other very often. Even though they lived about three hours away from each other and got busy during high school, they still talked on the phone or wrote each other letters often.

"Hey." I quipped as I stood up. "What are you doing here?"

"Nothing, I just saw you walk out here and . . . I

mean, I wasn't like stalking you or anything, I just…," she replied as she trailed off.

I cracked a little closed-mouth smirk with one side of my mouth.

"No, I know. What are you doing here, as in Mark's? Sorry, I didn't mean it like that. *How* are you doing?" I inquired.

I tried to make her feel more comfortable by inviting her to sit down. I shifted over to make room and sat against the boat canopy. She sat down and dangled her feet off the dock.

"I'm doing okay. Scarlett brought me here. I think she just wanted someone to drive her home, actually," she laughed a little to herself. "I'm actually here for the summer."

"Really?" I asked.

"Yeah. I got a job waitressing at Zivonz, so…," she continued.

"That's cool. You should make pretty good money there." I said.

"Yeah, I think it will be good. It will be nice to be at the lake all summer, too." She added.

"For sure. No better place to be in the summer," I said with a sarcastic tone, quoting the old motto you always hear in the area. "Where's your drink?" I inquired.

"Oh, I uh, I'm not drinking. I don't really drink

much, so . . ." She said uncomfortably as she pushed her hair behind her ear.

"That's cool," I responded as I nervously took a swig of my beer, not realizing the irony of doing so until I swallowed.

I changed the subject immediately in order to get past the awkwardness.

"Are you staying with your grandma, then?" I asked.

I knew she came to see her and Jenna's grandma, Lola, a few weekends every summer. Jenna was close with Lola, so I knew her well.

"Yeah," she said as she pointed in the direction of her cabin across the lake.

"Will! Will! Get your ass in here! I need my teammate!" Mark shouted as he popped out of the cabin without a shirt on and waved his arm for me to come inside.

I shook my head and smiled.

"Looks like I better get back to the party. Mark needs a partner for some sort of drinking game, I'm sure." I said, trying to talk down to the idea to try and convince her that I was somehow more mature than I really was. "But I'll probably see you around then, I guess," I added, not knowing why I was putting an end to the conversation so soon.

We started walking off the dock back onto shore

and stepped onto the grass.

"Yeah. I suppose, because you live here . . . or not here, but over there . . . or, yeah you know what I mean." She shook her head as she looked down, thinking she sounded dumb.

"Yeah, I knew what you meant. It's all home." I reassured her. "I'll see you around then?" I said in the form of a question, feeling like I wanted to talk more.

"Okay. See you around." She bit her bottom lip and walked back over to the bonfire.

I stood there for a moment and watched her walk back to the fire. I had a feeling of curiosity come over me. It was like a subtle shot of optimism. I tried to convince myself that it was the buzz from the beer as I finished it off and threw the empty can on the grass before walking inside. I could still feel Alisha's eyes on me, and she was probably wondering who the new girl was. Imagining her jealousy was actually kind of amusing. After a while I went back outside and casually looked around for Hannah. By that time, she was nowhere to be found.

I crashed at Mark's place, along with about a dozen other people. I told my parents I was going to stay there. Even though they knew exactly what was going on, they were cool with it. I was graduated from high school and, considering all that had happened to me in the past few months, quite frankly I could tell they felt sorry for me and were relaxed when it came to a curfew. We continued the party until about five o'clock in the morning and finally shut it down. We were still setting up for busy season so I had to work in the morning. All of us stragglers woke up to empty beer bottles and red plastic cups all over the place. The house wreaked of stale beer. We sat around in the living room reminiscing of the night before. I couldn't stop thinking about my conversation with Hannah. It was so random that she showed up. And I felt like I wanted to talk to her more for some reason. Maybe that reason was our connection to Jenna.

"I better get rollin', boys," I announced as I stood up.

"Aright, chill night tonight?" Mark asked.

"Much needed. I'll come over after work." I responded.

My dad was usually a little more flexible on Saturday mornings, so when I rolled in a little past eight o'clock, he didn't say anything. I mainly worked during the week, but I helped out occasionally on the weekends when needed. Mark had to work, too, since the store followed the same cyclical patterns as the resort. So both of us dragged ourselves to work on a couple hours of sleep with a couple pounding headaches.

Since Friday night was a crazy one, we settled on staying in and hanging out later on after we were both off work. Plus, he needed help cleaning the place up before his dad got home on Sunday. We agreed on Zivonz pizza takeout and a fire, maybe even some evening skiing. We loved skiing in the evening time because the water was calm and it was still somewhat warm outside. Mark was an incredible water skier. He could do it all – two skis, one ski, barefoot, slips – you name it. I was decent. Any kid who grows up on a lake usually has the fundamentals down at a young age. But I preferred to drive the boat or just sit and admire the artist on the water at work and the camaraderie on the boat. We lived like kings of the lake on those summer nights.

I escaped work a few hours earlier than expected with no hiccups. It was a good day. My headache went away by about lunchtime. I even snuck in a twenty-minute nap on the couch in my dad's office over the noon hour. I drove home, threw my dirty shirt into the hamper in the laundry room and peeled off my dirty jeans and threw them on the floor. I walked into our screen porch area and slid open the big wooden frame windows to let the breeze blow off the water into the house. It was refreshing after a long, hard day at work.

The screen porch was below the balcony patio. It was surrounded by windows giving view to the lake. It was decorated with nautical items including our best taxidermy fish. It had a TV reserved strictly for my dad. The screen porch was his man cave, if you will, where he would escape his wife and boys to watch the news, golf, or football. I loved joining him out there. It felt like a boys' club. I plopped myself on the couch in just my underwear. I was so tired and it was so hot out I didn't care about the exposure. Mark still had to work for another hour, so I had time to relax.

"Will! Are you eating supper?" My mom's voice echoed from the kitchen.

I had dozed off for a while and slowly opened my eyes, somewhat confused about what time of day it was.

"Um, no! I'm grabbing a pizza and heading to Mark's!" I yelled back.

I got up and got myself together with a shower and a fresh outfit. I called in the pizza order and talked to my mom for a few minutes in the kitchen as she cooked dinner for my dad. She was making steak and baked potatoes, which I was quite envious of as my stomach growled.

But nothing could beat Zivonz pizza. Zivonz was

an old, somewhat rundown restaurant and beach bar located on the small strip of public beach on Shoreham Lake. It was started by a married couple who were both teachers with Czech heritage. Not only did they need something to do during the summertime, they also wanted a place where they could grab a cold beer and a fresh slice of pizza on the beach without having to put on a shirt or shoes. After buying an old building and putting countless hours into converting it into a restaurant, eventually Zivonz opened its arms wide to the public. In their native Czech language, Zivon means "live well." And that's exactly the type of atmosphere they wanted to create. They spread the love and the patrons felt it. It was a seasonal establishment, only open from late April to usually early October, depending on the weather. It was a historical landmark in the area and had a very loyal cult following, a must-stop for all tourists. Zivonz was a place where everyone has at least one memory stored, whether it was a good one or bad. People of all shapes and sizes flooded the restaurant and patio throughout the summertime. If Zivonz had a no shoes, no shirt, no service policy, they would go broke. It was an escape for people. It was a place where, no matter what your age, you were allowed to act like a kid. The owners didn't guarantee any negative repercussions from your spouse, but it was fine by them. And everyone loved it. It was a family restaurant at dinner time and turned into a party spot at night as they moved the tables and chairs to the side to make room for the dance floor.

In a sentence, at Zivonz, every day was a vacation. You checked your worries at the door. No, really – they had a sign that said so hanging over the entrance. When you walked in, smells of pizza, suntan lotion, and beer mixed together, filling the restaurant and patio, and somehow smelled great. They had live music every Friday and Saturday, usually local bands. Mark performed there quite often. Thursday was karaoke night, where the true local stars were born. Names were written and carved on the walls and tables. Random memorabilia were hung on the walls in no particular order or reason – old skis, fishing nets, boat buoys, beer signs, street signs, fish taxidermy. Autographed dollar bills were tacked on the ceiling from guests throwing them up there. Pictures of people patronizing the restaurant draped in between, some not-so-flattering. It was a tribute to summer life on the lake and the tradition of Shoreham Lake.

Every summer, Zivonz hosted a golf tournament at our golf course. It was a four-person scramble. I played on my dad's team every year. When I was a sophomore in high school, we won the tournament in dramatic fashion. One of the prizes is a team picture with the trophy inside the restaurant, and that picture was hung up just above the bar with the other past champions. I always thought that was pretty cool. Local star athletes of past and present had their jerseys draped on the walls alongside an action shot of the player with an autograph addressing the owners.

The patio area overlooked the beach and the lake. Across the patio from the restaurant was an outside tiki bar attached to a pizza shack, where the magic pies were crafted. Aside from the relationships and hangovers it created, Zivonz was known for its pizza. The irregulars who visited Zivonz always took home their plastic cups as souvenirs. And the restaurant marketed themselves by replacing all words that contained "S" with their trademarked "Z."

I couldn't wait to eat, so I cruised over. When I walked towards the pizza shack on the patio, I spotted her. Call it a coincidence.

"Hey, Hannah," I interrupted her talking with the young man working the counter of the pizza shack.

She turned her head towards me, turned back towards him, and quickly turned it back towards me again. "Hi, what are you doing here?" She asked.

I smiled. It seemed like a strange question

considering it was a restaurant. But then again, I asked her the same question the night before at a party.

"I'm just picking up a pizza and bringing it over to Mark's," I replied.

"Cool. Well, have fun," she said.

Hannah hurriedly walked away towards one of her tables. The place was busy and they seemed understaffed.

"Will Camps." I told the boy at the pizza shack counter as he scanned the slots and pulled out my pizza. I gave him my money and dropped a dollar into the mug for a tip.

"So where are you playing next year?" The boy asked, bright and starry eyed.

"I don't know yet, still looking at some options." I responded, trying to end the subject.

"Cool. Well good luck, man." He said anxiously.

"Appreciate it, bud." I said as I raised the pizza box slightly towards him.

I started walking towards the door to the parking lot. I looked down at the pizza and stopped. I looked across the porch and spotted Hannah taking an order at a table. Then I walked over to her, waiting for her to finish the order.

"Hey, do you want to sit down and split this with me?" I asked her.

I had no idea where this was coming from.

"Umm . . . I uh, I'm working, sorry." She replied as she walked back towards the outside bar to put in the order slip to the bartender.

She seemed different than the night before, much less friendly. I started to wonder if last night even happened, or perhaps it was a dream or hallucination. Perhaps I just caught her at a bad time. Either way, I didn't care. I followed her and leaned up against the bar.

"Are you sure? Just one slice?" I tried again.

"Are you crazy? Can't you see how busy it is here?" She asked me.

"That's fine, I can wait. When do you get off work?" I responded with extreme persistence.

The bartender who prepared her drinks was eavesdropping.

"Everything okay here, Hannah?" He said with a macho tone.

I looked at him, furrowed my eyebrows, and leaned my head back slightly. I wanted to tell him to mind his own business. I didn't know him personally, but I certainly knew of him. He had been working at Zivonz for as long as I could remember. For all I knew, he was probably a good guy. But in that instance, I didn't care for him.

"Yeah, its fine, Jason." Hannah responded to him.

She quickly collected her thoughts and looked back at me. "Um, seven o'clock. If I'm lucky," she estimated.

She grabbed a few freshly made drinks and lined them up on a platter.

I looked down at my watch. It was a little after six-thirty.

"That's fine," I said. "I'll just wait over here. After all, I have an entire pizza to conquer," I said back with a cheesy smile. I couldn't believe how persistent I was being.

"Um…," she finally stopped, looked at me, and shrugged her shoulders. She was out of excuses. "Okay, sure."

I'm not sure if I've ever seen a more confused face, sprinkled with a little frustration as well. She quickly looked back at me with a bewildered look on her face as I sat down on the wooden table and cracked open the pizza box.

"Hi, my name is Hannah and I'll be your server tonight," she refocused on her work.

As I opened the pizza box, the smell of fresh cheese and oregano fumed from the box and wafted into my face. I sure loved that smell. I was a pretty fast eater. Even though I tried to slow it down, I was a growing boy and Zivonz pizza was by far my favorite. I threw down six pieces and did some damage to a seventh. I was ready to waive the white napkin in surrender.

I looked at my watch – eight more minutes. My hockey coach and his wife walked in and spotted me. He asked about how the decision-making process for the fall was going. I gave my standard non-answer. That conversation took up another seven or eight minutes. I walked up to the bar and ordered an ice water and walked back. I don't think Hannah looked over at me once in the meantime. She seemed to take her job very seriously. She was an extremely fast worker and quite the multi-tasker. I thought about how mad Mark must be with a growling stomach, but I didn't really care. After all, he had ditched me a fair share of times, especially for a girl.

I looked at my watch again – eight minutes after seven. Suddenly I saw a lady, probably around forty years old, rush onto the porch while trying to put on her fanny pack around her waist. She went and touched Hannah on the shoulder and Hannah immediately looked more relaxed. Hannah walked away, pulling the drawstrings of her fanny pack behind her back and walked towards the bartender. They talked for a few minutes. I kept waiting, tapping my toe over and over. Should I leave? Does she even remember that I'm waiting for her? Maybe she was stalling so I would leave. Suddenly, I felt pretty stupid. *This is crazy*, I thought. I got up, bruised with embarrassment, picked up the pizza box and threw it in the garbage and started walking out into the parking lot.

"Hey!" I heard a shout from behind me.

I stopped and turned around.

"Is there something you wanted?" She asked, putting it out there for me to make the next play.

"No, I was just…would you like to go for a walk or something?" I asked.

She squinted her eyes a bit in confusion.

"I mean, if you have to be somewhere, that's fine, I just thought I'd ask. I could use the company, that's all." I said, all but giving up completely.

She put her hands on her hips, turned her head and looked to the side. She was hesitant and even a little skeptical. She let out a deep breath and looked back at me.

"Sure. Why not?" She said, her guard lowering slightly.

"Great." I responded.

"But I rode my bike here," she added.

"Um, okay. Wait a second." I said.

I jogged back to the restaurant, went around towards the dumpsters, grabbed her bike and walked it over.

"Don't worry, I got it covered," I assured her.

I started pushing it along as she walked empty handed.

We started walking down the road, first covering the same things we talked about the night before. I asked her how work was, if she prefers it when the place is busy or not, and what her favorite thing is on the menu.

"Yeah, it's going well so far. I'm getting the hang of it. The pay is good, so . . ." she answered.

God bless her as she remained patient with me and pretended to be interested in my questions and bland comments to her answers.

"Well they definitely have the best pizza around, that is for sure," I commented.

We both seemed to be in agreement. We kept walking a few more steps without talking. The pause was a little awkward as I kicked a rock off the road and tried to think of something else to say to break the silence. The feeling was different than the night before. It was stuffier. She seemed guarded. It seemed like she had much more to offer the world, but, for some reason, wouldn't let us see. I tried to think of some more small talk.

"So do you miss her?" She asked.

I stopped in my tracks. Hannah's momentum kept her walking a couple of steps in front of me before she stopped to look back. She became a little worried that perhaps she crossed a line with the question. She thought about apologizing. I folded my lips in and gave a courtesy smirk as I looked at her to ease her concern. The question was simple, but it was heavy. I let out a deep breath out of my nose.

"All the time," I admitted.

It felt so good to say that. It was as if a weight was lifted off of me.

"Me, too," Hannah allowed with a closed-mouth smile as she nodded her head indicating her ability to relate.

We both immediately felt more relaxed with each other after broaching the subject. The ice was broken and the conversation flowed. Surprisingly, it felt good to talk about Jenna. Since the funeral, it seemed like people had been purposely avoiding the subject, constantly walking on egg shells around me. Or people would simply give their sympathies. They never asked.

I was surprised how open and honest I was with Hannah. I had no reason to be. I wasn't that transparent even with my best friends or family. But she had a presence that was disarming. I felt safe laying down all of my weapons, whether it was fear, anger, or some other defense mechanism. I obviously knew her and had spoken to her on occasion in the past, but she was a mere acquaintance through Jenna.

When we talked in the past, it was usually a casual greeting of some sort or comment on whatever Jenna said. I knew Hannah's parents the same way. Her dad was a very outgoing guy who enjoyed asking me about hockey when we ran into each other at Johnson family functions.

"I bet the past few weeks have been surreal for you." Hannah said as we continued walking.

"It's been a whirlwind. Almost like a dream, a blur. At the same time, it was so real." I said in agreement.

We came to the walking bridge over the coulee connecting Shoreham Lake and Lake Melissa. I walked over to the railing and sat down. Hannah followed suit. We sat in the middle and dangled our feet off the edge. The water was just a few feet below and was barely flowing, content just where it was. I was jealous that it could remain so still, something I never seemed to experience. The sun mirrored on the water. The bridge was curved with wooden side rails painted white. I rested my arms on the lower rail.

"I remember the smell of the flowers at the funeral. That scent has stayed with me. I don't know why." Hannah continued.

"I honestly don't remember much from that day. I was sort of in a daze." I said.

"Well your eulogy was great, by the way." She

countered.

"Thanks," I said as I shrugged my shoulders trying to play it off. "It was never something I thought I would have to do, that's for sure. She was doing so well the last few weeks, the best she had in a long time. It was such a surprise," I went on.

"When did you see her last?" Hannah inquired.

"The night before. She was tired, but she was happy. Her voice was relaxed. When I was leaving she said to me, 'I love you more than you love me. Always remember that.'" I recalled.

The tone unintentionally took a serious turn. I stared forward off into the distance.

"Wow." She said, treading lightly not really knowing how to respond.

"Yeah, it was strange – eerie when I look back on it now. I mean, we always told each other 'I love you,' but it was different, the way she said it. It's almost like she knew her time had come and was telling me goodbye without telling me, if that makes sense," I added.

"That's so like Jenna to do something like that." Hannah said with a smile, looking at me to find out if it was acceptable to inject a little humor into the situation.

"Yeah, it is, isn't it?" I responded with a smile of my own while shaking my head.

I picked up a rock lying on the bridge and side armed it into the water as it skipped once and disappeared under the water. I could tell she had been waiting to talk to someone about this just as long as I had. She was guarded at first, but after the initial awkwardness, she was honest to a fault. She was a great listener, as she listened with her eyes as well as her ears.

For the first time, I noticed how pretty she was with the sunshine on her face. Maybe I just never thought of her in that way because she was Jenna's cousin. She had a natural beauty and you could tell she didn't put much effort into it. Except for her eyes. Her eyes had an exotic look – a mix of green and turquoise, depending on the angle. She had defined cheek bones and dimples when she moved them. Her hair was dirty blonde like all the Johnsons, which got lighter in the summertime. She wore it up in a ponytail for work, but a lot of times let it down as it waved and followed the contours of her face. She didn't necessarily turn heads like Jenna had, but she had a different kind of beauty, more innocent may be the right word. She didn't have the curves and bouncy curls like Jenna, but she made up for it in other ways. She had the body of a gymnast or dancer, thinner and more defined. I don't know why, but I found myself comparing the two.

I draped my arms over the lower rail and put all my weight against it, limply dangling down towards the water. The sun danced on the coulee and warmed my back.

"Well, I suppose I should get to Mark's. He's got to be freaking right about now." I said, breaking the conversation and bringing it to another premature end.

"Yeah, and I should get home to Grandma Lola. I told her I'd play cards with her after work." Hannah replied as she stood up.

I tried pulling myself up and slipped a little. Hannah stuck out her hand. I looked up at her face and then down again and grabbed her hand as her body acted as a beam to pull me up.

"Well . . ." I said as it got kind of awkward.

"Well . . ." she replied with her eyebrows raised slightly.

"It was really nice talking with you. Let's do this again sometime," I said with a hesitant grin.

"Let's," she replied with a sweet but unassuming smile. "You know where to find me," she continued as if she was challenging me to act on my suggestion.

She appeared more comfortable and confident. She hopped on her bike and started peddling away down the gravel road. Her heart was beating fast and it forced her to pedal faster. She didn't want to make it seem like she was rushing away, but at the same time didn't want to give the impression she wanted to stick around. I started the walk back to my truck.

I laid in bed that night, awake but with a slightly different feeling. I thought about Jenna, as always. I thought about my sorrow. But I couldn't help but think about my time with Hannah. I laid in the darkness of my room, but I could see a small light under the door shining through from the hallway. It was just a glimpse, but it was enough to guide.

***

Over the next couple of weeks, I met her at Zivonz and made the same walk about half a dozen times. The first couple of times, I made it seem like a coincidence. The next few were somewhat planned. We'd pick up the conversations where we left off the time before. The talks were noticeably lighter each time. We would share stories of Jenna and her family over the years. She told me stories about when Jenna was young, before she moved to Shoreham Lake. I would share stories of her in high school. It was interesting piecing the stories together and finding patterns that she had as a young girl and continued as she developed into a young woman. I found talking with Hannah therapeutic. And she felt the same way. She was relatable. Each time we would stop at the bridge, with each stop seemingly longer than the time before. And each time, Hannah would ask how I was coping.

"I've had a ton of support from people," I responded, "yet I've never felt more alone than I have these past couple of months," I continued.

Then I looked in her direction.

"But to be honest, talking with you reminds me that I'm not in this alone." I said.

After a while, the conversation gradually turned from the past to our lives in the present. She would occasionally ask questions about my future which I always successfully dodged. June was approaching and the weather was starting to heat up. I talked about the summertime and how Jenna and I, along with our friends, would go on the lake all day and well into the evening – cruising around, skiing, listening to music, and watching the sunset without a care in the world.

"I haven't been on the lake yet," Hannah said.

"Oh man, you have to, it's the best." I added.

"It sounds fun. I'm sure I'll get out there soon," she said, seemingly searching for an invitation.

I thought about inviting her with us some weekend, but for some reason I was still leery of hanging out with her in public or getting too close to her. I didn't quite trust her enough to let her in our little world of lake life. It may sound juvenile, but it was exclusive and special to me.

"Yeah, I know Lola likes to drive her pontoon still," I said.

"She does," Hannah confirmed.

"Well, big plans for the weekend?" I asked, changing the subject.

"Yeah…it sounds like there's the water carnival in town? I think Lola wants to stop up there and check things out." She said.

"Cool. Yeah, I'll be there most of the weekend. I'm sure I'll see you there," I proposed.

We got up and went our separate ways once again. The water carnival was just a couple days away. Before talking to Hannah, I wasn't that excited for it. For some reason, I was kind of looking forward to it now.

***

Shoreham Lake was full of activities in the summertime. For those of us who lived there year-round, it added some spice to our small town. And it attracted the seasonal lake-goers and tourists, giving them something to do. The water carnival was every year during the first weekend of June. Along with Memorial Day the weekend before, it was the official kick-off to summer. Most of the activities took place in the park just off the public beach. It was a big event, with a picnic, live music, vendors peddling everything from jewelry to paintings to quilts, and countless water activities. There were trampolines and other toys set up in the lake's public swimming areas and water balloon fights for the young kids. Of course, there was a beer garden in the middle of it so the adults could cool off their taste buds.

Every year Jenna and I would form a team for the fire hose tournament. The local firemen donated two large fire hoses for the event. There were four people on a team, each holding the long hose. Two teams at a time would face off with their hoses pointed at the other. In the middle was a balloon tied to a long clothesline. The goal was to spray the balloon with the hose and back it up passed the other team's goal line. It was just a friendly game, but it got intense. Our team never won in the past but we always had a blast. The top teams were always the police and fire departments. Tons of people cheered on the teams, while occasionally getting wet themselves. This year, like everything else, was a first without Jenna. It was yet another reminder that she wasn't there. And like everything else, my first reaction was to skip it. But my mom and dad continuously told me that I couldn't stop living, and it wouldn't hurt to try and have some fun. So, I put together a squad with my friends. We made it to the finals against the fire department team. Before the match, we huddled up.

"Here we go boys, one more match and we're champs," I said as if we were getting ready to play a hockey game.

Even though it was meaningless, it felt pretty cool to compete again, especially with my buddies. We fell behind early, with the balloon pushing back towards our goal, but we pulled through and mounted a big comeback victory. We all cheered like we just won the Stanley Cup and hugged each other all soaked and wet. In good sportsmanship, we lined up and shook hands with the runners-up. It felt good to get a win.

After we finished, we peeled off our wet shirts and dried off with towels and each put on our water carnival championship t-shirts. People came up to us and congratulated us. Some kids even asked for our autographs, which was pretty funny. We rewarded ourselves by getting slushies, burgers, and fries from the street vendors.

"Hey," I heard from behind me.

I turned around.

"Hi," I responded with a smile.

"Nice job out there. Big win." Hannah said.

"You saw that, huh? Yeah, it was huge." I replied sarcastically, "it was fun, though."

Lola was off to the side, talking to a group of ladies.

"Do you want a slushy? I got a free one since we won." I offered.

She looked over at Lola and saw that she was preoccupied.

"Sure," she said as she shrugged her shoulders and sat down next to me.

We sat for a while and watched the other activities in the park. Hannah was noticeably quieter than with our usual conversations. Maybe she was shy because of all of the people. Plus, my friends could be intimidating to someone who doesn't know them.

"Hey, kids," Mark said as he hopped down the bleachers and sat right above us.

"I'm sorry for my friend's rudeness. He forgot to introduce us." Mark flirted with her as he stuck out his hand.

I just shook my head, "Hannah, this is Mark," I said.

"Hi, it's nice to meet you," Hannah said as she shook his hand.

"The pleasure is all mine, trust me." He responded.

I shook my head again.

"And where did you come from, Hannah?" He asked.

"You know Hannah," I interrupted, "She's Jenna's cousin....or, *was* Jenna's cousin." I added, which made it even more awkward.

Mark had a surprised look on his face, but quickly shrugged it off.

"Will you be joining us for the party at my place tonight?" He asked.

Hannah seemed flattered yet nervous with the question.

I interrupted again, "No, its fine. You don't have to."

"Excuse me, but I believe the young lady can speak for herself, William," said Mark as he turned back towards Hannah for an answer.

She smiled at both of us, "No, I don't think I'll be able to make it, but thank you," she said politely.

Lola wrapped up her conversation with the ladies and looked around for Hannah. She saw her and stood up.

"Well, I better get going. Thanks for the slushy." She said.

"You're welcome, Hannah," Mark chimed in as if she was talking to him.

"Bye Mark," she said to humor him as she smiled and walked away, glancing towards me.

"See you later," I said and waved.

I could feel Mark's eyes upon me.

"Don't." I said in anticipation as I watched her walk away.

"What?" Mark asked as he raised his voice.

"She's Jenna's cousin," I added.

"*Was* Jenna's cousin. And I didn't say anything," Mark responded as he threw up his hands and walked back up the bleachers.

He was right, he didn't infer anything. Maybe I was just trying to convince myself.

Just like the previous times I had talked with Hannah, I found myself wanting to talk more. Something came over me. I saw that she and Lola got stopped by another lady to small talk. I hopped off the bleachers and jogged towards her.

"Hannah!" I yelled as I waived.

She turned around.

"Hey...I didn't mean to sound like I didn't want you to come tonight, you are definitely more than welcome." I clarified.

"Yeah, no, I know what you meant, its fine." She responded.

"It should be pretty fun, you should swing by," I encouraged.

"Okay, well maybe I'll see what Scarlett has planned," she said.

"Cool, well then maybe I'll see you tonight then."

"Maybe," she said.

I was excited at the prospect of seeing her at the party. I didn't realize it, but I hadn't been excited for something in quite some time. Given my recent overindulgence in alcohol, I made a conscious effort to go easy that night as the party approached. Plus, I didn't want to be a mess if Hannah happened to show up. I wanted to have fun with the guys, but I decided to hold back. We stayed at the carnival for a while, then we all went our separate ways to grab dinner and freshen up before the party. Per usual, I met some of the guys over at Mark's early on.

Throughout the party, I was preoccupied with watching the front door to see if Hannah would walk in. I tried to enjoy myself, but I was distracted the whole time. A few of the guys asked why I wasn't drinking, but I played it off as unintentional.

I got stuck in a conversation with TJ about playing hockey in the fall. TJ was a super big hockey fan. He never played the game, but he loved to watch. He would've played, but unfortunately his parents couldn't afford to put him in hockey at an early age. But he turned out to be one of our biggest fans all throughout high school, and he was one of my best friends. He kept pestering me about playing junior or college hockey. He gave me a lecture of how I had too much talent to let it go to waste. I chimed in with a few nods and short answers, but it was mainly him doing the talking. Not only was it a conversation that I didn't want to engage in, I was also distracted by watching the door. He asked me what teams were interested, how I was going to make my decision, when I was going to make my decision, and so forth. All of a sudden, the door opened and Scarlett walked in. I felt a butterfly in my stomach. She closed the door and no one was with her. I was immediately let down. Hannah must have declined the invitation. Out of frustration, I grabbed TJ's beer and took a big swig. *It was time to party*, I thought. She wasn't coming.

All of a sudden, the door opened again and Hannah stepped inside. The butterflies returned. She walked in and looked around, sort of hesitantly. She still didn't know many people, and Scarlett and I were probably the only ones she felt comfortable with.

"Hey man, I'm going to grab a beer," I interrupted TJ and walked away towards the door.

The slight worry on Hannah's face vanished when I caught her eye.

"Hey there," I said as I approached.

"Hey," she responded.

I didn't know whether we should hug, shake hands, or do nothing at all. We exchanged pleasantries at the door and eventually left the safe zone and ventured around the party together. I offered to get her a drink and she accepted, which was kind of a surprise since she told me she wasn't a big drinker. She only had one beer, but it seemed to relax her a little. We didn't talk much, just made our way through the house as I introduced her around. As the night went on, it started to get late and she indicated a desire to go home.

"Yeah it doesn't look like Scarlett is going to leave anytime soon," she said with a little laugh.

We looked over and saw her and Mark attempting to dance together between falling over and taking drinks. It appeared they were heading for another relapse.

"Well, I can give you a ride home, if you want," I offered.

"Are you sure? I don't want you to miss out." She said with hesitation.

I laughed, "Trust me, I'm not missing anything I haven't experienced before."

We walked out of the house, and I was somewhat careful to look and see who saw us leaving together in an attempt to quell any potential rumors. It was just an innocent ride home, but I knew how rumors started in a small town. The drive was only a couple of miles, so I intentionally drove slow to prolong the trip. We talked about the party mostly, and touched on our plans for the next day. The conversation was shallower than our previous ones.

"Just up the road here," she instructed.

"Yeah, I know." I responded.

"Oh yeah, of course," she added.

I had been over to Lola's cabin on many occasions, and Hannah felt a little foolish that she forgot that. I pulled into the yard and shut the truck off. We both traded some transition words. I could feel some tension in the car. I was a little nervous and I could tell she was as well. We avoided eye contact and didn't know how to say goodnight.

"So, does Lola wait up for you?" I asked, breaking the ice again and nodding towards the house.

"I'm not sure. I sleep in the bunk house," she nods to our left.

I looked over. It was located behind Lola's cabin close to the road. It was nothing special, but it gave her personal space, something that was valuable to an eighteen-year-old girl. It included a small bedroom and bathroom, with a small living room area. Hannah mainly just used it for sleeping and spent the majority of her time in the cabin, which had more amenities, including a kitchen with an abundance of homemade food.

"That's nice to have a space to yourself," I commented.

"Yeah, it works out well. But there are still lights on inside, so I'll probably go see if she's still up." She said.

"Well…" I continued.

"Well…" she repeated.

You could cut the tension with a knife. I put my hands on the steering wheel.

"Have a goodnight," I said.

"Have a goodnight, Will," she responded.

She climbed out of the truck and walked confidently towards her front door. I sat there and watched curiously before I shook my head and drove away. I immediately regretted what I didn't do.

***

Once Hannah got inside and shut the door behind her, she peered out the window and saw the taillights disappear into the distance.

Lola, who was patiently waiting up for her, quipped from her living room chair, "When did Scarlett get a truck?" with a sarcastic tone.

Hannah knew that she was caught. She quickly thought of a believable excuse, but nothing came out. Lola looked up from her book she was reading with a big smile.

"Goodnight, sweetheart," she said as she got up and walked out towards her bedroom.

"Goodnight, grandma." Hannah replied.

Hannah dropped her purse on the bench by the door and walked into the living room. She felt light-headed as she stumbled across the floor and threw herself on the couch. Her hair was spread over the pillow like a windmill as she stared at the ceiling. She had a thousand different feelings rushing through her body, feelings that she had never felt before. It was almost unbearable. At the same time, it was a sensation she desperately wanted to explore further. She had voices on each of her shoulders – one saying it was wrong, one saying it was right. Paralyzed with emotions, she struggled to decide which one to believe.

***

I should have walked her to the door. I should have tried to give her a hug, or something. At that moment, a part of me even wanted to kiss her, as crazy as that sounded. I should have at least told her that I was glad she came to the party. That was one part of my mind. The other was telling me that I was absolutely crazy. It was too soon. She was Jenna's cousin and best friend, and that just wasn't right. There were voices on each shoulder, both with seemingly reasonable arguments. As I shook my head, I started the truck and put it in gear and slowly drove away into the darkness of her gravel-covered driveway. It was still fairly early by our summer weekend night standards, so I thought about going back to the party. Instead, I decided to just go home and go to bed.

I was infected with a flood of feelings as I drove back home. Hannah had an allure about her – a mystery that I wanted to explore further. I could feel a sense of optimism softly burning inside of me. I couldn't decide if I wanted to fight the feeling or not. It was becoming apparent that I didn't have a choice. It was out of my hands. It was in my heart.

6

My alarm clock went off like an ambulance siren the next morning. The sun was still asleep. I quickly rolled over and pounded my fist on the button to make it stop. I rolled back over onto my back and closed my eyes again for a moment and opened them again. Staring at the ceiling, it was illuminated just slightly by the faint light from my window. I let out a deep breath and hopped out of bed. I turned my nightstand lamp on and dug through my drawer for some clothes, then threw on an old shirt and sweatpants, turned my lamp off, and walked out of my room.

Tiptoeing through the kitchen and into the entryway, I tried not to wake my parents. I shuffled through the front closet in the dark and felt around for my shoes, then plucked both of them with one hand and closed the door. After lacing them up, I quietly opened the front door and closed it shut behind me. I walked out on the driveway towards the road, stretching and bending my arms and legs to loosen up. It was still a little dark outside, with the sun now peering out in the distance trying to start its job for the day. It was sort of cool outside – perfect temperature for a run. I stopped and let out a deep breath just before I approached the road. I started to jog.

Every summer and fall, I would run to train for the next hockey season. I would run all the way around Shoreham Lake, which equated to about ten miles. I preferred to run at odd hours of the day, either very early in the morning or late at night. I figured my competition was sleeping at that time and I was gaining an edge. People who saw me thought I was crazy, but I loved the challenge. It was more than just physical exercise. It was mental exercise, perhaps even mental therapy. I did some of my best thinking when I ran. For some reason, it seemed to clear my cluttered mind and ease any stress I had, at least temporarily. I savored the process from start to finish, pushing myself to places I didn't know were possible and surrendering to adrenaline along the way. There is nothing like the feeling of making it back to my finish line, covered in sweat, out of breath, and the challenge conquered.

I hadn't run at all since last fall, save when I had to get my car after Cliff's party. And I hadn't done any physical exercise whatsoever since hockey season ended months ago. The joints in my knees were rusty and achy. My back was stiff and my calves were tight. After about a half mile, I started to break the rusty shackles as I loosened up and found a groove. Thoughts and emotions swirled in my head with every step I took. After the first few miles, I was exhausted and was about to give up and walk back. All of a sudden, I saw a girl jogging up ahead of me. She looked around my age and had dirty blonde hair in a ponytail bouncing behind her. As I got closer, I recognized her – it was Hannah. I gained a little energy and caught up to her.

"Hi," I said as I approached her and slowed down to her pace.

A little startled, she put her hand over her heart and replied, "Oh my goodness, you scared me. Hi."

She was out of breath. It appeared that she was towards the end of her run.

"Are you a runner?" I asked as we continued on pace together.

"Yeah I am." She replied, out of breath.

"Cool. I'm trying to get back into it," I said, "Looks like next time I'll have to wake up earlier!"

She smiled and I could tell she couldn't talk much since she was breathing so hard. I figured I would let her be and stop annoying her. I sprinted past her and turned around while running backwards.

"Good luck the rest of the way," I said as she acknowledged me and continued on her journey.

I suddenly forgot about my fatigue and got a burst of energy, determined to make it through my usual route. I was determined to start and finish something – to prove that I could accomplish something again, however small it may be. Above all, it was to prove that the determined and competitive side of me was still inside of me. I found myself wanting to give up a few different times, especially when I hit the huge incline along the east side of the lake, which was always the hardest because of the resistance and its location along the home stretch. My chest felt tight and I had troubles breathing as my ascent began. The side ache that was lingering for the first couple of miles flared up again. My brain sent messages to my legs to keep pumping, like the large pistons that powered the Titanic. Suddenly, I felt a shot of adrenaline. I made it, barely, up the hill and coasted down with a slight jog.

As usual, I passed our mailman on his route. He gave his usual two finger wave from the steering wheel. I was almost too tired to waive back. I passed my dad while he was driving his truck. He had a surprised look on his face when he saw me run past. I was completely out of breath as I made the turn onto the south shore drive. My cabin was in sight. I worked through the side ache, but my calves were burning and my right shoulder was nagging from an old hockey injury. Digging deep, I started to pick up speed again. Almost there – just another half of a mile. *Keep going,* I told myself. I imaged the moments when Jenna encouraged me to keep going. Sometimes she would even bike along side of me. I had tunnel vision towards the finish line. By then I was speeding as fast as I've ever ran. The feeling was exhilarating. Exhaustion was overtaking me, but I refused to stop. Just a few more yards. I pushed on harder and harder. As I reached my driveway, I let out a loud grunt and raised my arms in victory as I tried to slow down to stop. I made it. Thank God, I made it.

Drenched in sweat, I could barely breathe. I gave a huge fist pump in the air in celebration, not before I looked around to see if anyone was watching. I put my hands on my hips and paced back and forth a few times before walking around the house towards the lake. Since it was so early, there were only a couple of small fishing boats out on the water. I walked onto the dock and paced back and forth again, trying to catch my breath. I was amped up on a high and I didn't want to come down – not yet. It was like a drug. I wanted to savor that feeling a little longer. I got down on my hands and toes and did some pushups. My sweat dripped down from my forehead through the small spaces between the wood panels of the dock, which rippled the calm water slightly. After squeezing in a few more pushups, I finally gave in and dropped on the dock. I rolled over onto my back and just laid for a minute. What a feeling. I closed my eyes and wiped the sweat from my face with the back of my hand. That was such a great feeling, physically sweating out toxins from my body and demons from my mind. I got up, exhausted, and walked inside the cabin.

My mom, dressed in her robe with her coffee mug in hand, peered through the window at me on the dock. She quickly sat back down at the table and resumed reading the paper so I didn't suspect her watching when I walked in. Her and my dad were both just happy to see me do something normal again. So was I. It felt great.

It was Saturday in June, and it was supposed to be a hot one outside. The radio said it could reach ninety degrees. For a guy who lived on a lake and didn't have to work, that was pure sweetness to my ears. That usually meant getting the boys together and loading up the boat for the day. I was expecting a call from at least one of them in a few hours when they got up. We usually took my family's boat because it was the newest and biggest. We would pack it with so many people that the boat often took on water because of the weight. We would cruise around, listen to music on the radio, and usually end up stringing up next to all of the other boats at the sandbar. On that day, I had a better idea.

A few hours later, I picked up the phone. One ring, two rings, three. My heart was beating fast and I suddenly got a little nervous.

"Hello?" Said a familiar voice.

"Lola, hi . . . uh, good morning," I fumbled.

"Well hello, who am I speaking to?" She asks, knowing full well who it was.

"This is Will Camps. Is Hannah there?" I finally got it together.

"She sure is, let me go get her," she replied.

My nervousness increased. I started to re-think my decision. Could I hang up? No, I already told her it was me. Do I make up another reason for my call? I quickly thought of different excuses, but they all sounded stupid. I was stuck. I had to go through with it now.

"Hello?" Hannah asked.

"Hannah, hey . . . Will, here," I said.

"Hi," she replied reluctantly as she looked over at Lola and turned her back.

"What are you doing this afternoon?" I asked.

"Um...my grandma and I were planning on going

to the flea market," she replied.

"Oh, ok. I was calling to see if you wanted to go for a boat ride," I offered.

She paused and turned her head to look at Lola.

"We can go to the flea market anytime dear," I heard Lola say from off in the background.

"Count me in," she replied into the phone, a smile evident in her voice.

"Great, be at the end of your dock at noon," I instructed.

Hannah hung up the phone and quickly rushed to her room. She stood in front of her mirror, letting her hair down as it laid on her shoulders. She was unimpressed. She then rummaged through her drawer to find a bikini, none of which had been worn since last summer. She went into the bathroom and put on her best makeup. It seemed silly to put on makeup before a day on the boat, but she wanted to make a good impression. Meanwhile, I walked outside onto the dock and checked the boat for gas, picking up some empty cans from the floor. I peeled my shirt off and jumped off the dock. The water hit me instantly, first shocking, then refreshing. During the summer months, we always kept a bottle of shampoo and bar of soap in a basket at the end of the dock. I loved bathing in the lake. It made me feel more in touch with nature. After packing a cooler with a few sodas, I threw on my hat and sunglasses, grabbed a towel, and hopped on the boat.

I fired up the engine and it roared to life. Hannah's place was across the lake, so I opened up the throttle at full speed. I stood up to see over the dashboard with the wind blowing in my face. What a feeling of freedom. I zoomed past a fisherman, undoubtedly angering him by creating waves that rocked his boat and scared his catch away. As her cabin came into sight, I saw her silhouette standing on the dock, coming into focus more as I got closer. I slowed down as I got within a few hundred feet and coasted in. There she stood, with cutoff jean shorts and a towel hanging around her neck. We both couldn't help but smile as I approached the dock. I quickly walked up to the front of the boat and stuck my leg out to catch the dock. Then I reached out my hand and she grabbed it tight as I pulled her onto the boat. Her hand was soft and the touch radiated through my body like a lightning strike.

We picked up right where we left off. Our conversation was seamless. We talked a lot more about Jenna – old memories, the early days when we were kids, the last days of her battle. We eventually talked about each other. I asked her question after question, a habit I inherited from my father. I was captivated by her words. She had a certain humility and authenticity about her. I was genuinely interested in what she had to say and it appeared she was the same with me, or at least she was good at pretending. We drove around the lake one time and then just floated in the open water. It was a peaceful day, hot sun with very little wind. There was nothing to interrupt us.

"Jenna loved it out here, didn't she?" Hannah asked, already knowing the answer.

I paused for a moment and looked out at the water.

"Yeah...she did." I responded.

Hannah could tell her question brought a somber tone to my voice. She then tried to lighten the mood a bit.

"Remember when you missed the big Johnson family picture because you were....in the bathroom?" She asked as she giggled.

"I have no recollection of that, no," I responded sarcastically.

"Sure," she said with sarcasm of her own.

I changed the subject and asked, "Do you want a Coke?"

"Sure," she responded.

She just smiled. Her smile was contagious. Her eyes lit up at the same time. It was probably the first time in weeks that I genuinely smiled. It was definitely the first time since Jenna passed that I didn't feel guilty for smiling. I was doing something for me, for my enjoyment. For a few moments at least, I wasn't thinking about Jenna or the stress in my life. I was just enjoying myself. And I don't care what anyone said, there was nothing wrong with it.

We floated around for a while longer. That turned into another hour. We continued to chat until the sun started to descend, losing track of the time. What started as a simple boat ride turned into an entire afternoon on the lake. By that time, the lake was glass. The pontoon stood still without an anchor.

I took a swig of Coke and kicked my feet up on the dash as I looked out. A group of birds flew over us in a perfect formation. There was silence for a bit as she looked at me.

"What are you thinking about?" she interrupted.

I kept staring out for a few seconds and turned my head and looked at her.

"I'm thinking I want to take a dip. What do you think?" I asked.

I noticed she didn't take off her shorts or swimsuit cover-up all day.

"I should probably get going soon, actually. Lola is making dinner, so…," she countered.

"Oh ok, yeah, it's probably about that time. I'll bring you back." I said.

I started up the motor and opened up the throttle. She stared off into the distance with her chrome aviator sunglasses on her eyes as the wind blew through her hair. She started gathering her stuff as I pulled into her dock slowly. I ran up to the front to catch the dock before the boat hit. As I kneeled down to hold the dock, Hannah's legs crossed my eyes, her skin glistening from the suntan oil, and hopped out of the boat. She turned around.

"Well, thanks. That was fun." She said.

"Definitely, we'll have to do it again sometime," I responded.

"I'll meet you at the end of the dock," she said with a smile.

I pushed the boat out from the dock.

"You got it." I said.

She turned around and started walking towards her cabin. I stole a look for a second before I hopped into the driver's seat and put it in reverse. That was the best time for a boat cruise, when the wind died down, the sun and the temperature were dropping, and everything was still. There's something about a boat that frees your mind, it allows you to leave it all back on shore. It somehow unites with the water to calm a restless soul. I cranked the radio and opened the throttle. I stood up and felt the wind blow in my face. There was greatness in that ride home. As I flipped on the radio, I cranked up Bob Seger's "Like a Rock" and sang it at the top of my lungs. The sun was dropping and the sky was lit up in layers of purple and orange, with a couple of dark clouds that looked like smoke. It looked like the sky was on fire. I felt some of that fire inside of me. For the first time in a long time, I could say it was a good day. Not quite great, but good. And that was a great start.

***

I picked Hannah up again the next Saturday and we soaked up the sun. This time, she shed her cover-up and shorts, revealing her black bikini underneath. I was more than impressed, as she was in great shape. She had a slender body with defined arms and thighs. After she took off her cover, I had trouble focusing in on what she was saying.

Eventually, I became more comfortable sharing her company with others. I picked up some other friends to join the next week and we spent the days at the sandbar – drinking beer, listening to music, playing catch with the football, and living the summer life. All of my friends were kind and welcoming to her. They knew she was Jenna's cousin, so I think that helped. A week later, I pulled up to the dock once again and Hannah was waiting.

"Beach it! Lola wants to see you!" She yelled.

I immediately got nervous. Even though I figured this day would come, I didn't know how to handle it. I hadn't seen Lola since the funeral. She obviously knew I had been hanging out with Hannah. Even though we were just friends hanging out, I had no idea what Lola thought about it. I was about to find out. After I plowed the boat into the sandy beach, I hopped out and walked with Hannah to the porch. Lola was sitting with a big hat on and a tall icy margarita on the table next to her.

"Well, hello Will!" She said as she stood up and walked towards me.

She gave me a big hug and kissed me on the cheek, just like she always used to do.

"Hi, Lola," I said.

"It's so good to see you, how have you been, darling?" She inquired.

"I've been alright," I answered.

"Well, I bet you have. You get to hang out with this girl a lot from what I hear!" She added.

I blushed a little bit.

"Yeah, I've been showing her around a little," I responded.

I wanted to make it very clear that we were just friends. Besides, that's really all we were.

"I've known this boy since he was about this tall, and he's been driving that boat around this lake from about the same time," she said as she picked up her glass and took another sip.

"That's probably true," I admitted.

We sat on the porch for about a half hour and chatted. Lola was such an interesting lady. She was wise beyond her years, but often masked it by her sense of humor. She was constantly joking around, and even a little too blunt at times. But that's why everyone loved her. She was a jokester, but served as a matriarch of the community. Her husband passed away years ago when Jenna and Hannah were young. Consequently, Lola was a very strong and independent woman who provided for herself ever since. Instead of giving up and withering away – a hazard for many widows – Lola pulled herself up by her bootstraps and plugged away. She was busy all the time. She was involved in basically every organization in town, from school board to P.E.O. She was also head of the parish council at the church. She was in card-playing groups and book clubs, which consisted of dozens of women gathering to drink wine and gossip, and occasionally they played cards and discussed books. In the middle of it all, the ring-leader was Lola. I always thought Jenna got her outgoing personality from Lola. And I was quickly finding out Hannah did as well. Lola had been through a lot over the years, but time hadn't laid a glove on her physically. She was a pretty lady – like all of the Johnson girls.

"Well, I better get to watering these flowers since this young lady spends all of her time carousing with the lake boys," Lola said with her familiar sarcasm. "You all have fun, now," she continued as she stood up and walked towards the cabin.

I grabbed Hannah's bag and threw it in the boat. I hopped up on the bow, grabbed her hand, and pulled her up. We started off talking about Lola. Hannah told me about how Lola encouraged her to go out and socialize and meet new people when she got to town. She would tell her that summer is what you make of it. Hannah described herself as somewhat sheltered in a new town, reluctant to go out and meet new people. She wasn't a shy person by any means, but a new place can be intimidating if you don't know anyone. We met all of the others at the sandbar and partied the day away. We shook dice and played cards. I was too preoccupied to apply sunscreen, and I could feel the burn all day. Around dinner time, boats started to scatter. I kicked up my feet on the dash and relaxed. The sun drained my energy. It's amazing how exhausted you can get when you're just relaxing and having fun. Pretty soon it was just my boat and Mark's. He and a few of the boys were still in the water talking with Hannah. They seemed to like her, and she seemed to like them. That made everything more comfortable.

"Champ, we're rolling out," Mark said as he and the boys piled into his boat.

I raised my beer in the air as they drove away. Hannah walked over to my boat.

I leaned over the edge and put my chin on the boat.

"What are you thinking?" I asked her.

"I'm thinking you should come take a dip," she responded.

I immediately threw my sunglasses off and hopped into the water. She laughed as I splashed her. She scampered away from me through the water. Her hair was wet, and she threw it to the side and wrung out the water with her hands. She stood up and I could tell she was cold, her arms folded in and her hands clenched together towards her chin. I approached her and stopped. The magic of the lake was too much to overcome. I pulled her in close. She got up on her tip toes in the sand and we both leaned in.

Our lips touched, our tongues met and weaved together slowly. All of a sudden, my soul was set on fire. My whole body filled with chills and my heart fluttered. She dropped back on her feet with her eyes still closed as we separated. She opened her eyes and smiled. We smiled at each other and I hugged her to keep her warm. I rested my chin on her forehead. We stood still for a minute. We were both thinking of the meaning of what just happened. At that point, there was no turning back. And I don't think either of us wanted to turn back.

***

The next morning, I woke up early as usual, losing another battle to insomnia. I couldn't stop thinking about that kiss and what it meant. I got dressed and went out to the garage. I grabbed my old bike and hopped on. I loved biking around the lake. Jenna and I did it together often, but I enjoyed it alone just as much. It was good exercise, but I used it as a time of reflection and appreciation of the beauty of lake country. That's what I loved about lake country in general – the constant feeling of escapism. Every one of us has a place of solace where they can go and be themselves; in fact, the best version of themselves. It's where we are tried and true. For me, that place was the lake. You won't find more smiles anywhere in the world. It doesn't matter what you do for a living, where you've been, or where you're going. At the lake, time stops and worries are washed away. Everyone is equal, with the wealthy no happier than the poor, as long as there's a beach and a boat. The wealthy man may have a bigger boat, but the measure of happiness is equal.

On this particular ride, I had a destination – not so much a place, but a person. I slowed down as I approached the bunk house, as I didn't want to wake the neighbors or more importantly Lola. I gently set the bike on the dewy grass and approached the door. I had been in the bunkhouse before so I knew the back window was in the bedroom. I saw a light on. Hannah was wide awake and sitting up in bed. The sunlight shined through the window and bounced off her hair. She was in an old t-shirt and attentively reading a book. I quietly knocked on the window to get her attention. She was startled a bit as she looked up and immediately cracked a smile as she marked her page. I pointed towards the door and she waived me in.

"Hi," she said softly as she stretched her arms.

"Hi there," I said softly back.

"What are you doing here?" she asked.

"I don't know, I was just going for a bike ride around the lake and figured I would drop in," I said, which was a fabrication. "What are you doing up this early?"

"Just reading and relaxing," she responded.

"Are you a morning person?" I inquired.

"I'm an all-day person," she answered.

I must admit I was pretty impressed with that answer. I sat on the foot of her bed. She had a vibe about her that made me feel comfortable and uncomfortable at the same time. I was kind of nervous given our kiss the day before. I was still sweating a little bit from the bike ride, so I used my arm to dry off my forehead.

"What are you doing today?" She broke the silence.

"Just going to church with my family this morning and then probably nothing." I answered.

I looked over at the clock next to her bed.

"I'm actually running late, so I better get rolling back soon," I said.

"Yeah, and Lola will be up soon, too, so...." She said.

"Yeah, you're right," I agreed.

I put my hands on my legs and looked around a little bit. A picture of Hannah and Jenna was on her dresser. They were in their cheerleading uniforms. It was taken after the game where we played Oakwood. I suddenly got a weird feeling in my stomach. Hannah saw that I saw it. I raised my eyebrows and stood up.

"Will, about yesterday. I don't know what got into me, but I'm sorry. It won't happen again." She said.

That weird feeling in my stomach grew more

prevalent. I was sort of surprised with her straightforwardness.

"Yeah, no, yeah, I know. Don't worry about it. It was nothing." I fumbled as I pretended to shrug it off. "I'm sure I'll see you at church, then," I added.

"Yeah, sounds good." She affirmed.

After that, the dynamic changed. I was grounded back to reality. I got on my bike and pedaled fast back to my cabin. Being late for church was unacceptable in our household, so I certainly didn't want to be the reason. My thoughts were swirling wild in my head on that bike ride home. I agreed with Hannah, and I felt guilty about what happened the day before. It seemed right at the time. But now it seemed all wrong. It was an uneasy feeling. Yet I also got the sense that something was left unfinished, and I was left with a sense of curiosity. The question was whether I wanted to finish it. Either way, she made it clear she did not.

That day was excruciating with uncertainty. I couldn't stop thinking about Hannah. I couldn't stop thinking about that kiss. It was an otherworldly type of kiss. Was it just the magic of the evening? Did she really have feelings for me? Did I really have feelings for her? I also couldn't stop thinking about Jenna. I wondered what Jenna would say if she knew about what happened. I wondered if she did know. I've heard the idea of those who have passed away as "looking down" on us. I wondered if it was true. Are they constantly watching our lives like a movie? The confusion was overwhelming. And the thought of Jenna knowing made me feel uneasy.

Our neighbors came over and played yard games and grilled out that afternoon. My dad ran the grill and played host. I spent most of the day laying on a lawn chair with my shades on, day dreaming and looking out towards the water. It was active on the lake with boaters. I declined every invite to play horse shoes or bean bags. I wasn't that hungry, but I managed to take down half of a burger and a few potato chips. I stared across the lake, wondering what Hannah was doing. I thought back to grade school, when we read the book, *The Great Gatsby*. I remembered Gatsby's fixation with the light coming from the dock of Daisy's house across the bay. The author of the story, F. Scott Fitzgerald, was originally from Minnesota. Perhaps he went through the same thing and drew on personal experience for that part of the story, because that's how I felt. Was she busy having fun or was she preoccupied with thinking about me, too? I decided there was only one way to find out.

After dinner, I hopped into my truck and drove. I knew where I was going, but I was terribly nervous so I took my time. As I slowly pulled alongside the road, I parked so the bunk house was blocking my car from the view of the cabin. I almost abandoned the mission and turned around, but I couldn't. The feeling was too strong to overcome. I walked up to the bunk house. This time, I knocked on the door. I looked back at the cabin to see if anyone was outside. The door opened and Hannah stood there. She was in a Zivonz hooded sweatshirt and shorts. She had a confused look.

"Hi," I said.

"You can't make a habit of coming around here," she said as she peeked outside to see if anyone saw us.

"I know, I just . . ." I trailed off. "Look, it wasn't nothing."

Our eyes were saying something that our voices couldn't, or maybe just didn't want to. It was if there was a magnetic field between us. With every fiber of my being, I tried to fight it. We suddenly succumbed to the temptation and came together and kissed. We made out passionately as I closed the door with my foot behind me. She hopped up into my arms as I lifted her up, her legs wrapping around me. I carried her into the bedroom and we crashed into the sheets. I gently bit her bottom lip and she sighed. We continued on for quite a while. For once we didn't talk, we didn't think it through. We just acted on raw emotion. And it felt amazing.

When we happened to pull away for a moment, we looked deep into each other's eyes. We started to smile together. I leaned in again and kissed her one more time.

"What are we doing?" She whispered hysterically. "Is this wrong?" She interrupted before I could answer.

I paused for a few seconds. She looked to me for an answer.

"If this is wrong, I don't want to be right," I said.

I kissed her softly again as she closed her eyes.

We laid in bed with my arm around her and talked for hours, her head snuggled on my chest. In the middle of the story about the source of the scar under my chin, she stopped responding. I looked and she was fast asleep. I didn't want to wake her, so I just laid there and closed my eyes.

I woke up the next morning to the sun rising through the window. My neck was sore and my right arm was completely numb. I glanced over at the clock and suddenly panicked. It was Monday morning and I was already an hour late for work. I hadn't slept in this late in months. Hannah woke up as well. She didn't have to work since she had the dinner shift. I scurried towards the door and threw my sandals on. She followed me to the door as she put her hair up in a tie.

"Wait, go out the window! Lola is up!" She said in a loud whisper.

I pulled her waist towards me and kissed her goodbye. Although I did my best to sneak out, Lola happened to be washing dishes and probably caught the view of my fender from the window. All she could do was smile.

"Oh boy," Lola said under her breath to herself.

And even though I knew I was in trouble for being late, that's all I could do is smile as well as I drove away.

For the next couple of weeks, Hannah and I hung out almost every night after work. The weather was warmer than normal for June. Usually lake weather doesn't really kick in until July, but we got in a full month of boating, skiing, and swimming. I found myself anxious all day, every day waiting to see Hannah at night. If she worked, I would often pick her up after. We would throw her bike in the back of my truck. I even skipped men's golf night with my dad two weeks in a row because I didn't want to miss a night with Hannah. As much as we could, we kept our romance a secret. When anyone asked, even my friends, we would say that we were just friends. When my mom inquired about the amount of time we were spending together, I just told her that I was making her feel at home in her new town. It wasn't a complete lie.

The Fourth of July was just a week away. Nothing says summer like the Fourth of July. In Shoreham Lake, it was easily the most celebrated holiday of the year. The festivities started with a golf tournament to benefit high school athletics, then days filled with street fairs and nights filled with street dances with live music and parties. It all culminated on the Fourth with a big bash on the public beach that ended with a huge fireworks show. It was a magical time where the whole area came alive.

It was my favorite weekend of the year. The anticipation of the weekend grew when I received word that my parents were going to be out of town. Although my parents loved the Fourth, they purposely planned a vacation to Florida for that week. I think after forty years of working and celebrating it in Shoreham Lake, they needed a break. It had been a tough year on them as well, with Jenna passing and realizing they would soon be empty-nesters. They gave me the standard warning about having parties and getting into trouble and I gave them my standard promise not to. In fact, I had no interest in throwing a party at our house. There were plenty of parties going on throughout the area, plus we had no problem getting into the beach bars on those busy nights.

My dad felt comfortable leaving everything in the hands of his trusted employee, Ryan Baker. Ryan was in his forties, and he had worked at Shoreham Hills since he was in high school. He started off as a bus boy and dishwasher at the restaurant, eventually graduating to bartender and then manager of the restaurant. When my dad was gone, he filled in as general manager of the entire resort. He was a tall man and his head was bald as can be. He always wore some type of Hawaiian type button-down short-sleeve shirt. He talked fast, walked fast, and made drinks like a scientist. From what I heard, he had a rough childhood, if you could even call it that. His father was abusive and kicked him out of the house in high school. My dad took him in and gave him a job and some direction. He even let him live in a hotel room until he found a place. My dad did that with a few different people over the years. Ryan had also made glaring mistakes throughout his life. He didn't seem to enjoy his work pouring drinks, but he was one of those guys who took his job more seriously than he probably should. He didn't seem to enjoy much of anything else either. But perhaps that kind of work caused him the least amount of pain. Or perhaps he had a case of learned helplessness, and that line of work actually caused him the most pain. Either way, he was a great employee and had been loyal to my dad since day one. Quite frankly, he was just grateful for the job. He earned everything he had, and consequently my dad treated him well.

My parents took off on Tuesday morning for the whole week. The forecast was hot and sunny all week and weekend. With the freedom of my parents gone also came more responsibility at the resort, especially since it was our busiest weekend of the year. Tuesday and Wednesday flew by. I worked days and Hannah worked nights, so we didn't get to see each other. I would wait up for her to get off work and we would talk for hours on the phone. We'd go from deep conversations to something as simple as the weather or the neighbor dog barking. We didn't care what we were talking about, we just wanted to be connected.

It got up to ninety degrees by Friday. I spent all day on the ranch. My t-shirt was soaked from sweating. The veins in my arms were sticking out as my biceps pumped. Hannah didn't work that day, so I told her I would call her right when I got off work. We were planning on staying the night at my place after the street dance since we had it all to ourselves. It was our weekend, and I couldn't wait.

Apparently neither could she. As I stacked bales of hay one by one on top of each other and went back for more, I felt hands from behind me cover my eyes.

"Hey!" She said as she snuck up.

I turned around. She was wearing a white tank top and cutoff jean shorts. She looked gorgeous. I hadn't seen her in way too long. It is a crazy feeling to always want to be with someone. I flinched towards her and tickled her stomach as I chased her over to the stack of bales. She playfully laughed and ran away. I grabbed her from behind and turned her around. She hopped up and wrapped her legs around me. I picked her up and sat her down on the bales. We both just smiled at each other. She wiped some dirt off my cheek. I flipped my ball cap backwards and leaned in for a kiss. As I pulled back, I could see my sweat and dirt rubbed off on her face. All I could do was laugh. She grabbed my cap and put it on her head. I lifted my shirt up and wiped the sweat and dirt from my face. My work was done for the day.

We went back to my place so I could get ready, and I decided to take a bath in the lake.

"You going to be okay in here all alone?" I asked.

"Go, you are filthy," she said as she pushed me away.

As I was in the lake, Hannah looked around the living room. She caroused down the hallway, looking at various pictures on the wall – me and my brothers catching our first fish, family portraits, and playing hockey. Then there was the collage of me and Jenna – pictures of us skiing, laying in the hammock, and baking cookies. She came towards the end of the hall as she came across my junior year prom picture of me and Jenna. She stopped and stared at it for a moment.

"Wooo!" I exclaimed as I slid the patio door closed.

Hannah, startled, jumped a little bit.

"What are you up to?" I asked her casually as I dried off my face with my towel.

I peeked over to see what she was looking at.

"Nothing, just looking around." She responded.

"You ready?" I asked.

She stared at me for a moment and thought about the question.

"I am." She confirmed.

"Great, I'll throw on a shirt and we'll get rolling." I said.

We walked out onto the driveway towards my truck.

"Shotgun," she said quietly.

I stopped in my tracks and looked at her. I remembered how Jenna used to do the same thing.

"What?" She asked.

"Nothing," I answered as I shook the cob web

from my head.

I walked with her over to the passenger side and opened her door. She looked at me with a strange grin. I closed the door behind her and quickly walked across the front and over to my side. When I hopped in the truck, she still had the same look on her face.

"What?" I asked again, this time louder.

"Nothing, it's just...no one has ever done that for me before." She admitted.

I thought to myself, if I had it my way, she would never have to open the door for herself again. We drove downtown for the street dance on the strip. The whole street was blocked off all the way down the beach. Live music was playing as people danced in the street and patronized the bars. Beach volleyball was rocking outside and there were carnival games lining the beach. We started off at Zivonz with all of my friends, who were waiting at a big table when we walked in. Over nervousness, I reintroduced Hannah to everyone and we quickly blended in. I went and sat with the guys and the girls took her to their side of the table. I tried my best to engulf myself into the conversations, but I couldn't stop worrying about Hannah across the table. After a while, we all gathered around the bar for drinks.

"You alright?" I shouted over the loud music.

I touched her arm but then quickly backed away

after remembering we were in public.

"I'm great," Hannah responded.

We had a few drinks and then joined the party out on the street. While some of the others made their way to the dance area, I stayed back and people-watched. Hannah found Scarlett and they seemed to dance all night. I actually became a little jealous after a while when she wasn't paying attention to me. But I was also glad that she was fitting in and having a good time. As the last song wrapped up, we all met up in the street.

"After party at my place?" Mark asked the group.

The group obliged. We piled into some cars and took the party to Mark's house. We played some card games and drank more for hours. I was still preoccupied by Hannah. A few of the guys flirted with her. It was a weird dynamic – I didn't want to make it public that we were an item, but at the same time I wanted to tell everyone else to back. Eventually, I motioned for her to meet me outside. I walked out on the patio and looked out towards the water and the dock. I waited a few minutes for Hannah to join me, but still nothing. I walked out over the lawn and onto the dock, where I sat down on the end. I thought about when Hannah came out to meet me on the dock at the first party of the summer and how fateful that moment turned out to be. I thought about how I was in such a better place at that moment than I was just a little over a month earlier. I slipped my sandals off and dipped my toes in the water.

"Hi there," I heard Hannah's voice as I felt the dock shake by her footsteps.

I smiled out towards the water and then turned around.

"Hi there," I responded as I scooted over to make room for her.

She sat down close to me and snuggled in. I put my arm around her. The party was fun, but I would choose this moment any day of the week. We hitched a ride back to my house a few hours later and spent the remainder of the night making love in my bed.

Hannah had the lunch and afternoon shift the next day, so she only got a few hours of sleep. Mark came and picked us up to bring me to my car. We dropped Hannah off at her cabin first. I got out of the car with her and gave her a kiss goodbye. When I got back into the car, Mark fired away.

"So that's happening, huh?" He asked.

"Just drive," I responded.

"I thought you guys were just friends," he said, mocking my previous assertions.

"Just shut up and drive," I responded as I laid my head back and shut my eyes.

"Alright, I'm going to back you on this," he said with a smirk.

Even though I hid it from him, I smirked, too.

Mark and I grabbed a big corn dog and fries from a street vendor on the strip for lunch. We went back to my place and took the boat out for a while with the boys. Hannah got off work around dinner time and I dropped them off and then picked her up on her dock. The sun was setting and the wind was still. I cranked up the radio and sang at the top of my lungs.

"Stop please!" Hannah yelled from the front of the boat.

She still had a headache from the night before and the loud music didn't help.

I walked to the front of the boat, still singing the lyrics, and grabbed her hand and pulled her up. We swing danced as best as I could in the middle of the boat, applying some of my lessons I picked up from watching her the night before. I picked her up off her feet and laid her on the ground as I hovered over her. I grabbed the back of her neck and guided our lips together. We made love as the waves gently swayed the boat. The rest is between me, her, and the summer sun. But if that boat could talk, we'd be in trouble. On the ride home, she sat on my lap and steered the boat.

"So, when do you want to go to the dance?" I

asked her as we walked back onto the beach and sat down on the patio.

"Don't be mad, but honestly, I think I'd rather just stay in tonight." She answered.

"Honestly, I was kind of hoping you would say that." I admitted with a smile.

Instead of joining the big party on the strip, we decided to spend the rest of the day on the beach and then planned to spark a campfire. As we sat staring at the red orange sunset slowly dropping into the water, it was pure tranquility. It looked like an exaggerated painting. I grabbed her cheek with my hand and turned her head to the side. I kissed her slowly and gently.

We packed some graham crackers, marshmallows, and Hershey's chocolate bars. I threw on sweatpants to get more comfortable. She was still in her bikini and cover-up.

"Do you want to stop at your place and get some clothes?" I offered.

"Do you have anything I could wear?" She asked.

"Sure, my sweatshirts are on the shelf in my closet. Just grab one. I'll get the fire going," I responded.

I gathered the s'mores ingredients and headed outside to set up camp and start the fire. The fire pit was charred. With a spark and a little work, a flame lit and the wood started crackling and burning. Just as my spark caught the wood on fire, Hannah came through the door and slid it shut. I looked up. She was wearing my hockey sweatshirt – the same sweatshirt that Jenna had for a couple of years – the same one that Jenna's parents gave back to me after the funeral. Of course, I didn't tell Hannah that, but it made me look back just a bit. By the time she sat down next to me and snuggled in, I focused back on the present. I couldn't help but notice a hint of Jenna's scent still attached to it, unless that was just in my mind.

The fireworks usually started as soon as it was dark outside. We stuck two reclining lawn chairs into the sand next to each other and made some s'mores. I liked mine barely done, she preferred her's more burnt. We felt like we were the last two people in the world as we watched the fireworks explode among the stars. The colors lit up the sky. It was an electric atmosphere.

"It doesn't get any better than this, does it?" I said confidently.

"Yeah it does." She responded with a confidence of her own.

"What do you mean?" I asked.

She threw the blanket off of her and stood up. She lifted her sweatshirt over her head, and then pulled down her sweatpants to the ground and stepped out of them. My heart skipped at least two beats. She had nothing on underneath. She smiled, ran, and jumped into the water, completely out of character for her. I quickly tore off my clothes and ran as fast as I could and jumped in after her. When my body hit that water, all of my pain and worries washed away, at least for that moment. And for once, that moment was all I cared about. We submerged under the water as we held hands and swam out towards the end of the dock into deeper water. We both touched our feet to the bottom, with just our heads above the water line. I walked closer to her and grabbed her waist and pulled her in for a wet kiss. The fireworks finale above us provided for a magical scene.

After a few minutes, I felt a couple of random drops and a breeze blow through. I tried to pretend like I didn't because I didn't want this moment to end. The drops started coming quicker.

"Uh oh," she said as she looked up at the sky.

"Dammit," I responded.

The skies threatened as clouds raced across the sky. Suddenly, it started to downpour. Hannah let out a playful scream as we both swam for shore. On the way through the lawn, I scooped her up from behind and carried her in my arms as she let out another scream. I climbed the stairs on the patio and opened up the screen door as it snapped shut behind us.

We put our faces together and began to kiss. I could feel the rainwater dripping down on our faces. We continued making out throughout the house en route to the bedroom. I laid her down and we stared into each other's eyes. She ran her hand up and down the back of my arm. Her touch was healing. I caressed her side with my hand. I could feel her body tremble. My heart raced with no finish line in sight. We made love passionately as our bodies united into one. I had never experienced such ecstasy. Over and over, it was incredible. When we finished, I rolled over onto my side. We just stared at each other and contemplated the gravity of the moment. I saw her silver cross necklace dangling from her neck from the moonlight through the window.

"Do you ever take that off?" I said as I pinched it with my fingers.

"Never," she said emphatically.

"Why not?" I inquired.

"Because He never gives up on me." She responded as she touched it.

Everything she said mesmerized me. She was addicting. She was so spiritual, and I envied her relationship with God. As for me, I always considered Him more of a friend of a friend.

"I love you," I proclaimed as I touched her cheek.

She didn't respond, and her face looked like she had seen a ghost.

"I'm sorry. Was that too soon?" I asked her.

"No," she answered, "it felt like it took forever."

She wasn't only referring to me, but anyone. She always wanted to hear someone tell her those words.

"I love you," she said just before she closed her eyes.

She rolled over with her back towards me and snuggled in close. As we laid there, I could feel her heartbeat up against my body. I tried matching her breathing pattern as our bodies lied parallel together, but mine was too fast. I tried to slow it down to match hers, but I couldn't because I was too excited. I wondered if she could feel my heart racing and hoped she wouldn't relate it to my nervousness. My excitement prevented me from falling asleep. I had suffered from insomnia for months, but this was for a different reason. And I loved this reason.

***

We both got up pretty early the next morning, just before sunrise. The window was open, and we could hear the sound of the calm waves against the beach and the birds chirping in the trees. We snuggled in bed with no distractions. It was nice to play house together, not having anything on our agenda or anyone to hide it from. I ran my hand up and down her arm and kissed her shoulder sticking out of the covers. She turned towards me gently.

"Do you need anything?" I offered.

"I would love some coffee," she said.

"We can do that here at the Camps Café," I said sarcastically.

I made a pot of coffee and some peanut butter and jelly toast, pretty much the only breakfast I was capable of making. She put on my sweatpants and t-shirt and I threw on some comfortable clothes and we went outside on the balcony. We sat on the porch swing looking out towards the water. The water was like glass. The sun was warm and constant. It was pure serenity. But the most compelling aspect of nature's beauty was the person I was sitting with. It was a perfect morning.

"This is gorgeous. I can't imagine waking up to this every day," she said in complete admiration.

Her hands wrapped around her coffee mug as if she was molding pottery. The heat from the coffee spread from her hands and warmed the rest of her body. After every sip, she closed her eyes for a few seconds, taking it in and appreciating it like a drug flowing through her body. I'm not sure if she thought differently or simply had a different vantage point than others, but she certainly saw things differently.

She noticed things like the flowers, the trees, the lake, curves in people's faces, pain in people's eyes, and kindness in people's hearts. She had a quiet optimism. She beautified everything, even the little things.

"It is gorgeous, isn't it?" I agreed, finally realizing something I took for granted every day.

That's what she did for me. She opened my eyes to things that were right in front of me. She made me dig deeper.

As I looked over at her I inquired, "So what's your plan for the fall?"

"I'm going to State, for teaching." She said assuredly.

"Miss. Johnson, huh?" I said playfully as she smiled.

"I've wanted to be a teacher since as early as I can remember. It's what I was called to do. The opportunity to teach others, and at the same time sprinkle hope into their dreams. That's what I want. Plus, I've always loved kids." She explained.

She continued to talk about her passion. She was truly captivating. Her words were poetic. It was refreshing to hear someone talk that way. She saw the world as a whole, not just our little part that we see every day. She saw it for what it could be, not just for what it was. As cliché as it sounds, she seemed genuinely interested in changing the world. Better yet, she genuinely believed she could. She had a passion for something beyond what she could see, a world only she imagined in her mind. And her passion was infectious. The first eighteen years of my life seemed like it had tunnel vision. She took off those blinders.

"What's your plan?" She turned the question back on me.

"For dinner, or . . .?" I dodged.

"For life," she responded as she took another sip while keeping her eyes on me.

I paused and thought about the question for a moment. I had been asked countless times by everyone what I was doing in the fall. I gave them the standard press conference answers. With her, I didn't want to hide the truth. She had something about her that attracted honesty.

"I was a kid with big dreams. I can't tell you how many state championships and Stanley Cups that I've won – in my head, on the driveway, or out on the frozen lake in the winter. Playing hockey and chasing those dreams was all I ever wanted to do." I said.

"Can I ask you a question?" She interrupted reluctantly.

"Of course," I replied.

"Why aren't you playing hockey next year, then?"

She inquired.

"Wow, that's a loaded question," I answered.

"Well, you said I could ask!" She reminded me.

"Yeah, you're right," I surrendered as I twirled her hair with my two fingers. "I've told everyone that I just want to move on and go to college. The truth is, I don't love hockey. I love Spoiler hockey. There's a difference."

She nodded her head and squinted her eyes as if she was analyzing my answer.

"I mean, I loved playing for this town. I loved playing the role of hero for all the kids, because I was one of those kids. I loved playing for my teammates – they are like brothers to me. The tradition of Spoiler hockey is what I fell in love with, not the game of hockey itself. Playing somewhere else wouldn't be the same. It would just be hockey." I continued.

"Are you sure you're not just scared?" She asked like she was an interviewer on 60 Minutes.

"Scared of what?" I asked her to elaborate.

"I don't know, the future maybe," she proposed, which sort of sounded like a question. "You speak about chasing your dream, maybe you're scared of what would happen if you actually reached it."

I thought about it for a moment.

"I'm not scared of the future." I said.

"No?" She asked for clarification.

"No. I'm scared of the past." I finally admitted.

She had a puzzled look on her face. I could tell she didn't understand but truly wanted to.

"Okay, here it is. All I ever wanted to do was win a state championship. My dad won one when he was in high school. My brother won one. Since I was three years old, that is literally all I've wanted. And I worked harder than anyone ever has to get there. I wanted it more than anyone ever has. I sacrificed everything – blood, sweat, and tears. And three years I made the semifinals of the state tournament and lost all three times, the last two years both in overtime." I explained.

She squinted her eyes and looked away in contemplation.

"I guess what I'm trying to say is that I don't want to go through all of that again just to end up heartbroken again." I finished.

When those words came out of my mouth, I realized I was going through the exact same thing with Hannah. I had so much admiration for her but didn't know if I wanted to go through it all again just to end up heartbroken again. It brought my fear to my attention. I'm not sure if she made the connection. But she seemed to understand the surface of it. It was strange how I found myself telling Hannah things I never even shared with

Jenna. And I thought I told Jenna everything.

"So now? What's your dream now?" She pressed on curiously.

I gave a little smile in order to break up the seriousness a bit.

"I'm not exactly sure, but I finally feel like I'm moving forward instead of backward," I responded.

"It just seems like you have it all. What do you want that you don't have?" She asked.

"You." I said defiantly.

She smiled with her teeth and her cheeks blushed.

"You have me." She said as she blushed.

"And I'll never let you go." I said as I pulled her face towards mine and kissed her again.

She took another sip of coffee and looked out towards the water.

"I could get used to this," she said as she rested her head on my shoulder.

"I hope I never get used to this," I countered as I kissed the top of her head.

7

For the next three weeks, Hannah and I were inseparable. Our relationship was white hot. Being with
her gave me the feeling of a lightning bolt to my
heart, and at times I had shortness of breath when I
was with her. Her presence was like a drug injected
into my vein, and it rapidly spread throughout my
body like a love-like heroin.

We did everything together. We went on the boat
almost every day after work. I would pick her up on
the dock and we would float around for hours,
usually just the two of us. I would usually try sneak
onto the boat before my parents could ask me who I
was going out with. I never had a better suntan.
Sometimes we would pick up Mark and some others
and go skiing and swimming. I tried taking her
golfing once. She lasted about six holes, and then she
rode along on the golf cart and watched me. She
would smile when I hit a good shot and laugh when
I hit a bad one. We went fishing a few times, and she
caught her first walleye that we ended up cooking

when we got back in to her place. We would ride the horses at the ranch. She loved the feeling of connecting with the wild when she rode. We would cruise down lover's lane, a gravel road in the middle of the country with trees lining both sides, overhanging and enclosing above it like a tunnel. We spent some time with Grandma Lola, playing cards and talking with her. And on many mornings, we would run around the lake together. Sometimes we would meet at parties, sometimes we would go together. Once we were there, we'd often sneak away from the bonfire and find a quiet spot. She was all I thought about and all I wanted to think about.

On one night in particular, we were at a party at my friend Todd's house. Todd lived by the grain elevator which was right next to the railroad tracks. As we were leaving the party, we walked over to the parked train. It was a starry night with crickets talking on and off.

"Come with me," I said.

"Where are we going?" She asked.

"Don't worry," I assured her.

There was a rusty ladder down the back of the boxcar. I jumped up and climbed it halfway and looked back.

"Are you crazy?" She asked as she looked around to see if anyone could see.

"Probably," I responded. "Come on!"

She shook her head and grabbed the railing and started climbing. I grabbed her hand and pulled her the last couple of steps. We stood on top of the boxcar and looked around. It was a pretty cool view. I grabbed her hand and pulled her close for a kiss. After a minute, we were laying on top of each other on the roof of the boxcar. After about twenty minutes, we heard the noise of a door closing. A light flashed on and the train started rumbling. Both of our eyes opened wide.

"Oh shit!" I let out.

"Get up!" She whisper-yelled.

I got up and pulled her up with me. The train started moving slowly. I looked around, wondering what we were going to do. We couldn't jump off, as we were way too high. The train started to pick up some speed. I got on my knees and looked down into the boxcar. The door was open about a foot. I quickly pushed it open with all my might, groaning like a weight lifter. It slid open.

"We're going to have to jump inside!" I said loud enough so she could hear.

Her face was frightened.

"We don't have a choice! I'll go first and then help you!" I continued.

She nodded that she understood.

I got down on my stomach and slid towards the edge and slowly put my legs down the side. I crept down further, my midsection was now over the edge as I hung on for dear life.

"Okay, I'm going to jump inside! One...two...three!" I screamed as I jumped and threw my legs inward.

I tumbled into the box and made a loud banging noise. I shook it off quickly and went towards the edge and looked up.

"Okay, are you ready? Hang your legs off the edge and I'll grab them and pull you in!" I yelled.

She shook her head. She was worried. I was even more worried.

"Hannah, this is the only way! Trust me, I will catch you!" I tried to assure her.

She gathered up the courage and got on her stomach. I saw her legs appear and she started to slide down. The train was picking up speed quickly.

I yelled, "Okay, on three! One...two..."

All of a sudden, her body slipped down. I grabbed her legs as fast as I could, and with all of my upper body strength pulled her in towards me. I almost had a heart attack as she fell inside, her weight knocking me over as we both tumbled to the ground. She was on top of me and our eyes opened wide, both simultaneously asking if the other was alright. She burst out into laughter as she put her forehead down on my lips. I couldn't help but laugh as I kissed her forehead and wrapped my arms around her.

"Unbelievable," I said.

"I believe it," she responded.

We kissed again. Every kiss with her felt like a first kiss.

We then sat up and rested our backs on the wall. I put my arm around her and she rested her head on my shoulder.

"I like who I am when I'm with you. I'm fearless." She said.

"Me too," I responded, even though I had never been more scared in my life.

The train was pulling full speed ahead. We had no idea where we were going. We had no idea how we would get home when we got there. That feeling of uncertainty was kind of liberating. The train went just fifteen miles down to the next town, and we ended up hitchhiking back home.

We went on a lot of adventures like that. I loved how she was willing to explore new things, and we did a lot of activities together. I remembered how she came off as a little guarded at the beginning of the summer, but she turned out to be incredibly free-spirited. It turned out she just needed the right person to be a catalyst. She did the same for me - she awoke my soul that I thought never slept. On the flip side, I loved how we could throw on some sweatpants and just do nothing. We still kept our romantic relationship a secret as best as we could. We went out in public together, but we kept our intimate moments in private. By that time, most people knew Hannah, and they knew she was Jenna's cousin. Therefore, many people thought it was innocent that we were hanging out. In fact, some even viewed it sympathetically as some sort of therapy for both of us. There were a few detractors of course. In a small town, rumors run rampant. And those rumors were just beginning.

Every year during the first weekend in August, Shoreham Lake played host to a massive country music festival called Summerfest. It was a three-day festival full of concerts and camping. It was essentially a country version of Woodstock. Just a few miles south of Shoreham Lake was a massive ranch that had a big stage, concert bowl, and about a dozen different campgrounds. People from all around the country fled to Summerfest to see the best acts country music had to offer. It was one the biggest music festivals in the country and we had it right in our little town. For most, it was sort of the beginning of the end of summer, especially for lake-goers. Class reunions took place for ten, twenty, thirty, and forty years. Classmates got together for one weekend and had permission to act like they were seventeen again. Old teammates reminisced about wins and losses, the tall tales stretched further every decade. Old lovers awkwardly introduced their spouses to one another with a little feeling of what if in the back of their minds.

Years ago, when Summerfest was just starting, my dad was a big sponsor of the event. Because of his early loyalty, he was granted front row tickets for the festival every year. My parents went when we were little, but they eventually tired of the three-day party. The past few years they gave the tickets to me and my friends, and my brother if he wanted to make the drive. This year, there was only one plus-one that I had in mind.

It was our first public appearance together as a couple. We got a few weird stares for whatever reason, but mostly people were just happy to see me out and about in good spirits. Most welcomed Hannah with open arms. We joined in on a pickup volleyball game in the campground. Afterwards, she showed a random drunk guy how to do a back handspring from her gymnastic days. He didn't quite match her grace. I swung the hammer and rung the bell in the general admission pit. We both had a few casual beers as we loosened up. Meanwhile, concerts were in full swing by the time we ventured to our seats.

"We should dance!" She exclaimed.

I could tell she was a little buzzed from the beer.

"Ah. . . I'm not a big dancer," I replied.

I never danced in public. I hated any feeling of vulnerability and always strived to avoid it. I hated anything that I wasn't good at. When it came to dancing, I was worried about looking downright foolish. I knew that Hannah was a good dancer. She danced her entire life and was a dance instructor for young kids. That only added to the intimidation.

"Come on, I'll show you," she said as she reached out her hand.

I shook my head and took her hand as she led me to the open area that the VIP ticket holders used as a dance floor. We made our way past the other couples, dodging some and bumping into others. She held my hand and led me the entire way. A guy accidentally swung out right in front of me as I bumped into him.

"Sorry, dude!" I yelled over the music.

He turned around. It was Jenna's brother Rick. He shrugged it off and motioned hello. I said hello and stopped to talk, even though it was too loud. Hannah walked back and grabbed my hand and I was forced to follow her. I was uncomfortable when Rick saw us holding hands and then dancing. Yet, between the beer, music, and the dancing, I quickly forgot about it. We made our way to the front and found a spot. She started leading me in the two-step. She could definitely move, there was no doubt about that. I could tell she loved it. I think she was happy to be doing something that was familiar again. For the first time in a while, she wasn't the stranger. I was too preoccupied looking around to see if people were watching me, or worse, laughing at me. I was pretty stiff at first and she found it humorous. The music was loud, but I saw her mouth tell me to relax.

I took her advice and got more comfortable with the second song. I started taking the lead and swinging her around with no rhythm. It wasn't perfect, but at least I didn't look completely out of place. To the common eye, I could dance. Then the music suddenly stopped and a slow song came on next. We stood a few feet away from each other. The two-step was one thing, but an intimate slow dance in public was another. We were hesitant to take that step. I looked her in the eye and reached out and offered my hand. She smiled and took my hand. I pulled her in close and put my other hand on her lower back. We started swaying slowly back and forth as one piece. She rested her cheek on my shoulder.

"I love dancing," she said as she lifted her head and looked me in the eyes.

"Is it because you get to dance with talented partners like me?" I asked sarcastically as she chuckled.

"It just expresses things that I can't say," she responded. "I don't know, it's hard to explain, really."

I stared over her shoulder and thought about what she said. I related it to playing hockey, which was my instrument of expressing myself.

"No, I get it, believe it or not. I understand completely." I told her.

She put her head back on my shoulder and we swayed back and forth. It was as if we were the only two people dancing. We blocked everyone else out of our world. We were in our own love coma. My heart was fluttering with excitement. Hannah was a little buzzed. I couldn't tell if I was or not, I couldn't distinguish the buzz from the alcohol from the high of being with her. Being with someone you love is the best intoxication there is.

"I love this feeling." I said.

"What feeling?" She asked.

"Love." I responded.

We shared a long kiss in the moonlight with the

music playing in the background. We danced the night away, fast songs and slow. We danced with each other, our friends, and even complete strangers. We played air guitar with the little boys. We sang along with the little girls. We left it all on the dance floor that night. And we didn't care what anyone thought.

We went to a couple different after parties, one at Zivonz and then one at Mark's place. When we got to Mark's, Hannah and I snuggled on the couch. She sat on my lap as we shared a hand in cards. Around five o'clock in the morning Mark drove a handful of us to Grandma's Diner for a late bite to eat, or early breakfast, depending how you looked at it. We hopped in my truck and started driving up County Highway 11, which went uphill along the east side of the lake. It was early in the morning and the scene from the top of the hill was truly picturesque. It was spiritual with the sun rising over the water. It represented a new day, literally and figuratively. When Hannah made fun of my stiff posture while driving, I threw my arms up in the air. Of course, she didn't know that Jenna constantly made fun of me for it, too. When the others joined in and poked fun of me, I just burst out laughing. *What a life*, I thought to myself.

Grandma's Diner was the place to go in Shoreham

Lake if you wanted stale coffee, greasy hash browns, morning gossip, or eggs over-easy. I knew the owner of the café, and could probably give you a brief biography of anyone sitting in a booth sipping coffee and reading the local paper. Hannah and I snuggled in a booth together, not caring who saw us. After, I dropped everyone off before Hannah and I went to my house, with every intention of carrying on from earlier on the dance floor. My parents were home so we snuck in the house and up the stairs to my bedroom. We snuggled into bed right away and spooned. I wrapped my arm around her and she held my hand tightly. We were too exhausted to do anything but sleep.

I woke up a few hours later in the same position and immediately felt nervous. I was a little worried about having Hannah sleep over with my parent's home. They were strict in that way, and probably wouldn't approve of any female houseguest. Besides, I wasn't ready to tell them about our relationship. I didn't know what they would think.

"Hey, you better go before my parents see you," I whispered into her ear.

She motioned her shoulder and groaned a little as she woke up. She rubbed her eyes and scratched the back of her head.

"What time is it?" She asked.

"Eight-thirty," I responded.

"You can take my bike home," I added.

"Okay, I'll sneak out." She said.

We stood up and I opened the door and looked down the hall. The coast was clear. Downstairs was quiet, so I assumed my parents must still be sleeping. I walked her to the top of the stairs and kissed her goodbye. She walked softly down the stairs. I felt a little relieved getting her out of the house without being seen. I crawled back into bed and laid on my back. I thought back on the past few months – all of the ups and downs, the roller coaster of emotions. It was quite the summer, and we still had a few weeks left. It was the first time where I thought about the prospect of summer being over. Before I thought too much into it, I switched gears and closed my eyes to try and get some more sleep.

A few minutes later, I heard people talking downstairs. I tried to lay still and listen, but couldn't quite make out the voices. With my curiosity sparked, I got out of bed and opened my door. I walked down the hall and stopped at the top of the stairs to listen.

"How is Lola?" I heard coming from my mom's voice.

I got nervous. Was she talking to Hannah? Who else would she be asking that to?

"She's doing well, keeping busy as always," I heard in response.

It was definitely Hannah. I didn't know what to do. I paced back and forth a few times. I didn't want to face the music, but I also didn't want to leave Hannah hanging by herself. Reluctantly, I started walking down the stairs. I heard them switch the topic to me. I stopped walking and started listening. The conversation was casual. They talked about my summer, how the dance was the night before, and my love of the lake life. My mom eluded to how much of a rollercoaster the past few months had been for me. I sat down on the stairs and just listened. I couldn't help but smile a little bit while listening to the two most important women in my life talk about me and share stories. It was an odd feeling, a feeling of appreciation that I rarely experienced. I finally walked downstairs and Hannah and my mom were drinking coffee and eating muffins together.

"Well, look who is up," my mom said with a smile.

"Yeah, yeah," I responded as I ran my hand through my hair, a little embarrassed.

I got over my initial embarrassment and I walked over and put my hands on Hannah's shoulders for a moment before grabbing a strawberry from the bowl on the table. I popped it in my mouth and sat down.

"Can we help you, Will?" My mom asked

sarcastically.

"Yeah, can we?" Hannah repeated in conformity.

The two seemed to have immediate chemistry.

"No," I said with a smile. "You've both done enough already," I finished as I grabbed another strawberry.

We sat there and talked for another half hour. I think it felt good for my mom to have another girl around for the first time in a long time. My mom loved her boys more than anything, but it was good for her to have a girl to talk to. Hannah handled herself very well. I was nervous for her with every question my mom threw at her. She seemed so comfortable, especially under the circumstances – the immediate and the big picture. It only made me fall further in love with her. I kept looking for a flaw or some sort of excuse not to, but couldn't find one. The conversation eventually slowed as it was time for my mom to get ready for the day.

"Well, I better get this day started," my mom said.

"Yeah, I better get going, too," Hannah added.

I walked her to the door and opened it for her. We walked outside together.

"Sorry about that," I said as we walked towards my truck.

"For what?" She asked.

"I don't know, having to talk to my mom," I said.

"No, I loved it. She is so sweet." She said.

I nodded my head in agreement. I walked around my car and opened the passenger door as she hopped up into the seat. I closed it behind her and walked around the front and hopped in the driver's side. I drove her home and kissed her goodbye before watching her walk inside.

I got back home and parked my truck. Even though my mom was cool about it at the time, I fully expected to get an earful when I got back. I was a little worried and thought about driving away and putting off the lecture. But I figured I had to face the music sometime and I might as well get it over with.

"Hi mom," I said as I walked into the kitchen.

"Hi honey," she responded as she stopped what she was doing.

Here we go, I thought. I sat down and braced myself.

"You know the rules . . ." she began.

"I know, I know," I interrupted. "I'm sorry about that, I messed up." I continued.

She was about to go on with the lecture, but something stopped her. She held back and stopped talking. She looked at me for a moment and I could tell she was thinking.

"Okay, just don't let it happen again," she said.

"I won't," I answered.

I stood up and started walking away. Before I reached the stairs, I turned around.

"Thanks, mom." I added.

"You're welcome," she responded.

I resumed walking towards the stairs.

"Will," she said.

"Yeah?" I asked.

"She seems like a really sweet girl." She continued.

"Yeah, she's nice," I responded as I shrugged my shoulders.

I tried to play it off that she was just a friend, that there wasn't anything there. For some reason, I still wasn't ready to admit it publicly. Sure, I admitted it to myself a long time ago. But I wasn't ready to say it out loud to anyone other than Hannah. I knew my mom knew better. She was a smart lady and she knew me better than anyone. It was a relief how she held back on me and didn't institute any type of punishment. Perhaps it was because I was eighteen and graduated from high school. Perhaps it was because I've never broken that rule before, at least that my mom was aware of. If you ask me, I think my mom still sympathized with me. I think she was so happy to see me happy again and she didn't want to do anything to jeopardize that.

***

Later that morning, I walked into the Corner Convenience Store, with the smell of last night still permeating from my body. The annoying bell hanging from the door bounced and banged up against the glass. I walked through the aisle between the peanuts and other salty snacks to the back of the store towards the refrigerators. I shivered a bit from the cool sensation of the refrigerator as I opened the door and grabbed a cold glass bottle of milk. On the way back, I moseyed slowly through the candy aisle, scanning all of the options and settling on two chocolate candy bars because one just wasn't enough. Nothing really went together like chocolate and cold milk. As I walked towards the counter, the man in front of me in line looked familiar.

"Hey, Rick." I said, sort of peering over his shoulder to get his attention.

He turned his neck to the side and eyed me behind him before turning back towards the counter.

"Will," he acknowledged. "Pump number two," he informed the clerk.

I found his passivism a bit surprising.

"H-How's it going?" I mustered.

He turned around and glared into my eyes.

"Will, to be honest, no one in my family has anything to say to you." He said with a tired demeanor.

"Rick, w-what . . ." I tried to respond as he walked away and out the door.

I stood there stunned. My heart sunk to my stomach. I immediately felt sick.

"Sir, is that all?" The clerk asked.

No response.

"Sir. Are you ready to checkout?" He asked louder.

I snapped back and raised my eyebrows.

"Yeah, I am. Sorry." I said as I set the items down on the counter and reached for my wallet.

"Any gas out there?" He asked again.

"What's that?" I responded.

"Did you pump any gas or no?" He reiterated.

"Oh, no gas, sorry." I finally caught on.

A wave of anxiety hit me hard as I walked out of the store and hopped into my truck. The anxiety quickly turned into full-blown regret and shame. What have I done, I thought? And better yet, what was I thinking when I did it? It was clear that Rick, and everyone else for that matter, saw me dancing the night away and kissing Hannah at the concert. It had only been about four months since Jenna passed away. At the time, I was so caught up in the moment, preoccupied with Hannah's charm and the buzz from the beer. That was the first time I showed signs of life from my love coma. The gravity of the situation was setting in. I think I messed up, and I think I messed up bad. My dad always warned me that it takes a lifetime to build a good reputation and a split second to ruin it. Chalk another one up for dad.

I picked Hannah up on her dock about an hour later. Saturday of Summerfest was the bash to end it all. It marked the start of the end of summer. It was one of the best nights of the year. The next day was one of the worst, since summer was in the rear view and it was time to get back to school and farmers prepared for harvest. On that Saturday afternoon, I wasn't thinking about the end of summer just yet. We continued our charmed lake life - skiing, tubing, drinking, and catching sun through it all. We chilled at the sandbar which eventually turned into an impromptu football game. But the confrontation with Rick earlier in the day was on my mind. The original plan was to have Hannah come with me again that night. But as the day went on, I began thinking it wasn't a great idea. Things were happening too fast. And I started to question again whether it should be happening at all.

"Alright, we'll see you guys at the concerts," Mark said as I dropped him off.

"You know, I don't think I'm going to go tonight," I responded.

"Very funny," Mark said.

"No, seriously. I don't feel very good." I proclaimed.

Mark was baffled by my decision, but he didn't let it bother him. As usual, I dropped off Hannah last.

"Are you sure you don't want to go tonight?" She asked.

Hannah had a blast the night before and was looking forward to going again. She was finally comfortable and having fun in her new town, and she didn't want to stop the momentum. She was skeptical about my sudden change of heart. She knew how much I looked forward to Summerfest.

"No, I just don't feel well," I said.

"Okay, that's fine. What do you want to do then?" She asked, assuming we'd hang out just like we normally did.

"You know, I think I'm just going to stay in by myself tonight. I think I need some rest." I added.

That only furthered her skepticism.

"Oh, okay." She said with a surprised look on her face.

She leaned in for a kiss and I gave her a peck goodbye before I watched her walk into her cabin. She turned around when she was halfway up the beach. It was like she was asking if I was sure of my decision. The answer was that I wasn't.

I ended up staying in that night. My parents found it strange as well, but given everything they witnessed the past few months, strange was the new ordinary, so they didn't second guess it. I spent the night lying in bed listening to some of my favorite records. When it got dark out, I heard a voice from downstairs.

"Will, there's someone here to see you!" My mom yelled from downstairs.

I was surprised. I really wasn't in the mood to talk to anyone, even Hannah. I quickly stopped in the bathroom to fix my hair before I walked downstairs.

"Hi, Will." She said as I appeared down the stairwell.

A feeling of utter shock came over me.

"Alisha...hi." I responded hesitantly.

I looked at my mom as she raised her eyebrows and walked out of the room.

"What are you doing here?" I asked.

"Can we talk?" She asked.

"Um...sure. Let's go outside." I recommended.

We walked through the room and outside onto the patio. Sitting down, she spoke like I had never heard her speak before.

"Will, we were meant to be together." She began.

It was strange seeing her that vulnerable. She always had it all, and she always got what she wanted. Usually she didn't even have to ask. There she was, humbling herself and putting herself out there. It was a reminder that all of us are human and all of us have emotions. No one is perfect and no one has it all. I couldn't help but feel somewhat sorry for her, something I never thought would happen.

"Alisha, I'm sorry. But I just don't have those kinds of feelings for you," I responded to her after she professed her love for me.

"And Jenna's cousin – you have feelings for her – really?" She asked in a snarky voice.

My sympathy for her quickly disappeared with the comment. I decided to ignore it.

"Look, I am sorry for that night at the End. It was a mistake. I wasn't thinking clearly. I was in a really dark place at that time, and I don't know..." I explained.

"So, you were just using me?" She asked as she started to get more visibly upset.

"That was not my intention. All I can say is that I'm sorry. But I can't be with you." I said as I stood up, signaling for her to leave.

"You're making a mistake," she threatened as she stormed off the porch and around the house.

I let her have the last word because, quite frankly, I was too tired to argue with her. I was in shock over what had transpired over the course of the day, facing a few more dips in the seemingly endless rollercoaster. I couldn't believe how complicated my life had become.

***

Meanwhile, Hannah was at home playing cards with Lola, who was also a bit confused why Hannah wasn't at the concerts. Her mind wasn't into the card game. It was on me. Lola could sense that she was preoccupied. Eventually, Hannah grew tired of the game and decided she would make a surprise visit to see how I was feeling. Because our relationship was essentially outed that morning by my mom anyway, she garnered the courage to come over. She hopped on her bike and pedaled towards my house. The thought was in the right place, but the timing couldn't have been worse.

As Hannah pulled up to our driveway, she saw Alisha's red Mustang parked out back and immediately became alarmed. She began to slow down pedaling. Then, she spotted Alisha walking around the house. Hannah stopped her bike and hid behind a tree. She saw her get in the car and drive away. Hannah's heart sunk. A wave of anxiety hit her like a tsunami. She immediately thought the worst. Things were starting to brew as I went to bed that night, but it was really just starting.

***

The next day was busy at Zivonz for the dinner crowd. Hannah was bustling around from table to table, taking orders and demands from patrons. She would rush through the wooden French doors to the kitchen and they would swing back and forth behind her. She was in one of those moods where she was frustrated but focused. She was sweating and her hair was beginning to look like a mess.

"Sorry for the wait, guys," Hannah said as she approached the table and grabbed the pen from behind her ear.

She looked around and saw Alisha and some of her friends. She became nervous.

"Yeah, we'll start with an order of fried pickles," Alisha said as a few of her friends nodded in agreement.

Hannah jotted it down in her notepad.

"What would you guys like to drink?" She asked the table, trying to act as normal as possible.

"So, did you have a good time at Summerfest?" Alisha asked as she smiled while her friends snickered under their breath.

Hannah's face turned red. She all of a sudden felt even more uncomfortable.

"What do you mean?" Hannah replied as she stopped writing and dropped her arms.

"At Summerfest. I saw you at the concert, our seats are just down the aisle from Will's. It looked like you were having a good time," Alisha continued.

Her friends tried to hold back their laughter, but didn't do a very good job of it. Hannah noticed Scarlett at the end of the table, who seemed to be avoiding eye contact with her. But it was apparent which side she was taking. Hannah stepped back and had a confused look on her face. She scratched the back of her head.

"Umm, yeah, it was fun, I guess," Hannah responded as her shoulders shrugged.

She was suspicious of the motive behind Alisha's questioning, especially since she saw her leaving my house the night before.

"Yeah, you aren't the only one who has fun with Will Camps, just figured I would let you know," Alisha said while she looked Hannah in the eyes.

"And Alisha would know," said one of her friends as their laughter got louder.

Hannah's embarrassment started to turn to frustration and anger.

"Um, do you guys want anything to drink?" Hannah asked, trying to put on a face to ignore their comments.

"No, we're all good," replied Alisha with another smile. "Will the fried pickles take long?" She followed up.

"No, they'll be right out," Hannah responded with a sarcastic, snippy tone.

She snagged the menus from the table and power walked back into the kitchen. She walked into the back storage room to catch her breath for a second. Her heart was racing. She threw the menus onto the counter and paced back and forth as thoughts were swirling around her head. When she got mad, or even worried sometimes, she had a small vein on the side of her forehead that would bulge. She could feel it pulsate as she put her hand over it to make it stop. She didn't want to go back to work, and she especially didn't want to go back to that table. She filled up her cheeks with air and let out a deep breath, trying to gather herself.

She gathered herself and went back and forth between her tables, including Alisha's. Her and her friends would smile when she came by, but Hannah kept plugging away working. After they were done eating, Hannah was anxious for them to leave.

"So, are these separate checks or one?" Hannah asked the table, looking away from Alisha.

"Just put it all on one and I'll take it," Alisha responded.

Alisha handed her a credit card. As Hannah took it back to run it in the machine, she noticed Alisha's dad's name on the card. When she returned to the table most of the people were standing and ready to go, a few talking to the neighboring table. Hannah put down the bill on the table and Alisha signed for it.

"I left a good tip. I'm sure you could use the money," Alisha said as she handed it back to Hannah.

"Can I ask you something?" Hannah said as she garnered some courage. "Is there something between you and Will?" She fumbled through the question.

"Depends what you mean by 'something,'" Alisha answered with a malicious smile.

Hannah became visibly upset.

"Well you didn't think you guys were like, 'something,' did you?" Alisha asked in a bitchy tone.

Hannah just looked at the floor. Alisha stepped closer to her face.

"Don't get your hopes up. You're just a rebound fling. Everyone knows he'll always be in love with Jenna." Alisha added.

"Ma'am?" A man said from the next table, trying to get her attention.

"You better get back to work, you have more tables to clean or whatever." Alisha said as she walked away, brushing Hannah's shoulder.

Hannah's heart almost stopped. She had trouble

breathing. Her eyes went blank. She stormed through the restaurant as she tore off her apron and threw it in the corner. She exited out the back door, hopped on her bike, and pedaled away in a haste. When she got home, she went straight into the cabin and plopped onto the couch. She didn't know what to do. She had never been in a serious relationship, let alone been cheated on or lied to. A part of her was in denial because our love was so strong, so genuine, that I couldn't possibly betray her. The other part of her thought Alisha had no reason to lie to her. Alisha wasn't Will's type, she thought. But she was beautiful, so perhaps she is every guy's type, she thought again. The feeling of uncertainty was killing her inside. It was her worst nightmare, finally opening up her heart to someone and having it broken.

***

I spent that day in contemplation. One minute I was convinced I wanted to be with Hannah, and another minute I was convinced it was a mistake. Either way, I thought she deserved an explanation. I couldn't wait any longer, so I decided to stop by Zivonz to see her. I walked around the patio area and inside, but she was nowhere to be found. I asked one of the bartenders where she was.

"She left a few hours ago," he responded.

"I thought she closed tonight?" I asked.

"She left early without saying anything. She looked kind of upset." He answered.

"Why? What happened?" I asked.

"No idea, bro." He answered again.

"Alright, thanks." I said, hesitantly.

I suddenly got a weird feeling. What could possibly make her so upset that she would leave work early? She was the responsible type who followed the rules, and that was out of character. *Maybe she just felt sick*, I thought. But then again, maybe this had something to do with me. I made the drive around the lake to her place. I pulled in the driveway and saw her bike leaned up against the bunk house. The lights were off, so I peered into the window. She wasn't in there. She must be in the house. As I approached the house, all of the windows were dark as well. I knocked a couple of times to no answer. I tried turning the doorknob and the door was locked. I thought that was very strange since most people in Shoreham Lake didn't lock their doors. My suspicion raised. As I walked back to my car, Lola pulled in the driveway in her baby blue classic Chevy Malibu. She smiled when she saw me.

"Hello, Will!" She said as she got out of the car.

"Hi, Lola," I responded, trying to act normal.

"You're here early, aren't you? Isn't Hannah working tonight?" She asked.

"Yeah, I thought so, but I stopped by Zivonz and they said she went home." I explained.

"Oh, I didn't know that. Is she inside?" She asked.

"No, I knocked and no answer. Your door was locked, so…" I continued.

"Oh. I locked it before I left. She must be at Scarlett's or something." She suggested.

"Maybe," I agreed skeptically.

"Well, I'll tell her you stopped by," she said as she walked towards the house.

I finally gave up and started the drive home.

***

Lola waited for me to pull out of the driveway before she reached for the door handle. She found it locked as well. She walked around the house and lifted a moss-covered rock beside the house and grabbed a spare key. As she entered the house, she walked into the living room to find Hannah lying there in the dark.

"Baby girl, why did you lock the house? I didn't even have a key with me." Lola said.

Hannah didn't say anything. Her eyes were swollen and red, and Lola could tell that she had been crying.

"Sweetheart, what's wrong?" She asked with concern as she sat down next to her.

Hannah couldn't say anything. All she could do was cry. Lola pulled her head onto her shoulder and rubbed her arm. Lola closed her eyes. Sometimes grandmas don't need to say anything. Sometimes they just need to be there.

***

I tried calling the house that night but no one answered. I finally convinced myself it was too early to panic or feel uneasy. It was just so unusual that she wouldn't call me. I tried thinking of how I could've done something wrong, but came up with nothing. It was a little harder to fall asleep that night, but I kept telling myself there was no reason to panic. *I'll talk to her tomorrow*, I thought.

My mind was preoccupied at work the next day, still wondering why she left work and never returned my calls. It just wasn't like her. We hadn't gone an entire day without talking all summer. It was very possible I was overreacting, and I hated the thought of being the obsessive and smothering guy. But still, I couldn't help the way I felt. I went through the motions at work while I mostly daydreamed. When I got done for the day, I went home and washed up for dinner, the smell of which was the best thing I'd experienced all day. I debated whether I should call her. Would that come off as overbearing? I called twice last night and drove over there. But what if something was actually wrong? She would want me to call. I picked up the phone and dialed.

"Hi, Will," Lola said, her tone a bit less friendly than usual.

"Hi, Lola," I responded, "Is Hannah home?"

"She's at work actually," she responded.

"Oh, I didn't know she worked today," I said.

"She decided to pick up an extra shift since she left early yesterday." She explained.

"Okay. Well, tell her I called?" I asked.

"Sure. Goodbye, Will." Lola said before she hung up.

The phone clicked. Something was definitely wrong. Lola was never that short with me. She was never that short with anyone. The uncertainty was killing me, so I decided I had to go find her and find out what was going on.

I didn't want to bother her at work, so I waited for closing time. It was dark by that time, and I drove up to Zivonz and parked towards the back of the gravel lot. I put it in park and shut my lights off. I parked facing the restaurant so I could watch people come out. Waiting and watching made me feel like a stalker, like an obsessive boyfriend who was keeping an eye on his girl. I hated that feeling. But I tried to justify that this situation was different, that I wasn't that guy. About a half hour passed and she still didn't come out. I decided the only option was to go in and investigate. I needed answers. I got out of the truck and started walking towards the restaurant. I was nervous.

I walked onto the patio area and a couple of servers were wiping off some tables and stacking chairs onto the tables. One spotted me.

"Sorry, but we're closed," she said as she continued working.

I ignored her and walked inside. I passed by some more workers. Hannah was standing at the bar talking to Bobby, the bartender. Bobby was a couple of years older than me and I knew him pretty well.

"Will, we're closed man," Bobby said.

Hannah turned around and appeared startled. I raised my arms and shrugged my shoulders as to show confusion.

"What's going on?" I said to her.

"I'm working. I'm sorry." She responded as she started to walk back towards the kitchen.

"What the hell is going on?" I asked with a raised voice.

Bobby walked from behind the bar and began to

walk between us.

"Will, come on, man," he said as he put his arm out towards me in an attempt to block me from following her.

I looked at him suspiciously. My blood was boiling.

"What the hell is going on?" I asked him.

"You can't do this right now. You need to leave." He said to me.

I was completely baffled. I felt as though I was being treated like some psycho criminal. All I wanted was an explanation.

"I just need two minutes. I have no idea what's going on." I pled with him.

"Not tonight. You need to go." He demanded.

I looked over his shoulder back towards the kitchen. Meanwhile, Hannah stood behind the door listening. She was worried. She had never been in this position before. She wasn't used to drama.

"This is unbelievable," I said as I turned around and started walking out. "Unbelievable," I repeated as I shook my head and slammed the door shut and walked out on the patio towards the parking lot.

Hannah was so nervous. She was conflicted. A wave of anger finally came over her and she sprinted out of the kitchen, through the bar, and outside.

"No, you know what's unbelievable?" I heard her

yell from behind me.

I quickly turned around.

"Hannah, what the hell is going on here?" I demanded.

She walked briskly towards me and stopped about five feet away.

"Alisha Anderson," she said assertively.

I closed my eyes and turned my head to the side.

"That's what this is about?" I asked.

"So it is true?" She asked back.

"No! I mean, it is, but it's not. That was before I knew you. I mean, not before I knew you, but before we were together," I fumbled my words with the appearance of guilt.

"Well, she came in here and told me all about you two. In front of everyone." She said furiously.

"She told you what?" I asked. "There is nothing between us." I insisted.

"I saw you two on Saturday night. You lied to me." She said.

I sighed and shook my head.

"Hannah, she came over to talk, but it was nothing. I didn't even know she was coming. She just showed up. And I told her I didn't have feelings for her." I insisted.

"This is exactly why I don't do this." She continued as she threw her hands up.

"Do what?" I asked in desperation.

"Whatever this is, or whatever this was." She answered.

"So that's it? After all we've been through? You're taking her word over mine?" I asked.

She looked at the floor in silence. She was shaking. I was anxiously awaiting her response. After a moment, she looked up and into my eyes.

"Do you still love her?" She asked.

"Alisha?" I asked hysterically, "What are you talking about?"

"Jenna," she clarified.

My face winced with confusion. *Where did that come from*, I thought?

"Jenna?" I asked. "What does she have to do with this?"

"She has everything to do with this," she repeated. "Do you still love her?"

My instinct was to start talking. But I couldn't get anything out. I shrugged my shoulders.

"It's true, isn't it? Don't lie to me again. If you ever really cared for me, don't lie to me." She begged.

Her anger was palpable. I had never seen her this assertive. My face was white as a ghost. I thought the question was extremely unfair.

"How do you expect me to respond to that?" I asked.

"With the truth," she responded.

I swallowed my throat. I just shook my head and looked to the side. The question was impossible to answer. It was far too complex for just a yes or no response. And I refused to give such a simple answer to such a loaded question.

"That question is not fair," I suggested.

"Well, you not giving me an answer isn't fair." She countered.

I nodded my head and looked away again.

"This was a mistake," she said, "I knew it from the beginning. I was reluctant to get into this with you in the first place. Girls like me don't date guys like you. Girls like Jenna and Alisha date guys like you."

"What does that mean?" I asked, wondering if I should be offended.

She wanted to answer, but held back. I became turned off by her rush to judgment. A feeling of regret creeped into my mind. Something just wasn't there that was before. Maybe she was right. Especially if she couldn't trust me enough to take my word.

"Yeah, maybe this was a mistake." I reluctantly agreed.

A moment of silence overcame us.

"Well, I guess that's it then," I continued.

"I guess it is." She responded.

Her words were absolutely gut wrenching. I shrugged my shoulders at her again and shook my head. I turned around and started walking away with my boots kicking up dirt in the parking lot.

"You know what," I said as a turned back around, "I've made a lot of mistakes in my life. And I never thought you were one of them. And I could have dated Alisha Anderson years ago and I always turned her down, including Saturday night. And as far as...you know what, you are right. This was a mistake." I said firmly.

You could hear the pain and frustration in my voice escaping after being held in for so long. I turned back around and walked towards my truck. Hannah just stood there with her hands on her hips, she had tears welling in her eyes and goosebumps on her skin. She was overwhelmed with anxiety. She didn't like that side of herself, and she didn't play it well. It was uncomfortable for her.

She was always reluctant to get serious with guys. She had seen guys before me, but she never had been in love. She was especially reluctant to become close to me, given our connection with Jenna. She also saw me initially as an arrogant sports jock who loved the attention from everyone, including other girls. In the beginning she had the mentality that girls like her didn't date guys like me, and she always kept that sentiment in the back of her mind. All of her fears were realized. She was upset over Alisha, yes. But I think she was always insecure about Jenna, and that was finally brought to the forefront. She pretended Jenna's presence wasn't there for months, but she was always in the back of her mind. Truth be told, I pretended as well, and she was always in the back of mine.

I drove home that night in shock. I believed firmly that I had done nothing wrong and was being falsely accused of something. I was angry about the accusations about Alisha. I didn't know exactly what Alisha said, but I knew it was a lie. I don't know what possessed her to do it, but I'm guessing it was a combination of envy of Hannah and revenge against me for denying her. I was a lot of things, but I was not a cheater. That part I vehemently denied. The other accusation thrown my way – essentially an emotional cheater – wasn't so easy to totally deny.

I pulled into the driveway and slammed the truck in park. I rested my head against the seat and stared at the ceiling, having no idea what to do at that point. I walked inside the house and went upstairs to my room, closing the door behind me and resting my head and back against the door, then I slid down the door and sat on the floor. My head dipped down as I put my hands on my head. I was exhausted. I didn't cry, because I didn't have any tears left. I was just simply exhausted. At that moment, I didn't have any fight left in me.

8

"*Oh my goodness!*" Jenna exclaimed as she tore open the present.

All of her family members around the room stopped opening their gifts and turned to look. Jenna pulled out the sparkling necklace from the box and placed it on her neck.

"*I love it! Thank you so much, baby!*" She continued as she gave me a huge hug.

I had worked all summer to be able to afford it. That moment was worth every penny saved. Jenna skipped across the living room to show her cousins, especially her favorite cousin, Hannah. They crowded around each other and admired her new treasure, undoubtedly comparing it to the underwhelming gifts they had received. I sat back down on the piano bench that brushed up against the Christmas tree. Later when it turned dark, we went back to my place and skated on the vast frozen lake. It was serenity. It was our first Christmas together as a couple, and I didn't know anyone. But I made a great first impression.

***

I woke up with familiar feelings – a mix of depression, anxiety, and loneliness. My depression made me feel lousy and I was always tired. I had no energy or ambition. I felt as though I was cursed and hopeless in this world. I had a pessimistic outlook on everything, having trouble seeing the good in anything. My anxiety prevented me from any sense of enjoyment since my mind was in a continuous state of worry. I was constantly scared. I would wake from the limited sleep I got in a pool of sweat. On one hand, I cared about nothing. On the other, I cared about everything. The loneliness was an obvious one. I had no interest in being around people because I thought they had no interest in being around me. Before, I was always a person who surrounded myself with people and immersed myself in activities. Plus, I had someone who loved me since I was in the eighth grade. I never had a chance to be lonely. Now I always wanted to be alone, but the prospect of being alone scared me to death. Finally pulling out of a love coma is a very sobering feeling. The strangest part about it is that I was aware of all of these feelings. I wasn't in denial, like an alcoholic or addict may be. I knew I had a problem. I knew I needed help. But I thought I could self-correct. The problem was that I didn't know how.

I was back to square one, arguably even further

behind. The tide had turned low again. Hannah had helped me make immense progress these past couple of months. She distracted me from my underlying feelings and blinded me from reality. A part of me regretted it. Another part of me realized if she hadn't come into my life when she did, only God knows how I would've ended up. She helped give my life purpose again, and I wondered if I should fight for that purpose again. I wondered if I should fight for her again. I wondered if I wanted her. I wondered if my feelings for her were genuine in the first place, or if I was desperately grasping for someone or something to save me from completely falling off the cliff. Perhaps it was just a way to hold on to Jenna. Perhaps after my time with Jenna was cut short, I was trying to extend it somehow with Hannah. We were both so vulnerable at the time. We were both reaching for something. Ironically, the same reasons we were together were the same reasons why we couldn't be. Because of that, our relationship may have always had limitations. Perhaps we were just kidding ourselves – maybe it wasn't real after all. Maybe it was a deceiving mirage in the distance, and once we got closer, it disappeared.

We loved like summer would never end. In what seemed like an instant, it was ending. So many questions. So many justifications. Back and forth, one contradicting the other. At that point, I selfishly thought that God owed me one. He took my future from me when Jenna died. He tore up my plans. I felt like a boxer taking punch after punch. I grew weary of those feelings. I was tired of all of it.

For the next couple of weeks, I found myself daydreaming at work. I avoided conversation and I went through the motions with my chores. When I would get home, I retreated back to lying in bed mostly, listening to music, and trying to fall asleep to push the pain down the road. The music soothed the pain but couldn't quite cure it. The thoughts in my head were random. I thought a lot about what happened with Hannah. I would analyze it like a mystery case. The catalyst on the surface was definitely Alisha. But there was nothing going on with Alisha, and there never was. I could see how it looked bad, but besides one night, there was nothing there. Besides, that was before I became involved with Hannah. And I was surprised how Hannah took Alisha's word over mine. It made no sense. She put so much trust in me early on, and let it go so easily. It had to be a distraction from the true motive.

But what was her true motive? It had been bubbling just below the surface the whole time, and the ordeal with Alisha blew it open. Her question about Jenna was revealing – her memory laid dormant for months, but erupted like a volcano. I think she always had Jenna in the back of her mind, and I think she was always insecure over it – perhaps because she thought that she wasn't my first choice. But the truth is, with both Jenna and Hannah, I didn't have a choice. Your mind is no match compared to your feelings. Her allegation about Jenna was beyond my control.

I considered myself innocent of all charges. After all, what did she expect from me? It was an unreasonable expectation for me to completely forget Jenna. She was the love of my life and it had only been a few months since she unexpectedly passed away. In the end, maybe it was just the impending end of summer, and our love was burning out with the summer sun. Summer love is a dangerous thing in that way – eventually the season ends, but the feelings can last forever. It was one of the most exhilarating and at the same time perilous feelings I had ever experienced, because I knew that sooner or later it had to come to an end. The spring sparks, the summer burns, the fall wind blows, and the winter freezes those memories forever. Maybe that's all it was – just summer love.

***

Hannah spent those days working and wasting

the last days of summer away. She reverted to her old lifestyle, working hard and spending time with Lola. She tried to have some fun at the encouragement of Lola, but she was often distracted. She had never been in love before, so she wasn't aware of its mighty power and lasting effect. Even though she was angry about how it ended, she couldn't just turn it off. Love isn't a feeling that simply disappears immediately. It takes time to wither away, and sometimes it never fully does. A part of me hoped that the experience would make her sympathize with my lingering love for Jenna.

***

The next weeks were excruciating for me. I knew it was over, but I had a glimmer that maybe it wasn't completely. It was a game of who was going to blink first. I didn't want to reach out to her since she's the one who broke it off. I didn't want to appear desperate, even though I probably was to some degree. As each day went by, the potential dimmed more and more. Perhaps it was simply time to move on. The past few months had been such a rollercoaster and I was just tired of it all. My emotions had been through the ringer and I decided that it was time to get back to a normal life.

The summer had been a fantasy, I convinced

myself. On one of those days, I finally decided it was time to get back to reality. It rained on and off that day, so I did a lot of work in the shop, mainly working on golf course equipment. I took a couple of breaks with the other men, guzzling down some soda and candy bars to add a boost of energy to make it through the day. When the greens mower needed a couple of parts, I volunteered for the errand.

I pulled up to Laker Sports to a group of regulars on the picnic table. I said hi, and they were noticeably less friendly than usual. I wasn't naïve to the idea that rumors were spreading around town. I lived in Shoreham Lake my whole life, although I had rarely been the subject of the negative rumors, so that part I was not used to. I walked in as the bell banged against the glass door.

"Champ," Mark said as he looked up briefly from his purchase orders.

"What's up?" I asked.

A couple of people at the counter said thanks and quickly left.

"Just trying to pay the bills, you know," he responded. "Been a while," he added.

"Yeah, I've been pretty busy," I responded, and he knew I was lying.

I gave him my order and he wrote it down and tore off a receipt.

"Party at Larson's Farm tonight," he said, "probably the last one of the summer before everyone leaves. You in?"

I thought about it, my initial thought being there was no way I wanted to go to a party. I decided to change the subject.

"Are people talking?" I asked him with a serious tone.

"People are talking." He confirmed.

I was surprised by his bluntness.

"What are they saying?" I asked curiously.

"You were cheating on Jenna with Alisha. You were cheating on Hannah with Alisha. Hell man, I didn't know you were such a ladies man," he said with a joking tone.

I looked at him seriously and shook my head. I wasn't in the mood to joke around.

"Sorry. Look, I heard you had a big fight with Hannah over something. And no one has seen you in weeks," he explained.

"You believe them?" I asked, almost daring him to test me.

I was looking for a fight at that point.

"No, I don't believe them." He said, pledging his loyalty.

I just looked at him and nodded.

"And some people have been talking about you

dating Hannah so soon after Jenna. But that has been going around all summer," he continued. "Maybe it's time to move on from it all, brother," he recommended.

I thought about it. If I wanted to get back to a normal life, going out in public was a part of it.

"Alright. I'll go. I'm in." I gave in.

"We'll pick you up." He assured.

I grabbed my receipt and walked out, looking around like I had some sort of target on my back. Mark was sort of suspicious as to why I was so short with him. But I just didn't feel like I had to explain myself to anyone, especially my friends who I felt should automatically understand. People were indeed talking around town. The rumors escalated and became more exaggerated by the day. People said I was a cheater. People said I was psychotic, trying to hold on to Jenna by somehow reincarnating her through Hannah. People said our families were feuding. People even thought I was consciously pushing off my future and quitting hockey because I was having a mental breakdown. I found it very distasteful how some people treated me differently after it was obvious that I decided to give up playing hockey. It's a different dynamic when people aren't praising you all the time. When you're on top of the mountain, everyone stretches out a hand. When all the glitter and confetti blow away and the champagne goes dry, people change. It revealed the character of people if they treated me differently or not. The rumors also revealed to me who my true friends were. I felt like a different person. My arrogant mystique had faded and people could tell by looking at me.

I finished off the day and Mark and the boys picked me up in Nick's truck, a cooler full of iced down beer in the back. I was so tired of the drama. I just wanted to kick back and have a good time with my buddies. They were the one constant in my life – no matter what I was going through – hurt, heartbreak, hangovers, hockey, girls, and even family drama – they were by my side. Over the years, we had been through a lot together. I laughed, cried, prayed, and cursed with those boys. We had been through the best times and the worst times together. Through all of it, we were always by each other's sides.

I got off to a quick start, chugging beer after beer on the drive to the party. I wanted to let loose and forget about everything. I didn't want to worry about a girl. I hadn't had that freedom in years. And besides, if I were to face some people, I couldn't do it sober. When we got to the party, most people acted normal towards me. I noticed a few weird stares, but nothing significant – until a couple hours later.

"Excuse me," I said as I brushed past a few guys on my way to the keg.

"Hey, superstar," one of them said as I walked past.

I turned around and looked around a bit. I confirmed that he was talking to me.

"What's up?" I asked.

"Are you going to say sorry or what?" He asked.

I didn't think it was that big of a deal, so I played it off.

"I said excuse me, sorry, dude," I responded innocently.

He got a big grin on his face as he took a few steps towards me. He took a swig of his drink.

"You don't get it, do you?" He asked. "I don't give a shit about that. I'm talking about what you did to Rick's little sister."

I looked over at Rick in confusion.

"Look, I don't know what's going on here guys, but I'm just trying to get another beer." I said, trying to defuse the escalating tension.

"Alisha Anderson?" He continued as he took another step closer.

I'm assuming he heard about the rumors, but I had no patience to address it. I closed my eyes and shook my head.

"Look, man, let's just relax here," I recommended.

"So, you admit it, you were with her while Rick's little sister was sick." He accused.

"That is not true. You have no idea what you're talking about." I responded.

"It looks like the golden boy isn't so golden after all," he added.

My blood was boiling and my hands were shaking. I suddenly stepped towards him and we were toe to toe. I could smell the whiskey on his breath. His eyes were glazed over. It seemed like he was doing more than just drinking.

"Are you going to hit me, hockey star?" He challenged. "That didn't work out for you either, did it?" He continued with another low blow. "Go ahead, give it your best shot," he said as he turned open his cheek.

The place turned silent. People gathered around. I clenched my fist, at that point it was sweaty. My nerves and blood pressure were at an all-time high. I wanted to punch him. I had never hit anyone before. It wasn't my nature. But he was testing my limit. I thought about it. Just as I was about to raise my fist, I looked over at Rick and I saw Jenna in his eyes.

"I'm better than that," I said about his invitation to fight. "*She* taught me that." I said as I looked over at Rick.

I turned around and started to walk away. A small crowd had assembled around us.

"And what about her cousin – you like to keep it in the family, huh?" He yelled.

I stopped in my tracks. My blood boiled higher than ever. I quickly turned around and marched towards him with my fists clenched.

"No, but I do!" Mark yelled as he came flying through the crowd and punched the guy square in the nose. He flew backwards and landed on his back in the dirt.

"And Will's my brother!" Mark yelled again.

Chaos immediately ensued. A couple of guys started attacking us. One of them broke his beer bottle over a tailgate and charged towards Mark, who successfully dodged him. The aggravator got up and hopped on my back and tried to choke me. I quickly flipped him over onto the ground. We fended them off enough to run towards Nick's truck. On the way, Mark tumbled to the ground and quickly popped back up. Nick and TJ hopped into the truck and Mark and I hopped into the bed just as we peeled out of the party and sped down the dirt road.

Once we were in the truck, Mark and I laid down in the bed. Mark winced in pain and he tried to clench his fist. Blood was dripping down and dirt was mixed into his wound from his fall. His hand looked mauled. We were both sweating and worried about what was about to happen next. I sat up and peeked outside of the truck bed to see if anyone was following us. No one was. I laid back down in relief. Mark and I looked at each other and both started to laugh.

"What the hell was that?" I asked through my laughter.

"That was a hell of a right cross – that's what it was." He said.

We both sat up against the cab and looked at the road behind us.

"What a trip," Mark said as he tilted his head and looked up at the midnight blue sky.

I think he was referring to our road trip that night, but he very easily could've been talking about our entire lives together up to that point.

"Mark," I said as I looked over at him.

He turned his head towards me.

"Thank you." I said.

"I'm the champ, now." He said with his cocky grin as he raised his bloody fist in victory.

We spent the next day on the lake – just us boys. It was relaxing to be with them and have no drama. I spent most of the day in reflection, sitting on the back of the boat quietly with my shirt off and sunglasses on. I admired the boys as they drank and sang songs while Mark played his guitar. We floated around until dark. That day made me appreciate my friendships more than ever. It was another silver lining – a glimpse of hope after everything I had dealt with. It was a moment of appreciation.

Both Jenna and Hannah taught me that.

***

During the next week, I reverted back to exile. My attitude was a roller coaster. Labor Day weekend was approaching, which was the benchmark of the end of lake season. It was the last weekend before people returned to the city and students went back to school. I spent that week listening to music in my room. I read a couple of books and even wrote some of my thoughts down as I thought about my past. And for the first time all summer, I seriously thought about my future. The deadline for some junior and college hockey teams had passed. There were a few remaining, and I considered getting in touch with them. For whatever reason, I never garnered the courage. I still held what I told Hannah as true – I wasn't scared of the future. Truth be told, I just wanted my old life back. I loved everything about it. But I knew that was impossible. Coming to that realization only exacerbated my depression and anxiety.

My mom definitely noticed the dip in the rollercoaster, since I was no longer hanging with Hannah or my buddies very often. I cut off communication with everyone for the next few days. That turned into a week and then the weekend.

When Saturday of Labor Day weekend came, I stayed in my room pretty much all morning and early afternoon instead of going on the lake like usual. When I missed out on a beautiful afternoon out on the lake, my mom knew something was seriously wrong. This time she walked in my room without knocking.

"Hi, Willy," she said as she walked in and sat on my bed.

She hadn't called me Willy in years. That's a name that my older brothers gave to me when I was little, and continued to use as I got older to torment me. That's what I was known as to them and their friends. My parents and their friends followed suit.

"Hi mom," I responded as I sat up a little.

"Aren't you going on the boat today?" She asked.

"No, I don't really feel like it," I said.

She saw right through me. She was my mom, and at times she knew me better than I knew myself. I couldn't hide anything from her.

"It's over with Hannah, isn't it?" She asked,

already knowing the answer.

I looked down, not really knowing how to portray it.

"I don't know if anything was ever really there in the first place," I answered.

I went on to explain to her the dynamics of everything. I told her the circumstances of how we became romantic, how innocent and pure it was. It wasn't preconceived. We acted on raw emotion. Neither one of us intended to hurt anyone, especially each other. We didn't try to fall for each other. In fact, we fought it as hard as we could. But human imperfections are no match for the power of love. You can control your mind, but you can't control your feelings.

I told her about Alisha and how that came about. I never intended to become involved with her in any capacity. To be blunt, it was one drunken mistake. I was at rock bottom at the time, and it was foolish. But she made me feel good for a brief moment in time, and at that time I was starving for a feeling like that. At the time, I was vulnerable. I wondered if I was ever going to feel affection again, and I thought Alisha may be my only shot. I spent the majority of my life following the rules and trying to be a good person, but I made one mistake. Once again, I'm only human. I told her about how Alisha confronted

Hannah, and how she made up lies about me to extract some sort of revenge for turning her down in the end. My mom knew what kind of person Alisha was. She knew something was going on when Alisha came over, and maybe she jumped to the same conclusion as others did. I wanted to make sure my mom knew the truth because she was one of the few people whose opinion really mattered to me.

I told her about Jenna's family and how they clearly disapproved of me and Hannah. I told her about the conversation at the gas station and the fight at the party. She knew about my desire to be liked by everyone and knew how much the situation must have bothered me.

Finally, I told her about my feelings of guilt. I felt like I gave up on Jenna, or as though I left her for someone else. I never wanted to leave Jenna, but she was taken from me.

My mom mainly listened, and she was surprised about how transparent I was with her. My mom and I had a very close relationship, but rarely did we talk about deep feelings. Then again, up until the past few months, I had no deep feelings to share as my life was pretty great. Nonetheless, I told her everything. I bottled up everything for such a long time. Eventually, I had to release.

"Do you love her?" My mom asked me.

"Hannah?" I asked for clarification.

"Yes," she answered.

I paused for a moment, not because I didn't know the answer, but because I didn't know how I *wanted* to answer. You can lie to other people, but it's impossible to lie to yourself. And I couldn't fool my mom.

"I *did*," I admitted.

"Then you have to hold on to that. You can't let others tell you who to love and when." She responded.

"But then again, maybe I was just trying to grasp at something as I was falling. Maybe I was trying to hold onto Jenna in some way." I continued.

My mom continued, "You know, a lot of people in this world just settle for someone, for whatever reason. Some people have to convince themselves that they are in love. Nothing is more telling than when someone has to try and convince himself that he's not."

That's exactly what I was trying to do.

"And honey, you did not give up on Jenna. You stood by her until the end. You still are," she added.

She went on to explain some history. I always knew that Jenna and her family were from Oakwood and that they moved to Shoreham Lake the summer before Jenna and I entered eighth grade. What I didn't know was why they moved. Apparently, Hannah's dad and Jenna's dad, who are brothers, used to farm together. After a few difficult years in farming, Walt started drinking. He would drink with a group of other farmers in the area almost every night. That eventually spilled over and started to affect his family life. Mary blamed it on the farming lifestyle and also the influence of the people around him in town. Hannah's dad became extremely upset about Walt's drinking, as it affected his work and the family name around town. Their relationship eventually became so strained, that the only solution to save Walt's marriage was to move to Shoreham Lake. At that time, Lola was already living in Shoreham Lake full time, which was spurred on by her husband's death. They had a lake cabin and she decided that she wanted to live there all year round. Walt and Hannah's dad stopped talking, and that had an effect on Jenna and Hannah's relationship. They were inseparable as kids until the fallout. Their moms tried their best to keep their relationship together, and would often arrange for them to have play dates as often as possible. Lola often served as the mediator. As they got busier in high school, it became more difficult and less frequent. My mom explained to me that the fact I was seeing Hannah could have opened some of those old wounds. I shook my head in disbelief.

"Jenna never told me about any of this," I said.

"She probably didn't even realize what was going on, she was so young," my mom explained.

It made sense, and actually put some pieces together for me. But as you can imagine, this didn't help my feeling of guilt. Exacerbating a family conflict was not something I had in mind. I didn't have any of this in mind. I always appreciated what I had. I don't think I took anything for granted. But never does one appreciate things so much than when they are taken away. And that is only intensified when everything is taken away.

"I'm just so tired of losing. I've lost everything," I said as I shook my head in disbelief.

She squeezed my shoulder.

"But this is something you can win," she replied.

She gave me a hug and got up and walked towards the door.

"Remember, you're my little engine that could," she stated.

"I think I can," I responded, quoting the famous passage from the book.

She smiled at me from the doorway and responded, "I *know* you can."

When she walked out the door, I laid back down, facing my night stand. My prom picture with Jenna was still on display. I stared at it and my reflection in the glass came into focus. I found myself staring into my own eyes. At that moment, I challenged myself. Just like that train, I thought I could keep going, but at that moment I didn't quite know I could. I always made the mistake of caring too much about what others said about me. But every person comes to a point in their lives in which they need to choose between what others want and what they want themselves. If this life is meant strictly to please others, you fail to truly live your own life. Selfishness is not always selfish. Sometimes it's essential for survival. I was faced with the decision of keeping a good reputation or potentially tarnishing it by fueling the fire of the allegations. Even though the allegations were false, perception is reality in a small town. On the other hand, maybe it was time to cut my losses and move on, as hard as that was to realize.

On Sunday, I went to church with my family. I caught a quick glimpse of Hannah and Lola across the church as we walked in. I spent the entire hour wondering if her eyes were upon me, but I didn't dare look for fear of getting caught. The tension was thick in the room, at least from my perspective. I wondered if she could feel it too, or if I was simply an afterthought in her mind. I tried not to think about her, but it was impossible. Like most Sundays, I sat in the pew and went through the motions. I used the time for occasional reflection but mostly just thought about my everyday life – hockey or school work. The first reading at the service was from the book of Job. During the reading, my attention turned to Father Mike.

Job was a man who had it all – a wife, many children, abundant wealth, and good health. Job was also an extremely faithful man to God. Satan asked permission from God to test Job's faith, and God agreed. Satan took everything away from Job, yet Job's faith did not waver. Father Mike touched on this reading in his homily as he analyzed the question so many people have as to why God can let good people suffer. The priest inferred that the passage teaches us that God lets evil in our lives in order to test our faith. If we pass the test, God will reward us, either in this life or the next. For probably the first time in my life, I was captive in church. I felt as though he was speaking directly to me. And as I peeled back a layer I felt as though God Himself was speaking directly to me by having this passage read on that day and at that moment. And there was that pesky word again – faith.

***

I hadn't talked to Mark again for a while, and he

grew concerned for me once again after my breakup with Hannah and everything that followed. He knew my situation better than almost anyone. He wanted to help me. After all I had done for him throughout his life, he felt obligated to return the favor.

He knocked on the door. Moments later, it opened.

"Mark, what are you doing here?" She asked with surprise in her voice.

"Well it's nice to see you too," he responded sarcastically.

Hannah let her guard down a little bit after his comment. She smirked and looked over his shoulder outside.

"Sorry, but what are you doing here?" She asked again.

"I came to talk to you about Will." Mark responded seriously this time.

Hannah shook her head, "Mark, just..."

"No, just hear me out," he interrupted.

"Look, I know you don't take me very seriously. I know that, and I get that. And if there was someone better to come testify on his behalf, believe me, I would want that person here. But I'm his best friend in the whole world, and no one knows him better than me." Mark said.

Hannah listened as she walked inside and sat

down. Mark followed and remained standing.

"He didn't cheat on you with Alisha." He added. "I know him."

Hannah looked down and didn't respond.

"He loves you, Hannah." Mark continued.

Hannah looked up and thought about what he said.

"He loves Jenna. And I don't think that's something we could ever overcome." Hannah proclaimed.

"Of course, he does. Like I said, no one knows him better than me. But that's not something you can hold against him. He can't completely forget about his feelings for her, none of us can. We all loved her. He doesn't deserve that – especially after all he has been through. It's possible to love you, too." He said.

She nodded her head but remained silent.

"Just look at me, I fall in love with multiple girls every weekend," he said jokingly.

She laughed, but shook her head again. Mark walked towards the door and Hannah stood up and walked him out. He turned around before leaving.

"He's the best guy I know, Hannah. He saved my life on many occasions. And I have a feeling he did the same for you." Mark added.

Hannah closed the door behind him. She walked into her bedroom and plopped onto her bed. Laying on her side, she looked at the picture of her and Jenna on her nightstand. As she kept staring, she saw her reflection in the frame and stared into her own eyes. As she kept staring, she stared into her own soul.

***

I spent most of the afternoon laying in our hammock staring at the light blue sky. Thoughts swirled around in my head but I always came back to one conclusion: God was testing me. He was testing to see if I had faith. I found myself in Gatsby's shoes again, looking across the lake and wondering what Hannah was doing, what she was thinking. A part of me wished she was miserable and regretted letting me go. The other part of me wished she was happy, because she truly deserved it. I finally decided I had to consciously try to stop thinking about her. Summer was almost over, and if she was going to move on, so was I.

As Monday rolled around I got up for work. Even though it was Labor Day, I was tired of laying around. I wanted to keep busy. I wasn't motivated to work, but I was motivated to keep my mind occupied. I woke up extremely early while it was still dark outside. For the first time in my life, I woke up earlier than my dad. Because it was a holiday, there were no assigned tasks for me to complete, so I had to find some on my own. I decided to mow the out of boundaries grass, which was a pretty big project that usually took a full day to complete. About an hour into the job, just as the sun was coming up, a pickup pulled up alongside the mower. It was my dad on his way to the office. He rolled down the window of his truck.

"You okay?" He asked.

"Yeah, I'm fine," I respond as I shrugged my shoulders, "just trying to get some work done here."

He nodded as if he understood my motivation for working that day.

"Carry on," he said.

I took an extra-long lunch hour in order to stretch out the day. I got back to work in the afternoon as the sun disappeared and clouds started to roll in, the wind picking up. As the afternoon was coming to a close, I was just finishing up. Suddenly, I saw a shadow of a truck pull up beside me out of the corner of my eye – dad again, I figured. As I looked up, I saw a red truck with a Johnson Auto sticker in faded letters on the door. I recognized the truck. I got a feeling in my stomach and I became nervous. I stopped the mower as the pickup pulled up next to me. He manually rolled down the window. I turned off the lawn mower.

"Get in," Walt demanded.

I was frightened. My heart started pounding. What was this about? Did he hear the rumors? Did Rick tell him about the fight? I was reluctant to succumb.

"*Get in,*" he repeated.

Out of respect, I walked around the back of his pickup, slowly opened the door and hopped in. I never was more speechless. He stared forward. It was dead silent, no radio on or anything.

"What's going on?" I asked as sweat dripped down my nose.

I looked down and noticed a liter of whiskey on the floorboard, almost half empty. I could smell the booze on his breath. Knowing his history, this was alarming. His hand reached into his inside coat pocket. I was so nervous I started shaking. My heart started pounding harder. My breathing got louder. I reached for the door handle. His hand stopped inside his coat pocket for a moment as if he was reconsidering. He seemed nervous himself. I was downright scared. He slowly pulled his hand from his coat as he pulled out a piece of paper. It was folded in half and he looked down at it for a few seconds. I let my guard down a bit and my shoulders loosened.

"We found this," he answered as he held it up, his head remained looking down.

My fear turned into anxiety with my heart racing uncontrollably at that point.

"What is it?" I asked.

"It fell out of her book," he added.

Walt's face tightened up and, as I looked into his eyes, I could tell he had been crying, which seemed like an impossible thought. His lips quivered. He tried to talk and was interrupted abruptly by tears. He looked away from me and out the driver's window. He started shaking violently. He rested his arms on the steering wheel and dropped his head onto his arms. He dissolved into tears. Never in my life had I seen a grown man cry like that. It was incredibly moving – a cold, unemotional man with absolutely no control over his emotions. My level of speechlessness spiked. My eyes were stuck wide open. I was completely stunned. I didn't know what to do. Should I console him? Should I leave? Confusion paralyzed me.

"Walt, what is that?" I repeated, my eyes still stuck wide open and my nerves bursting.

He wiped his eyes and nose with the back of his hand. He collected himself to some degree and looked over at me. He handed the piece of paper to me.

"You just need to read it," he said as he finally gathered himself together enough to speak.

I took it from him, the paper was a little damp and wrinkled from being in his pocket.

"Walt . . . honestly, I have nothing left. I can't afford another disappointment. What is this?" I asked.

I suddenly gained confidence, something that I never had around Walt. It seemed as if the dominance shifted from him to me.

"Read it." He said.

"I don't know if I want to." I countered.

"Don't do it for me, then. I know I haven't been the greatest...just...do it for *her*. Do it for my baby girl." He said as his voice cracked. "*...my baby girl.*" He repeated as his face winced.

He pounded the steering wheel with his fist. Inside, he was pleading with God as to why He took his baby girl.

I had no idea what it was. A part of me wanted to hand it back to him. I finally decided to try and move on from everything, and I couldn't afford any more heartbreak. One eventually gets weary of disappointment and unfulfilled dreams. I was at sanity's breaking point. I had seen more tears in a summer than most do in a lifetime, and I was still just a kid. I looked at him one more time before I reached for the door handle. I opened it as it squeaked, hopped out and closed it behind me. He quickly drove away as dust swirled around me. I looked at the paper. I didn't know what to do. Walt personally delivered it so it must be important. I was exhausted – mentally and physically, but, most of all, emotionally. The past five months had been the biggest roller coaster of emotions I could ever imagine. Whatever that piece of paper was, it could possibly do me in completely. I dropped down and sat on the grass with my back against the wheel of the mower. I lifted up my shirt to wipe the sweat off my face. I took off my ball cap and set it on the ground and then pushed my hair back.

My hands were shaking as I unfolded the piece of paper. My heart was beating uncontrollably. It was handwritten. I began to read.

Last Will of Jenna Johnson

I bequeath:
To my sister Stacey, my jewelry and clothes.
To the nurses who took care of me at the hospital, all of my money.
To my cheer teammates, my never-ending spirit.
To my cousin and best friend, Hannah, to find a new best friend.

Finally, I give my love, Will, his heart back
– so that he may give it to someone else.
To them both, that they may find true hap-
piness.

I never felt a feeling like I did when I read those words. I didn't know a feeling like that existed. The emotions were too difficult to put into words. I've tried to put words to it – a combination of shock, guilt, excitement, and nervousness. No words do it justice. I looked up and I had trouble breathing. I became light headed. It made things clearer, yet also more blurry, it gave me closure yet everything still felt open-ended. Reading those cryptic words made it feel as if Jenna was present.

I looked at it again and noticed the date of the document – April 9. That was the day before she died. My feelings only escalated at that point. I looked up as my curiosity sparked. I quickly thought back to the last night I saw her, when I walked into her room. She marked her page in the book she was reading with a folded piece of paper, just like that one. She also put a pen down on her night stand. I didn't think anything of it since she always liked to underline passages in books or take notes in the margins. She knew that she was dying. I wondered to myself how she could possibly have known she was about to die. If so, why didn't she tell anyone? Why didn't she try? Did she finally give up? Or was she finally letting go? Maybe she was setting herself free – free from all of the pain here on earth – and at the same time, in a crazy way, she was also setting me free. She knew all too well of my obsessive personality. She knew that as long as I was with her, that is all I would focus on. This realization only escalated my feeling of guilt. I wanted to cry, but I simply had no more tears left. It's almost as if she knew this was all going to happen. She must have known Hannah was moving to Shoreham Lake for the summer. Her Last Will served as some sort of a love prophesy. Maybe she saw all of this coming.

I had a choice to make – burn this life down and walk away or get to work to salvage it. I was sick and tired of being sick and tired. After thinking about what the moment called for, I made my decision. It was time to end all of this heartbreak. I had to take the chance to be with her again. There was only one way to do it.

I drove home and walked into the garage, grabbing an old rusty boat anchor. It was heavy enough. I grabbed a ski rope. It was long enough. Finally, I opened my dad's liquor cabinet and grabbed a bottle of tequila, half empty. I was well aware of the deepest part of the lake. We sought out that area when we fished for walleye, especially late in the season. I gathered everything and walked outside. I finally decided that I didn't want to live in anguish anymore. I came to the point where I didn't want to live if I couldn't live without her. I wanted to drown the past. The only question that remained as I stepped on that boat was how I wanted my life to end.

***

Summer was drawing to a close, and all that goes along with it. The dog days were setting in. The tan on my skin was already beginning to fade. The leaves on the trees were beginning to fall. People were beginning to board up their summer cottages as the wind and leaves swirled around them. I always had a mixed sentiment about the cool fall breeze – one part refreshing and one part discouraging. Fall had a different feeling, even a different smell. It brought in change, which often does a person good. But it's always a somber feeling to watch the summer sun fade, even though it's necessary to truly appreciate its beauty. Yet I understood that in order to fully appreciate the uniqueness of summer, you had to go through the other seasons. Just as in life, in order to truly appreciate your blessings, you need to face adversity.

But summer is more than just a quarter of the seasons. It's more than just dates on a calendar. It's when we are at our best and on top of the game that we call life. Sure, it's the sun, sand, water, boats, and boards. Sure, it's the green grass, blue sky, longer days, and later nights. It's the tan lines and sweating longnecks. It's the photograph of you and her with that perfect sunset in the background. Its Friday golf, Saturday sandbar, and Sunday sunburn. It's all of that.

But that's not what makes summertime special. The most important things in life are the things we can't touch. They don't occupy space on this Earth, only in our minds. What makes summer special is the relaxing feeling when you're floating on the water. It's the humble feeling of appreciation when you see your family and friends enjoying the day. It's the feeling of camaraderie you get when you're playing games with your buddies. It's the buzz at midnight and the headache in the morning. It's the freedom while you watch an outdoor concert, even if it's just your buddy on the guitar across the campfire. It's the excitement of driving to the lake on Friday afternoon. It's the time for reflection on the Sunday drive home. It's the sexiness in the air, when people share more of their skin and more of their lives. It's the butterflies you get when you're spending time outside with the one person you love the most. It's the energy. It's the optimism. It's the anticipation in saying hello. It's the sadness in saying goodbye.

***

I looked around to see if anyone was watching. The coast was clear. I was nervous. I gently rested everything inside the boat and cranked the lift down. The wind had picked up and there was a misty rain that filled the air from the overcast clouds – a good thing so nobody could see me from shore. The waves were furious, crashing against the shore and up against the boat. I started it up and backed out into the water. The boat rocked back and forth. I cruised westbound. The waves were large and hit the boat, with water splashing inside. I had many contemplative moments on that boat in the past, none more than that drive. I thought about everything. I thought about how I was a kid with big dreams. At that moment, I realized that I never reached any of them. I was tired of broken dreams. I didn't want to live like that anymore. It was time to put it all to rest.

I reached the depth of the lake and stopped as the boat floated. I grabbed the bottle of tequila and rested it on my lap. I screwed off the cap. My hand was shaking. I shivered as I could smell the fumes from the bottle and the memories associated with it. There's something about the taste of tequila – it's an intimate drink that stings and lingers. I raised the bottle and tipped it towards the clouds. I leaned over the boat and poured it all out. After tying the rope to the anchor, I folded Jenna's Will and stuck it inside the empty bottle. Then I screwed the cap back on the bottle and tied the other end of the rope around its neck. Finally, I looked around to see if any boats were near. I gently dropped the anchor and bottle into the water, letting the rope slack go as it submerged. It sank in slow motion as the words on the paper came back into my mind. I watched it drop towards the bottom and eventually dissipate, leaving me with my reflection in the water.

I didn't want to live without her. It was time to go get her.

I continued driving west. The wind picked up and the waves got larger. I kept driving, trying to navigate my way through the waves and mist blowing in my face. Her cabin was like a lighthouse guiding me. Just a few hundred feet from shore, a silhouette appeared. It was an angel. It was my angel on earth. She was sitting on the beach and stood up. She was waiting for something. I hoped that something was me.

I killed the motor as the boat crashed into the

beach. Stepping on the bow, I quickly jumped on the sand and walked towards her.

"Hi," I said.

"Hi," she said in a quiet voice.

"You can't make a habit of coming around here, you know," she said, mocking what she said months earlier.

The wind blew her hair across her face and she pushed it back out of the way.

"There is nothing between Alisha and me, and there never has been. It was one mistake and it was before you and me," I explained.

"I know," she responded.

"But you don't know everything, and that's my fault. Listen, five months ago, my life was over. Everything I loved on this earth was gone. I had nothing left to live for. Then you came into my life. You made me want to live my life again. You woke me up from every broken dream I ever had." I explained.

"Will, Jenna will always be in your heart, though." She interrupted.

"You are right. She will always be in my heart. That's the truth. But from this day forward, only you will *have* my heart." I proclaimed.

Tears started to well in her eyes.

"This is not how love is supposed to happen," she

said as her voice cracked and she shook her head.

I interrupted, "I don't care. I've lost love before. I'm not going to let it happen again."

She shook her head again. I stepped towards her.

"I have faith. And I believe in fate. And when faith meets fate – that's love."

9

"What happens next?" He asks as we slowly pull in the driveway as the cobblestones crackle under the wheels.

I stop the car and we remain seated as I come up for air and take a breath. I was shocked about my revelations. I've never shared that much detail of the story with anyone. He hung on every word I said. He was captive. His hands are covering his mouth, almost as if he is in prayer posture. He stares at me, stunned and fascinated. I'm probably even more stunned that I just told him the story, something I consciously suppressed and avoided for so long. Perhaps, unconsciously, I was waiting for the right moment. It's quiet. I ponder his question.

"Well, what happens next is up to you," I tell him.

"What do you mean?" He asks for clarification.

"What I mean is that you choose what happens next. You can go in two directions – you can use this breakup as a source of bitterness or a source of motivation. If you use it as bitterness, I can promise you that you'll stop living in any meaningful way. If you use it as motivation, you *won't* stop until you find something to fill that void – better yet, someone." I say.

He seemed to grasp the consequences of his choices.

"There's just no one like her," he says.

"Of course there isn't. A part of you will probably always miss her, and that's human. But there's someone else out there. In this situation, probably someone better. And finding that someone will help you get over her." I add.

It gets quiet again. I reach for the door handle to get out of the car.

"Do you still miss her?" He asks, causing me to pause.

I haven't been asked that question in over twenty years, not since Hannah asked me when we took a walk together down the road on one of those early days of summer. It is such a simple question, the answer isn't so simple. Hannah wanted the truth the night she ended it between us. At the time, I didn't know how to put it into words. After years of contemplation, now I do.

The truth is, I do. I miss everything about Jenna. I miss her love. I miss her friendship. I miss her smile. I miss her touch. She still crosses my mind from time to time, even after all these years. I think anyone who has lost love for whatever reason thinks back once in a while. It's no slight on the person you are with now. It isn't some mental crime of infidelity. It's only human. When someone has that big of an impact on your life, you can't completely wipe away the memory. She still appears in my dreams sometimes, haunting to a certain degree. It was so long ago that sometimes I wake up in the middle of the night and wonder if the whole thing was just a dream. But when I wake up, I quickly realize that it was all too real to be a dream. The lasting impact was too powerful. Often times we forget the details of our dreams within minutes or hours of awaking, sometimes forgetting them altogether. On many occasions, I remember that I had a strange dream, but fail to recall the details. When I dream of Jenna, I always remember it.

The truth is that Jenna's memory will live with me forever. I never had any intention of abandoning that. I think that would be disrespectful to both her and myself. Yet, over the years thoughts of her have grown further and further between. See, I've always struggled to live in the moment. Far too often I live in the past, chasing ghosts and dodging skeletons around the closet. Far too often I live in the future, relentlessly chasing dreams up the road. And when both happen, I miss out on too many moments in the present. Then before I even know it, life has passed me by. As I've gotten older, I've made a conscious effort to live more in the moment. I've tried to savor the now. I've tried to appreciate the moments given, because I have seen how precious they truly are. But I'm still human. I'm not sure if we ever completely bury the past, no matter how badly we want to sometimes. Besides, in my case, I wouldn't want to. My past has made me the person I am today. I'm more thoughtful than I ever thought I could be. I see the meaning in things. I feel more. I'm a stronger man. I'm a more compassionate man. I'm a more appreciative man. I'm a better man.

Do I still love Jenna? Of course, I do. The truth is that Jenna will always be in my heart. She's my guardian angel in heaven. When you attach yourself to something so closely, it's something that you can never fully let go of. People try all sorts of things to get over heartbreak – friends, family, therapy, alcohol, drugs, food, work, working out, and the list scrolls on. I've tried close to all of them. But I have found the only true cure for heartbreak is new love. I don't think anyone ever gets over someone until they meet someone else to fill that void. It's not that the other person is replaced necessarily, but the empty feeling is filled. Of course, none of this is scientific, but it's more than just a hypothesis. It's coming from a guy who lived it. It's coming from a guy who almost died from it. It's coming from a guy who thought he had a once in a lifetime love, but turned out to be twice.

"All the time," I responded to his question honestly.

It was the same answer I had given Hannah twenty years prior.

"And not a day goes by where I don't thank God that he sent an angel to earth to save me. Your mom helped me carry the cross when I couldn't. She saved my life." I continue.

He shakes his head and almost has tears in his eyes.

"If Jenna wouldn't have died, I wouldn't be alive," he says as his voice cracks.

My heart skips a beat. It's a powerful statement. I can't blame him for having that thought, as I've had similar "what if" thoughts when I've encountered different things and people throughout my lifetime.

"I don't know if I truly would be either," I added as my voice choked.

In a harsh and cryptic way, the experience of losing Jenna made me appreciate the value of life. Going through that darkness has inspired me to help my son see the light. I just realized that right now.

315

God knew that all along. It was his way of lighting a fire in my heart, even if I didn't realize it until now. And there was no more fitting of a way for Jenna to pass away – her heart got too big.

"She must be your angel in heaven, too." I continue as I rub the top of his head and open the car door.

"Is the story over?" He asks.

"That's up to you." I said with a smile as I open my bag and hand him my old journal that chronicled my feelings twenty years earlier.

I close the door and walk inside the cabin. I hear a noise in the kitchen. I walk slowly down the hallway and peer around the corner. I breathe in the smell of dinner simmering. Wine glasses are poured with the bottle next to them on the counter. I approach her from behind, wrap my arms around her waist, and softly kiss her neck. Resting my chin on her shoulder, I gently rock her back and forth as if we are slowly dancing to a song that is in both of our heads. She closes her eyes and leans her head against mine. I don't speak a word and neither does she. We don't have to. We both know. We both emotionally exhale many years of stress and anxiety that wear on a relationship. All of the mistakes. All of the accomplishments. All of the failures. All of the successes. All of the sins. All of the greatness. All of the pain. All of the happiness. We know that, after all these years, although with callused hearts, we still have that feeling that so many others have struggled to come up with an alternative word for – love.

I spin her around so we are face-to-face, grab her legs and hoist her up so she sits on the counter. I put my hand around her neck and pull her in close.

"I love you," I whisper just before we both close our eyes as I kiss her.

***

"I love you too," she said with affirmation, her toes curled into the sand.

I looked into her eyes. My heart was racing. I could feel it beating out of my chest. I was so excited. The anticipation was off the charts. I could see into her soul and everything all of a sudden became clear. I put my hand in my pocket and dropped to one knee. I raised up a ring towards her.

"Will you marry me?" I asked as my voice cracked. "Take my heart forever."

She immediately burst into tears. She covered her mouth with her hands in shock.

"Yes!" She yelled.

That moment, that feeling, was so profound that it quite possibly could be the closest thing to heaven I will ever experience. I stood up and slid the ring on her finger while her hand was shaking. We embraced fully, and as I closed my eyes, tears fell. And for the first time in my life, they were tears of happiness. I grabbed her face and kissed her.

***

Hannah and I got married on Christmas Day of that year, and for the first time in fifty years there was no snow as temperatures reached sixty degrees. It was a perfect day, when my summer love turned into real love. It's easy to fall under the spell of summer, but the real tests are in the depths of winter, and she stayed with me. Many people were in my heart on our wedding day – all of the people who had an impact on my life. Jenna was in our hearts that day. But as I told Hannah that day on the beach, only one person had my heart from that day forward, and that was my bride. We got married in Shoreham Lake at the resort. We moved to Minneapolis and went to college together. Hannah became a teacher while I went on to law school. She still has a passion for teaching, and she relishes having time off in the summertime to spend time at the lake.

Hannah's grandmother Lola passed away about ten years ago. Hannah inherited her old cabin on Shoreham Lake. Instead of passing it down to Hannah's parents, she left it to her. Lola knew how much it meant to Hannah. We also thought it was her way to entice us to move back to Shoreham Lake, or at least to keep a presence there. Every time we drive back to the city after a summer lake weekend and find ourselves caught in traffic, I wonder why we ever left. I guess life brings you places you never thought you'd go, which, in my case, is a vast understatement. But you always leave your roots behind.

We held onto Lola's cabin for a few years. But eventually I made a deal of a lifetime with my old pal Andrew Swanson III. He got Lola's small simple cabin which was perfect size for him. It was easy for him to upkeep and he could still go fishing and play golf with his buddies down the road. And me? I finally realized my dream of owning that cabin on the top of the hill – punching my front-row ticket to the best sunsets in Minnesota. Of course, I had to throw in some extra cash and free moving labor to boot. At age eighty-nine, the old man was still stubborn as hell. As we got done moving all of his stuff into his new place, Hannah grabbed his arm gently and thanked him for everything. She walked towards the car, holding hands with our son.

"Well, that should do it," he said. "Now get off my property," he continued sarcastically.

"Thanks for everything, Drew," I said.

He stopped unloading the box and stood up,

looking at me in shock.

"You were right. Everything makes sense now," I told him.

While we helped him move, I figured out he was "Drew" who wrote me the note after Jenna passed away. He knew about Jenna, as he caught us in his yard. The note referenced his wife dying, and he had recently lost her to cancer at the time. He lived near The End, and I realized he was the man who asked me about Jenna that night. And he also wasn't far from our house, so he had the chance to drop it in my mailbox the next morning. The giveaway came as I helped him move and discovered some letters from his late wife. She called him Drew.

"Boy, I have no idea what you are talking about," he said.

"Forget it, old man," I said sarcastically and I smiled.

He smiled back and resumed unpacking.

Everything did make sense after all those years. All of the hard times I went through got me to that point – true happiness, just as Jenna had prophesized. Going through all of that made me appreciate everything that much more.

Sometimes when I sit on the porch at our cabin on top of the hill and watch the sunset, I do think of Jenna. I picture her in that white lace dress, dancing barefoot across the beach, with the water coming up and crashing into her legs. Her hair is partly blocking the sun as it reflects on her beautiful golden strands. She looks back briefly, smiles with one side of her mouth, and keeps walking down the beach towards paradise. The best thing about it is that I can tell she is happy – for me and for herself.

Then when I wake in the morning, the sunrise reminds me of a new beginning, which is assurance that the sun will come up the next day no matter what I go through in life. I've seen enough sadness for a lifetime, yet, in some ways, my life is just beginning again every single day. My experiences are unique, and I wouldn't change them for anything. Through the hustle and bustle of my life today, I'm searching for peace – piece by piece. I'll find it someday, even if I have to wait until the next life.

The great thing is that I can share her memory with Hannah. We still talk about her occasionally, usually in small talk about our families. We both went back for Mary Johnson's funeral a few years ago. I said a few words at the prayer service. I reconciled things with Jenna's brother Rick, and we remain good friends today. Walt and I haven't spoken on a substantive level since that final day of summer. I always wondered if he struggled with drinking after that day or just had the one setback, but I never asked. I didn't think it was my place to tell anyone. A part of me thought he deserved to indulge through grief that one time. I'm still best friends with all the boys to this day. Even through college, law school, marriage, and children, we all remain close. I cherish those friendships and I'm proud to still have them. The older I get, the more I realize how special and rare lifelong friendship are.

And my mistress? I still think of hockey from time to time as well. I don't miss the game per se. But I miss the camaraderie with the boys, the brotherhood that only teammates can truly understand. I miss the high of scoring a goal, or adrenaline of running onto the ice in front of screaming fans. I miss the relentless pursuit of the state championship. For many years after high school, I had constant dreams of hockey. Many of them brought me back to that semifinal game. And for many years I felt like I was cursed, one could say I had a bitterness about it. I haven't skated since high school. People assume since I played and had some success in high school that I'm still a fan of the game, but that's not true. I received many requests to play intramurals in college and law school or city league, and various coaching gigs. I politely declined all of them. It wasn't Spoiler hockey, so I had no interest. From that day, I never watched much hockey either. If I couldn't play, I didn't want to watch. I'd tell people I became burnt out over the game. The truth is, there is just too much heartbreak there. There are too many demons. That's something I never got over. Demons follow you everywhere. They pay no attention to time or geography. Some demons remain with you no matter what. But I came to realize throughout the years that even that heartbreaking loss as a senior happened for a reason. If I had won that state championship title, it may never have gotten better than that for me. I might have settled on that, resting on my laurels. At age eighteen, my ambition may have been over. But God had another plan for me – instead of taking my future, he was actually giving me a future. I know there is something out there, something bigger, that I am destined for. Losing that game was perhaps the best thing that ever happened to me. It kept me hungry. I've spent my entire professional life trying to avenge it, and that has made a huge difference in my success today.

My son never showed much interest in hockey, and maybe that was partly my fault. He is more of the creative, artistic type. He enjoyed school, he was in the school plays, and is a very talented writer. He was class president and editor of the school newspaper and also has his own blog where he logs his thoughts and ideas. As long as he is driven and active, I don't care what he is involved in. Now that he's graduated, he's planning on attending college for journalism. I couldn't be any more proud of him.

***

Hannah puts her hand down on the counter but slips a little on the newspaper as she hops down onto her feet, "Whoops," she says as she braces herself.

She grabs a glass of wine and hands it to me and then takes a drink of her own.

"What's this?" I ask as I pick up the newspaper.

It was the Shoreham Record, the hometown paper that comes out weekly around the area. We subscribe to it at the lake cabin so we can somewhat keep in touch with what's going on around the lakes area. A headline on the front page caught my eye and sparked my interest: "Shoreham Lake Hockey Seeks New Head Coach." For the first time in a long time, I felt that old fire inside. Maybe the pilot light was left on all this time.

***

Meanwhile, my son makes his way outside with his backpack on. He realizes how special the story was, how powerful it was, how it could inspire him. It made him think of how it could inspire countless others who have experienced heartbreak or loss. He also realized how countless others have experienced love and could relate, as love is the most universal thing that we have in the world. It's timeless, and it doesn't discriminate. Those who have it cherish it, and those who don't relentlessly strive for it, consciously or unconsciously. Those without love are tortured souls, constantly searching. For far too many, love is an elusive prize. For far too few, the feeling of love is all consuming. And in the end, for everyone, the only thing that endures more than pain is love.

It was a story that he needed to hear. He believes it's a story that the world needs to hear. He walks out onto the lawn and notices a big oak tree with a spot in front of it with the grass still worn. He sits down with his back resting against it. After staring at the red orange sunset slowly dropping into the water for a moment, an epiphany overcomes his soul and butterflies begin fluttering in his heart. He opens his backpack and pulls out his computer. He flips it open, turns it on, and opens a fresh white document and types:

"Love's Will"

It wasn't over. The story had just begun.

About the Author

P. Ryan Campbell is a writer and lawyer, born and raised on a farm in North Dakota and on a lake in Minnesota. He loves writing intriguing and inspirational stories for people to enjoy as an escape from their everyday lives.

His own way of escaping is spending as much time as possible on the beach and on his boat, where his life motto is to work hard, play hard, and pray hard.

The story isn't over.

Connect with him at pryancampbell.com.

68417591R00184

Made in the USA
Lexington, KY
10 October 2017